W F B

GETTING IT RIGHT

a novel

Also by WILLIAM F. BUCKLEY JR.

WILLIAM F. BUCKLEY JR.

GETTING

IT

RIGHT

a novel

Since 1947
REGNERY
PUBLISHING, INC.
An Eagle Publishing Company • Washington, DC

Library of Congress Cataloging-in-Publication Data

Buckley, William F. (William Frank), 1925–
 Getting it right : a novel / by William F. Buckley Jr.
  p. cm.
 ISBN 0-89526-138-3 (acid-free paper)
 1. Right and left (Political science)—Fiction.
 2. Conservatism—Fiction. I. Title.
 PS3552.U344 G48 2002
 813'.54—dc21
                    2002151632

Published in the United States by
Regnery Publishing, Inc.
An Eagle Publishing Company
One Massachusetts Avenue, NW
Washington, DC 20001

Visit us at www.regnery.com

Distributed to the trade by
National Book Network
4720-A Boston Way
Lanham, MD 20706

Printed on acid-free paper

Manufactured in the United States of America

10 9 8 7 6 5 4 3 2 1

Books are available in quantity for promotional or premium use. Write to Director of Special Sales, Regnery Publishing, Inc., One Massachusetts Avenue, NW, Washington, DC 20001, for information on discounts and terms or call (202) 216-0600.

For Javier

Que quedes, como siempre, en las manos de Dios

Preface

THIS IS THE STORY OF A YOUNG MAN and a young woman whose paths first crossed in 1960 at the founding conference of the Young Americans for Freedom in Sharon, Connecticut. He had one idea how to reshape national policy, she another. The story is of their adventures, touching on the development of the conservative movement, post-Eisenhower, pre-Reagan.

This book is a novel in which public figures are intimately portrayed. Liberties are taken in chronology, and of course, as is to be expected in novels, thoughts and sentences are given to individuals which, however true they are to character, were not actually recorded.

But there is no misrepresentation in this novel, certainly none intended, and to the best of my knowledge, none crept in. These were the thoughts and declarations, the acts and critical sexual activities, of the protagonists, making up their private lives as well as their public lives. Not one word is attributed to any public declaration by Robert Welch or other representatives of the John Birch Society that wasn't actually spoken or written by them. This is so also of Ayn Rand, respecting her thought and writing.

The fiction is imaginative joiner work, the knitting together of a story in which many people on the political scene from 1956 to 1966 were involved, from all of which conversation the author heard what he took to be the tuning fork of modern political conservatism.

In an appendix, the sources used in the text are cited.

—WFB, September 2002

GETTING
IT
RIGHT

Prologue

I HAVE NEGLECTED MY JOURNAL for several weeks. Not so long ago, Lucy would have reproached me, with her charming indirection ("Theo, have you done your journal today? Well, *get to it.*"). It was for many years a daily event, now more like a weekly event. The lapse this time is more than a month. *Theo. Be honest with yourself! You are deceiving nobody.* OK. My last entry was written the week of the Republican convention in San Francisco that nominated Dwight Eisenhower to serve another term, back in August. And now we are practically at election day. Ike is bound to be reelected.

Which suits me fine. Though not . . . well. I occasionally remind my dwindling body of students that idiomatic changes govern the meaning of language. What is said to suit me "fine" is, as often as not, less than fine. It is a compromise. "Can you come in at ten o'clock tomorrow?" Miss Ludwig asked me an hour ago. I replied that that suited me fine. It doesn't, really, suit me fine, no more than the reelection of President Eisenhower suits me fine. I have no reasonable alternative to going to the dentist tomorrow at ten, given my toothache; I have no reasonable alternative to voting for Eisenhower on Tuesday, the alternative—a vote for Adlai Stevenson—being intolerable.

Apropos of which, Lucy would have been pleased with my deportment at the faculty meeting this morning. Yes, I said to Dean Mills in September, I would agree to continue to attend the monthly meetings of the history faculty, even though I am formally retired, reduced to teaching one seminar. *Why did I say that?* Because I took subversive pleasure in denying Jonathan Mills such satisfaction as he would take from my absence from faculty meetings. I don't ever *say* much at them anymore—well, only every so often. Mostly anemic contributions to administrative questions. I did defend the Bradford history text for freshmen when it was proposed to replace that text next year with the work of that *imbecile* Stannard. But those who knew me in my fiery days would not have thought they were now listening to the voice of Theocritus Romney, waging battle with the faculty *à outrance*. They'd have thought I had lost either my voice or my spirit. Or, since Lucy is not listening in, my balls.

They'd have been right on one point. At age sixty-six my voice is lusty, but my disposition to raise it, slight. There isn't much spirit left, not even on the issue of the history text. Should Princeton continue using an introductory text which pays *some* deferential notice to high moments in American political history? Or replace it with the fashionable book by Professor Stannard (baptized, or rather, not baptized, as Stanoivski), who informs the freshman reader that the Revolutionary War was an act of economic opportunism, the Civil War a continuing expression of that economic aggrandizement by a wealthy and covetous northeastern alliance (you see, southern slaves were free labor, and the Yankees didn't want to compete with free labor)? Yes, and Stannard informs the student reader that the lateness of the constitutional amendment permitting income taxation betrayed the *"immaturity"* of the American nation (the mature nations, while this was going on, were working up to a world war that killed fifteen million people, but that's okay, they paid for it with income taxes).

But I will not work myself up on the subject here, and certainly didn't do so at the faculty meeting this morning. I just smiled a little. My St. Sebastian smile, Lucy called it. St. Sebastian, arms tied behind his back, looking at the archers taking aim. Mandy calls me on it, whenever I fall into that mood, which is every time she tells me she can't see me next week, for some reason or other, as though her son weren't old enough to look after himself; all I ask for is one night a week. I am contributing much more than one-seventh of the cost of her Gramercy Park apartment.

It was less easy to keep quiet when the dean asked for an informal, off-the-record show of hands: Eisenhower for a second term? Or Adlai Stevenson for president? I call just raising my hand for Eisenhower at the meeting the same thing as keeping quiet, because that is *all* that I did, just raise my hand when his name was given. There were twenty-one of us at the faculty meeting. Twenty recorded a vote for Adlai.

I don't blame them, in a way. In my book on the development of the West, I stressed the acuteness of the challenge to the American pioneer. It was that edge that fired their spirit, the raw cold, the hot sun, the daunting scarcity of meat and grain, the lurking Indian warrior, the unattended mother when the baby came, the need to save pennies to build schools and churches. That spirit is emaciated, and the Republican Party, which should be preserving it—should be carrying it forward—is lost in ambiguity. The radio reports *this very day* that in Hungary there is a credible popular movement to throw off the Soviet tyrant. The fight for liberty is coming to a head there. But its proponents will depend, finally, on . . . the United States. On President Eisenhower. On the leader of the Republican Party. What will we do? What pride does the party of Dwight Eisenhower— which repudiated Robert Taft, its organic leader, at the convention in 1952—generate? Not enough to get more than a single vote of the Princeton history faculty.

This is the Eisenhower who thinks that we cope best with the Communist leadership by international exchanges. The only time I did raise my voice at a faculty meeting was when President Eisenhower confessed at a press conference that when Marshal Zhukov told him that the Communist system appealed to the idealistic, Eisenhower said that—I'll never forget his words—"I had a very tough time trying to defend our position." Soviet *idealism!* The Russians are building missiles and exploding nuclear bombs. Our own secretary of defense admits that the Soviets' bomber capacity will exceed our own.

Ike's answer to all that?

More state welfare, more deficits, more guarantees to the farmers and to labor union leaders—never mind the enslaved people of Eastern Europe.

I may have one more book left in me. A short book. Maybe a long essay. My good Mormons in Salt Lake would be glad to publish it. It would address the conservative movement in America. Mostly Republicans, but a lot of Democrats, and I'd speak out about the listlessness of America, the same continental entity that subdued nature, the Indians, the French, the British, the Spanish, and the Nazis but can't come up with a foreign policy that smashes its fist down on Communist presumptions. On Moscow's challenges to our freedom and independence.

But we would need to define *what* that freedom is. What are the roots of it, and how can we nourish them while giving in to statist depredations, year after year?

Maybe it's a good thing that I am doing my journal more irregularly. Maybe I'll put it in a capsule to be read, oh, fifty years from now, 2006. To document that what we used to think of as America the land of the brave was, well, with us yet. Not just with me. But not much more than me in the company of scholars at Princeton University, which nurtured James Madison. What would he have done today for the equivalent—in Hungary—of the generation that gave us *our* independence? That was a haunting sentence Whittaker Chambers wrote to Buckley. I thanked him for sending me a copy. That's what I call despair. Chambers wrote him, "It is idle to talk about preventing the wreck of Western civilization. It is already a wreck from within. That is why we can hope to do little more now than snatch a fingernail of a saint from the rack or a handful of ashes from the faggots, and bury them secretly in a flowerpot against the day, ages hence, when a few men begin again to dare to believe that there was once something else, that something else is thinkable, and need some evidence of what it was, and the fortifying knowledge that there were those who, at the great nightfall, took loving thought to preserve the tokens of hope and truth."

I'll get back to my painting. I told the story of the Rocky Mountains with some success in my book, they tell me. I wish I could do them justice with my paintbrush.

BOOK
ONE

1

THE MISSIONARY TRAINING PERIOD began right there in Salt Lake City, immediately after Woodroe Raynor graduated from high school, nearing his nineteenth birthday in 1956. The training hadn't been extensive. The Mormon missionary outpost in Vienna was in a hurry, eager for stateside help. The missionaries in the field would superintend further training in the country in which Woodroe would be serving, doing his duty by his church.

The Vienna Mormon station, in July 1956, had a cadre of three Americans and four Austrians, rapidly put together after the May 15, 1955, State Treaty. This covenant with Moscow formally detached Austria from the military competitiveness of the Cold War. The new treaty had been denounced by a few conservatives in the U.S. Senate, notably William Jenner of Indiana. In his dissenting speech, Jenner made the point that to commit the Austrian state to neutrality forfeited the liberationist potential it might someday have exerted on Czechoslovakia to the north and Hungary to the east. Under the terms of the treaty, Austria could make no military covenants with East or West.

In the days before the treaty was concluded, there had been heated pro-Communist coverage in what professionals in the United States Information Agency handily called the "satellite press." "When Moscow decrees the correct line," Woodroe had been instructed in Salt Lake, "newspapers and radios in the satellite states serve dutifully as echo chambers." The Communist line, in the winter of 1955, had declaimed that Austria could not safely be permitted at any time in the foreseeable future to be free of military supervision by Moscow—given the enthusiasm the Austrian people had shown for Hitler when, in March of 1938, promulgating the Anschluss, he had declared that Germany and Austria were now a single state. In suddenly endorsing the hands-free treaty, Soviet leadership, under Stalin's successor, Nikita Khrushchev, was making a show of the regime's new, cooperative disposition. The satellite press got into line, celebrating the treaty as one more step toward a people's peace.

So it was that on May 15, 1955, in the great Austrian Gallery of the Belvedere Palace in Vienna, the treaty was signed. Mormon authorities in Salt Lake lost no time in making claim to the old house on Radetsky Street. Requisitioned by the Nazis in 1939, the Mormon property had served as a training barracks for the Austrian Gestapo. At war's end it was abandoned, sitting empty for ten years. Notwithstanding, the Communist occupying force denied the Mormons permission to reoccupy it for missionary activity—never mind that the Mormon enterprise abroad was resolutely nonpolitical. It was only after the 1955 treaty that Austria resumed sole registry, and quickly turned the property back to its prewar owners.

Woodroe was given quarters in the dormitory section of the building. He was lodged under the V-shaped roof and could enter his room only by stooping. During the day, he pursued his German study and sat in, to learn about teaching techniques, at the ongoing English-language classes hungrily subscribed to by young Austrians. On completion of his training in September he was informed that he would be doing fieldwork as an assistant at the Mormon missionary post in Andau, forty-five miles to the southeast, on the Hungarian border.

In pastoral Andau, Woodroe lived in the same house as his superior, thirty-five-year-old Andrew Goodhart, and Goodhart's Hungarian wife, twenty-five-year-old Hildred. Woodroe taught English, helped to provision and maintain the city library's English-language section, and did what he could as a carpenter and painter on the grand project of converting an adjacent barn into a schoolhouse.

There was always work to do around the house and in the garden, especially now that winter was coming. He wrote to his widowed mother, "It's this simple, Mom. I do anything that Andrew or Hildred ask me to do. He's nice, but you know, he doesn't smile much. We listen to the radio all the time, in German and in English, and you can't tell, looking at him, what he's thinking. In case you're curious, he graduated from Lively High in 1939—seventeen years ahead of me—and did a crash academic program at Salt Lake U. before the war, majoring in German and then doing intelligence work and meeting Hildred. With Hildy, who is ten years younger, he's very formal. I already told you, she's Hungarian. Her father was a railroad engineer. Actually, what he really was, was a Communist intelligence agent—I *think*. I'm not sure what the word stands for that she used about her father's past, and Andrew wouldn't like to be interrogated about ties of his wife's father to Communism, never mind that we're talking about when Hildred was only fifteen years old.

"We speak together in English because Andrew wants her to practice her English. Her German is, well, fluent: she was taught the German language during the Nazi occupation in Budapest. That's how come she met Andrew—doing translating when our people set up in Budapest, thinking to include Hungary in on the Marshall Plan. Mom, it's very beautiful in the Burgenland countryside. Not much like our part of the world.

"Send me your pumpkin pie recipe, will you? And, Mom, while you're at it, send me some pumpkins. Got to go. Much love, Woody."

Woodroe had been given a bicycle to use on his errands. He could now accompany Hildred when there was more than a single basket of articles to fetch. He took quick advantage of the bicycle to ride about, in the countryside, early and late in the day, marveling at the intensity of the green of the Austrian fir trees and the vivid richness of the meticulously cultivated farmland. Soon he discovered the spooky little bridge traversing the Einserkanal waterway to Hungary. He was entranced at the sight of it, a bridge not nearly wide enough for a car, nor sturdy enough. It was a footbridge of rickety boards with waist-high handrails, too high for little children to reach. At first it surprised Woodroe that a passageway, however little, between sovereign countries was irregularly guarded. Well, he remembered, why not think back to the Austro-Hungarian empire? A sole sovereign of the two countries. Both historic countries had received the Soviet armies and both had been under the direct control of Moscow up until the treaty with Austria loosened Soviet braces there. Meanwhile, the Russian military continued in tight control of Hungary. Maybe one day Woodroe would walk over the bridge!

But better to confide that ambition to Hildred. The next day, when Andrew was teaching class and Woodroe was helping her paint the kitchen, he told her of the bridge.

She smiled broadly.

Could he cross over on it?

Yes. "But better if you have a Hungarian guide. I will take you next Saturday. Better not to speak of it to Andrew. We'll just say we're going out for a ride. If the weather is good."

The weather was good, and in midafternoon they had got there by bicycle, a journey of only fifteen minutes, since they had chugged up the hill in between. Circling the hill was easier work but took ten minutes longer.

"Follow me." Hildred ran her portable stretch of chain around the tree, through the front wheel of her bicycle, and then through Woodrow's, snapping the lock.

They began the walk across the canal, she leading the way, both holding on to the handrails. He could feel the bridge's motions inclining to the wind. Looking down on the water, he saw the drift of the forty-meter-wide Einserkanal, several barges lazing their way eastward over the dark blue water. At the far end of the bridge a young couple stood, braced against the wind that funneled up the canal gorge. The man was dressed as a farmer might dress: a leather halter holding up coarse blue trousers; under the halter, a bleached white shirt with an open collar; a sweater of sorts hung over his shoulder.

He was very young, Woodroe observed, probably just into his twenties. His companion was of the same age, except that Teresa, as he would come to know her, was not dressed in farm clothes—her cotton skirt and shirt were studiously clerical in design. Hildred would learn after they began talking that Teresa worked as a clerk at the military unit nearby and today was strolling, after hours, with her cousin Anton, who worked on the farm at the river's edge.

Hildred quickly informed them that though she was herself a native Hungarian, she was married to an American who worked as a schoolteacher—"that's better to use than 'missionary,'" she said in English to Woodroe, whom she introduced. The two Hungarians had never before met an American, and Teresa, her braided blond hair tied around her head, turned eagerly to Woodroe. She was delighted to try out the English she had applied herself so studiously to learn for what seemed years. *Had he ever before been in Hungary? Were he and Hildred aware of the great changes that were imminent in Budapest? The great liberal measures being advanced?*

Yes, Hildred said, she was well informed about them, "but we have to get our news from the BBC. We can't get anything from our—your—Budapest radio. Just the same old thing."

Woodroe spoke to Hildred, keeping private what he said. "I keep ten U.S. one-dollar bills. Could we use one of them to buy them a beer or something?" Hildred agreed, and the invitation was happily accepted.

Two military jeeps were parked outside the little bar up the hill. Approaching it, they passed by stone benches on the green outside a small church of Gothic design, young men and women seated on them, chatting. On one bench a young man listened attentively to a portable radio. Inside the rustic tavern, Teresa beckoned them to a table in the corner. An attendant brought them beer and a nonalcoholic orangeade for Woodroe. Woodroe took a pencil from his shirt pocket and drew on the paper place mat a rough outline of the United States of America.

"Here is New York. Here"—he sketched a north-south line—"is the Mississippi River. There"—he moved his pencil left—"are the Rocky Mountains. They are *our* Alps." Hildred supplied the emphasis for the benefit of Anton. "And there"—he smiled broadly with pride—"is the largest saltwater lake in America. I am from . . . *there.*" He made a pencil dot on the north end of the lake.

They spent two hours together, speaking in German with spurts of Hungarian interpretation done by Hildred. It was after four in the afternoon that Hildred said, "We have to go. Our bicycles," she explained to Teresa, "are across the bridge, and we are then nine kilometers from Andau."

"I know how far it is to Andau," Teresa said sharply. "But maybe there won't be such a barrier between us after the government of Imre Nagy gets on with our reforms. Maybe one day here, in Hungary, it will be like over there"—she motioned toward the Andau Bridge—"in Austria. After the Soviets—" Hildred raised a cautionary finger to her lips, looking over to the Communist army officers at the other end of the room. Teresa took the warning and finished in a whisper, "After *they* get out."

They all swore to meet again, and Hildred wrote down an address. "I'm sorry we can't tender you an invitation to Andau. Someday soon, perhaps."

That night Woodroe wrote to Teresa. He had no sense of how long it would take a posted letter to travel from the post office in Andau to the post office in Kapuvar—a distance, as the crow flies, of about ten kilometers, but who knew how many bureaucratic postal leagues away. To his surprise, only four days passed by before he heard back from her. Woodroe didn't get much mail at Andau. His mother wrote every week, his sister every fortnight, and one or two Salt Lake City classmates occasionally rang in. But on Wednesday, when Woodroe returned from his daily bicycle ride to fetch the newspapers, Andrew handed him, without comment, the letter with the Hungarian postmark.

Woodroe stuck the letter in his pocket, opening it while waiting for his students to file in.

Teresa had replied that she would be happy to see him anytime she was not on duty, her duty hours being from 0800 to 1600. The military base was a mere ten-minute bicycle ride from Kapuvar. "I live in the barn at my cousin Anton's farm, right by the path going up from the bridge. We passed the barn on the way to the Grodka— the tavern." She wrote in small block letters, perhaps to take special care that, writing in English, she'd make as few mistakes as possible.

"The telephone at Grodka is 81540. Laszlo is always there and will take messages. It would be so fine to see you again. We must talk about all the things we are interested about. Nobody never guards the bridge, so you can come and you can go when you wish. I am supposing you hear a lot from Vienna, being so close. And I am living only seventy miles from Budapest, where things are very hot, very—heated. A thought. Do you have a light on your bicycle? In case you are returning to Andau after it is night?"

How to handle the matter at the mission?

Woodroe was excited by the letter. He needed to think about it all, but the students were now seated. He assigned them to read six pages from the book on George Washington he had distributed the day before. He would allow them a half hour. Then he would question them.

I have got to see her.

What the . . . *hell!* Mormons did not use profane language, but the forbidden word did cross his mind. He was speaking to himself, analyzing the question. His duties and obligations to the mission did not commit him to eremitical life when off duty. Whatever the paternalistic, not to say condescending, role of Andrew Goodhart, Woodroe owed him nothing more than dutiful attention to work at the mission. Woodroe Raynor was free to live his own extracurricular life.

He was in any case accustomed to exercising responsibility. He had begun doing that after his father's death. Woodroe Albert Raynor, at sixteen, was now the man of the house, assuming many of the responsibilities his father had exercised before his long, incapacitating illness. Woodroe could always call on Uncle Woodroe, his mother's brother, for advice, and did on such matters as insurance payments and the investment of his father's savings, but all of that was pretty straightforward.

At eighteen, Woodroe had been elected vice president of his high school class. The yearbook editor, under Woodroe's picture, had written, "Most likely to succeed. Because he looks like Elvis Presley." Woodroe had liked that. And after all, Elvis was only a couple of years older than he. Woodroe had academic honors, was referred to as a bright and able young man by his father's friends, and had pleased them all by deferring his Princeton education to serve his Mormon mission.

Yet—he repeated to himself—in his off-hours he was bound only by the responsibilities of his indenture to the church. It would not do to start drinking whiskey, or even coffee or tea, or to smoke cigarettes; or, in the immediate situation, to violate the diplomatic rules of the mission, which forbade alignment with any political movement.

He intended to do none of these forbidden things.

But he *did* intend to visit that lively, interesting, attractive woman, to spend a little time in her company, and also to learn something from her about Hungarian political developments.

During the break he bicycled to the post office. He used the public telephone, and asked the operator whether she could dial a number in Hungary.

"What number?"

He gave it.

Laszlo answered the phone.

Would he kindly leave a message for...Teresa?

"Teresa Molnar?"

"The young lady with Anton. We visited with you on Saturday."

"Ah, you are the American?"

"Yes. Yes, Herr Laszlo."

"What is the message?"

"That I will meet her at Grodka tomorrow, at 1730."

"All right. I will tell her."

2

NOTWITHSTANDING THE DECLARATION of independence he had made to himself the day before, Woodroe didn't inform even Hildred, when he set out on his bicycle, where he was headed. She could reasonably suppose that he was taking the train to Vienna again, maybe to hear a concert, or see a museum, have dinner at a coffee shop, perhaps run into other young Americans and discuss the exciting events in Hungary. Woodroe said only that he'd be gone for supper, not to wait up for him.

He measured the time exactly. Leaving on his bicycle at 4:45, he made it, in briskly cool autumn weather, to the Grodka tavern in Kapuvar twenty-three minutes later. Nothing to it, though the hill on the direct route was steep. About the same time required to travel from Salt Lake to Alta to ski, though of course that hike wasn't done on a bicycle.

He couldn't be certain that Teresa would be there or for that matter certain that she had got his message, so he put a paperback in his pocket, a novel by John Steinbeck. Arriving at Grodka, he walked up to the bar. Laszlo said yes, he had delivered the message, perhaps Teresa would be coming in soon. He nodded Woodroe to an empty table.

Woodroe had the problem of all faithful Mormons finding themselves in a saloon. How to justify using the space without patronizing the host's merchandise. His father had often had to meet with customers, or potential customers, at a bar of their choosing, so

Woodroe knew as a boy that the mere presence of a Mormon at a saloon was not scandalous. He looked about and ordered the orangeade Hildred had got for him on the first visit. At 5:45 he concluded, disconsolate, that she wasn't coming. The bar was filling up, the radio at high volume. If he stayed on, pretty soon he'd find himself hogging a scarce table.

But then she arrived, and her blond freshness made him a little giddy as he bounded to his feet and extended his hand. She had on more lipstick than the other day. Her braided hair seemed to have a special sheen. She wasn't wearing the dry garb of the last time around—instead, a pleated cotton blue skirt and a broad belt with designs in brass. Her gold earrings pierced her ears, and the scent was of the azaleas Woodroe's mother so painstakingly cultivated. She sat down. Without asking, Laszlo brought her a glass of the local wine.

Immediately they were talking animatedly about the great student procession of the day before in Budapest and of the revolutionary implications of the state police's firing on the students. "Now—who would know better than me, working right there at Camp Esterhazy?—*the military itself* is wondering, should they obey central command? Or instead support the students and back Herr Gero, who is now the acting prime minister? *Éppen ezen az éjkszákan*"—in her excitement Teresa had lapsed into her native tongue. "This very night"—she collected herself into English—"we will maybe know what is to happen."

Everyone at Grodka was silent, listening to the radio but with mounting frustration—the broadcaster was clearly bound by the dogmatic overhanging of what had been the Communist government. Every few minutes Laszlo would switch to the BBC, wrestling to understand and relay the highlights. After the second BBC bulletin, Teresa shot up her hand. *"Quiet a moment!"* There was a responsive silence from the twenty men seated about. "The BBC," she translated, "reports that the revolutionary government has announced that it will return the land to the peasants!" To Woodroe she said, "Some of that land will go to Anton!"

The radio went back to the Hungarian. Teresa listened for a few minutes, then got up. "We will go to my little house and listen there to the BBC. They are giving the Budapest news every few minutes."

Woodroe rose too. "How do I pay?"

"Do you have a dollar bill?"

He pulled one out of his wallet. She took it, waved it in sight of Laszlo, and dropped it down on the table. "Come with me."

They were seated in the room of the old barn with the high ceiling. The fireplace was lit, the room large. The bed with the red-quilted bedspread was tucked away in one corner, the lamp at its side unlit. Diagonally across were the sofa and two armchairs; on one windowless side, a refrigerator and stove and a row of cupboards.

The BBC gave reports every half hour, and Woodroe felt the national jubilation. Every few minutes Teresa would switch to the AM set and bring in the news from Budapest. The announcer seemed refreshingly liberated, she said, giving the news now free of government cant. She would relay what was said sentence by sentence. Watching her lightly freckled face, Woodroe felt the excitement of the historic event, and the electric excitement of her company.

Sometime after eight, she stood up and clicked both radios off.

"We will revolve them, the AM and the shortwave. And listen to the news . . . later. Now we will eat. And drink. To the revolution. . . . Woodroe, why must you not drink wine?"

"It's against the rules."

"But Woodroe . . ." The smile was enticing. Bottle in hand, she bent down toward the empty glass on the coffee table, all but baring her breasts to him. "Woodroe, don't you understand? *This is a revolution!* We are free now to do anything we wish! And what I wish is you. But first I wish you to drink to me. And to the revolution. And of course, Woodroe, it is *much* too cold for you to go back to Andau on your bicycle. You will spend the night with me."

At two in the morning she yanked her blanket away and dug her elbow into his side. "Woodroe! Wake up! The prime minister says the government of Hungary will address *all* the student grievances! We will have—you will have—one more glass of wine to celebrate."

Now she yanked the entire bedspread away, laughing.

Woodroe grabbed the blanket and drew it over his waist, lifting himself to his feet.

She was standing naked by the fire, opening a bottle.

All he could think to say was, "Teresa. It is very cold."

"Come closer to the fire."

The fire was roaring now. The BBC kept reporting fresh developments.

Once more she turned the radio off, and beckoned him back to the bed. "Once more, Woodroe. For the revolution."

She promised that if he slept, she would wake him in time to make his way back to the bridge and his bicycle. Later, kissing her and tightening his jacket against the cold, he set out, reflecting on what he had lost in those few hours, and gained.

3

H<small>E DIDN'T GET AWAY ON FRIDAY</small> as he had hoped. That morning, he had appeared, showered and shaved, in time for breakfast with the Goodharts. When the doorbell rang, Andrew left the room, and Hildred permitted herself a smile, mercifully abbreviated and unquestioning. "I hope you found adequate sleeping quarters in Vienna."

Woodroe nodded pleasantly and went back to perusing Vienna's *Der Standard,* which he could now read without any problem. Andrew returned, sat down with a second cup of bouillon, and told Woodroe that they would be conducting that evening an introductory session for six new students. "I haven't met them, but I'm told they know not a word of English." He sighed heavily. "Well, that is what the good Lord sent us here to do, to educate, and care for people."

"How old are they, Andrew?"

"The youngest applicant is fifteen. The oldest is thirty-five—her mother. The others are boys, teenagers. Like you."

God! Woodroe thought. *I'm still a teenager!*

The unscheduled evening session meant no excursion across the bridge that night.

It was hard to believe the news that came over the radio. Imre Nagy appeared to be forming a genuine political government, a coalition of Smallholders, Social Democrats, and National Peasants, as the parties called themselves. At noon Woodroe went to the pay phone, reached Laszlo, and gave word that he would surely be there on Saturday.

Immediately after lunch he took off in the cold rain for the bridge. It was teetering wildly from the heavy wind. He crossed it and walked briskly up to the tavern.

She wasn't there. Laszlo said he had delivered Woodroe's message.

Should he walk over to her barn? He asked Laszlo, Would Anton, tending his farm, be easy to find? No. Anton had left for Budapest. "He will reclaim his land."

Teresa must have been held over on duty at the military camp. He asked, struggling to come up with words Laszlo could understand, if the military was still—like—like *normal* military? Continuing to do routine work?

Laszlo shrugged. He didn't know.

Was there any way to telephone Teresa at work?

Laszlo did not know whether this could be done. He added that he had never telephoned her at work.

What would happen, Woodroe wondered, if he were simply to arrive at the military camp and ask for her?

It took only seconds to acknowledge that this was truly crazy-thought—he was embarrassed that the idea had so much as crossed his mind. *Walk into an army camp in a country governed by a hard Communist regime only three days ago? Whose national military might still be under Communist control?*

He asked Laszlo for paper, and wrote out a three-page letter. He told Teresa that he loved her with all his heart, that he could not sleep for longing for her. He said that she must on all accounts inform Laszlo when next he might come to her, never mind the hour of day or night. If she wanted him in the afternoon—or in the morning, or at midnight—he would simply leave the mission and explain later.

25

He walked over the field to her barn and slipped the letter under the door.

From Andau, he telephoned every day. Laszlo had heard nothing from her. "Perhaps she is in Budapest."

On Wednesday, Andrew Goodhart had a call from Vienna.

Putting down the phone, he informed Woodroe that the two of them would go to Vienna. They had been summoned to meet with the head of the Mormon mission for Austria, presumably to discuss the explosive news from Budapest. "*Just imagine!* The first occupied East European country to shake free of the Soviet Union!"

In Vienna the temperature was cold but the sun bright. A taxi took them to the Mormon mission on Radetskystrasse. The Mormon officials met for four hours. Woodroe was seated with two other young missionaries behind the principals, who were at a long wooden table. It was not too soon, the mission head said, to think ahead. At Salt Lake, the elders would want recommendations from Vienna on how to extend help to the new democratic state.

The seminar over, Andrew and Woodroe got a ride to the station. On the train, the passengers seemed unmoved by the historic events just across the border. They had had so much, these middle-aged Austrians. The takeover by Hitler, the war, the roundup of the Jews, the Gestapo terror followed by the Red Army terror, the awful scarcities, the ever-so-gradual return of life in the American zone, and then the peace treaty. Let Hungary fend for itself.

They were back at five. Woodroe said, simply, that he would not be there for supper.

Again, at Kapuvar, there was no word about Teresa.

Why had there been no letter? Had she received his own letter? He walked again to the barn and slid a penknife probingly under the door. He could tell that the letter left on Saturday had been removed. He wanted to leave a note but was without paper to write on.

He took from his wallet a one-dollar bill and wrote on the border: "Teresa. I must hear from you. I call Laszlo at noon every day. Love from me—and from the free world!"

It was on Thursday that Imre Nagy gave the electric speech announcing that Hungary would withdraw from the Warsaw Pact, the iron pact which bound the Communist satellites to a common defense.

That did it.

The next day the Russian tanks came. And then the terror: the shootings, imprisonments, hangings.

That same night the refugee flight began.

Late Saturday afternoon Woodroe was bound again for Kapuvar. But there were Hungarians flooding north on the bridge, making their wobbly way across with what they could bring with them on their backs. The men who brought suitcases needed to carry them over the handrail—the bridge was too narrow for bulk. There was barely room for Woodroe, struggling to make his way athwart the traffic. Reaching the Hungarian end, finally, he could make out in the last minutes of twilight what seemed thousands of men, women, and children pressing to get down to the crossing.

He bounded past them up to the Grodka. It was closed. He made his way by flashlight to Teresa's barn.

It was dark, but the adjacent farmhouse was lit. He banged on the door. Anton opened it, clutching a rifle.

"Where is Teresa?" Woodroe asked in German.

Anton spat on the ground. "Teresa is with the enemy. She is giving guidance to the Russians. I am going to the bridge. I am going to take my rifle. You can help?"

Dazed, Woodroe nodded. Anton pointed to a large sack. "You can take that."

Woodroe strapped it over his back. Anton took a second sack and, rifle slung over his right shoulder, said simply, "Let us go."

— *William F. Buckley Jr.* —

It was near dawn before they got to the head of the line and after seven when they reached the other end, walking inch by inch to freedom in Austria. There were thousands of refugees milling about the Austrian bank, many setting out on the nine-kilometer trek to Andau, the closest village center. Woodroe pointed to the bicycle chained to a nearby tree. "That is mine."

When they reached it, Woodroe said, "I know the road to Andau that goes around the hill."

"Good. You go if you want. I will stay here and watch."

Woodroe sat down with him. They would pause for a while and survey the bridge. Anton pulled a stick of bread from one of the sacks and broke off a piece for Woodroe.

It was near nine that they heard the shouts. Two armored cars could be seen descending the hill at the far end of the bridge, followed by a column of soldiers. Across the divide they could hear voices coming through megaphones, but not the words that were spoken. An armored car positioned itself at the head of the bridge, cutting off access to it. Two men in uniform wearing thick winter coats carried a supply of what seemed like logs in olive-green cases. They disappeared under the bridge's end span.

"They are going to dynamite it!" Woodroe said.

Anton raised his rifle. His shot felled a soldier standing by the armored car.

A shot fired back, hitting the tree trunk above their heads. A second fatal shot hit Anton between his eyes. A third entered Woodroe's hip. He dragged himself to the sheltered side of the tree. Moments later he heard the explosion. He edged his head around to see the bridge of Andau wrenched from Hungarian soil, swung down over the Einserkanal, hanging from the edge, fifty meters from where he lay wounded.

Somebody, one of those thousands on the Austrian bank, dressed Woodroe's wound. Sometime later, he didn't know how many hours later, he was transported through the throng to Andau. And later—on the same day, he had the impression—he was in the hospital. Several weeks after that he was learning to walk with a crutch when Vice President Richard Nixon, fresh from victory at the polls in the Eisenhower-Nixon landslide of 1956, was suddenly there with his entourage and the press, on a whirlwind visit in the bitter days after the Soviet army had done its work in Hungary.

Nixon made many stops in the refugee centers of Austria, where 200,000 Hungarians were being cared for. When he came by the hospital bed in Vienna, he clasped Woodroe's hand. A photographer recorded the moment and the embassy got a print. The next day Woodroe was given a copy.

Yes, Woodroe now knew what treachery was about. He had known since he was a mere nineteen-year-old. That wasn't, by Big Ben time, all that long ago; he was only twenty-five in 1962, but the bridge of Andau seemed forever ago.

After Andau had come Princeton; then, without even a pause, the John Birch Society of Robert Welch (Woodroe now addressed him, at his invitation, as "Bob," after a year of "Mr. Welch"). One small part of what happened to him in his lifetime had become, in a modest way, public knowledge: he could force himself to smile on that, that moment when Woodroe Raynor and Vice President Richard Nixon had shared a camera screen. The Birch Society had reproduced the picture, sending it to chapter presidents, when Woodroe joined the staff.

Nixon! Nixon was now, six years after the Hungarian revolution, reduced to running not for president—he had done that, losing to Senator Kennedy—but for governor. Governor of his home state of

California. The French called that, Woodroe remembered from his exposure to French maxims at Princeton, *"reculer pour mieux sauter"*— one step back, two steps forward. Get elected governor of California in 1962 in order to maximize your chances of running for president again in 1964. This, Woodroe thought reproachfully, was the Nixon who had thrown cold water on Senator Joe McCarthy. Yes, and the Nixon who, at a press conference in 1960, had thrown cold water on what everybody knew was the John Birch Society, though he hadn't mentioned the Society's name, just "Radical Right." Woodroe doubted Nixon had ever read Ayn Rand's *Fountainhead.* If he had, he might have learned something about the need to remain true to one's principles.

Nixon *of all people* had to know something about the depths of the Communist conspiracy. He had had a full taste of it when, going hard after Alger Hiss, he ran into that great stone wall of resistance—the people who *would not tolerate* the surrealistic idea that one of their own was *a traitor.* Alger Hiss. Pure-blooded product of the Establishment, Johns Hopkins, and Harvard, clerk to the august Oliver Wendell Holmes, rising figure in the service of Franklin Roosevelt's New Deal. The same man who wielded the very first gavel at the founding conference of the United Nations in San Francisco. Nixon had fought his way through the Hiss case; why didn't he continue to fight? Take on the next, hidden (and not all that hidden) layer of men and women whose torpor and treachery for fifteen years had been responsible for event after event that led to defeat after defeat—in China, in Korea, in Berlin, in weaponry, in space. Way back at age nineteen, Woodroe had learned about such things firsthand. A lifetime's education.

He kept the Nixon picture taken in the hospital. He didn't exhibit it, though at Princeton he had pulled it out one time to show to his roommate; and he had shown it to Robert Welch when he was being interviewed for a job with the John Birch Society, where he would try to advance the movement of the Hungarian freedom fighters, and continue to learn from his experience with Teresa.

4

WHEN LEONORA GOLDSTEIN was sixteen, she participated in a lottery ($1) sponsored by the Atlantic Longshoremen's Union, to which her father had belonged, and lo! she won it. Her surprise and her excitement overwhelmed her mother when she heard the news at the end of the afternoon, in the kitchen of the small Brooklyn apartment. Rachel Goldstein was seized by her daughter without being told immediately the reason for it all and couldn't maintain her balance, let alone open her mouth to speak orderly words. Leonora was at once kissing her, attempting to dance with her, pulling her on the ears, alternately pounding on her mother's shoulders. Finally Rachel Goldstein managed to pinion her daughter over the back of the sofa, grabbing her fists together and saying, in her accented English, "Lee, Lee, now *Yossel, genug shoyn*—You stop that now, you hear me! What have they done to you? Made you a Rhodes scholar?"

Leonora stopped. "Momma, before I tell you, can I have a—glass of champagne?"

She laughed joyously at her mother's astonishment.

"No champagne in the refrigerator? How come?" More laughter. "Have you *ever* had champagne, Momma? I know, I know. But can I have a Coca-Cola? Or—" What else did the widow Goldstein routinely keep in the refrigerator? Tomato juice? Club soda? Leonora was too excited to explore the question. *"Anything."* She was hogging the suspense. Rachel, a wink in her eye, would carry the game one step further: she would feign indifference.

"Well, Leonora. Let me see. Could I brew you some nice tea? That would take a few minutes. But who is in a hurry? Not Rachel Goldstein."

She had outwitted her daughter.

"*Wait a few minutes?* To tell you about the biggest thing that's happened in my whole life?"

"The biggest thing that's happened in your life, young lady, is that you were"—Rachel turned her head aside—"born in America."

"All right, Momma. And the second-biggest thing that's happened to me is that I won the lottery."

Rachel Goldstein looked up. Lottery?

"The union lottery. You probably forgot. They came in February. You gave them one dollar for one ticket. And wrote down my name."

Now Rachel joined in the celebration with her broad smile, cocking back her oval face with the gray hair tied trimly behind her neck, always convenient for a scrubwoman who spent time on her knees. She loosened her apron and threw it over the counter. "You won! My darling girl, you won! Your father would be smiling and laughing in his grave! Beat the longshoremen's union finally!"

They spent most of the evening poring over the travel folder. Leonora's first prize put her on the tour the Atlantic Longshoremen's Union, in company with the longshoremen's union in San Francisco, was sponsoring. The itinerary: London, Paris, Milan, Rome, Naples. Twenty-eight days, including passage eastbound on the SS *Continental*—a dazzling seagoing adventure—and back on Pan American Airways.

Rachel wore her glasses now and examined the folder. "I'm surprised they let you in."

"Momma, not everybody connected with the union lottery knows about Dad."

"His killers may remember him."

There was no point in going back into the fatal union brawl. Leonora revered the memory of her late father, and was faithful to his anti-Communist faith, about which she had been taught as soon as she could reason. Her father, the widow had taught the daughter, had been killed in the battle for control of the union fought by Communist "goons," as Rachel insisted on calling them. "They may be socialists also, but mostly they are goons."

But that was back in 1940, during the Nazi-Communist Pact, when the San Francisco longshoremen and selected union allies in New York and Philadelphia agitated against any munitions aid to the embattled Great Britain, Stalin having declared Hitler his ally. Leonora was a year old. She wanted, tonight, to talk only about her forthcoming adventure in Europe, and the evening was heady with excitement up until Leonora said in passing that she would need her birth certificate in order to get a passport.

Rachel was silent. There was the problem. The birth certificate was forged.

When Leo and Rachel, aged thirty-seven and thirty-five, applied for visas at the U.S. consulate in Gdansk, Rachel had gone to great pains to conceal her pregnancy. They had tickets on the *Vistula,* bound for New York. No woman bearing a child qualified for a visa: United States immigration laws were dodgy and restrictive. It was one thing to give out a ninety-day visa to the Goldsteins, permitting them to visit their cousins in New York, another thing entirely to have a visa holder give birth in the United States, entitling the progeny to full citizenship. Desperate to board the boat, Rachel filed by the visa clerk wearing a corset and a voluminous dress. She succeeded in making herself entirely amorphous—a pretty, chunky Jewish peasant woman, lucky enough to have a husband who could pay for a round-trip vacation.

The deception had gone well enough, except that three days before reaching New York, Rachel had given birth. The ship's purser dutifully recorded the birth as having taken place at sea, depositing a copy of the ship's paper with immigration officials at the Forty-second Street pier. In ordinary circumstances, the immigration authorities would have imposed strict surveillance on a foreign baby without any claim to U.S. citizenship, but these were not ordinary circumstances—Hitler had attacked Poland two days before the ship arrived. What exactly the SS *Vistula* would proceed to do had not been established, but there was no thought given to forcing the Goldsteins to return on it to Hitler-occupied Poland.

That settled that problem, but Leo Goldstein didn't want the little baby to go through life with ambiguous citizenship. His obliging rabbi in Fulton Street took the ship's birth certificate and devised another, certifying that Leonora Goldstein had been born on September 3, 1939, in Brooklyn, New York.

Rachel worried that sixteen years later, when Leonora presented the birth certificate to get a passport, an alarm would sound. Somewhere, extant, was the *Vistula*'s logbook, recording the birth at sea. If the worst happened, maybe she would write to Senator McCarthy and tell him her late husband had fought against the communization of the Atlantic Longshoremen's Union.

The mortal engagement between the band of New York longshoremen who had resisted the West Coast Communist-guided organizers had been papered over by the New York police. They set the fatal episode down to "an accident," precipitated by a person or persons unknown. Rachel Goldstein was befriended by Joe Silverman, a young lawyer. He promised he would do what he could, and attempted to enlist the aid of anti-Communist labor union leaders in the city. Harry Bridges, who controlled the dominant San Francisco branch of the alliance of longshoremen, decided to step in—now that Hitler was the enemy, the flow of war materiel to Russia must not be interrupted by labor union strife. He instructed the union managers in New York to negotiate. Leonora was just two years old when the union, now eager to help Great Britain and other allies of the Soviet Union, issued its finding—that Leo Goldstein had died in the course of duty and was entitled to a (modest) pension. In return, Rachel signed the release written up by Silverman. She would continue her work as a cleaning woman at the courthouse, but she knew now that Leonora would one day go to college.

Never mind the release, there was no language in the settlement that prevented Rachel from teaching Leonora about the Communists, who had now inherited all of Poland and much of the rest of Eastern Europe.

Rachel had emerged with Leonora from the passport office, breathing easily for the first time in days: no questions had been raised about the legitimacy of Lee's birth certificate. A month later, back from her tour, Leonora returned to her studies. Though still just a senior in high school, she was advanced enough to enroll in a class at Hunter College. She gave more than formal attention to her father's legacy and her mother's undeviating opposition to the Communists. But she went much further than Rachel. She had rather confused her mother when, a year ago, she put it to her that "the genus, not the species" was the cause for proper concern. Communism was simply the most virulent expression of what her father had fought against. The evil was socialism. Now, in 1956, just weeks after starting her class at Hunter, she came home one day to tell her mother that the college's undergraduate political organization was "a socialist front."

"What do you mean?"

Leonora explained. The majority of the students, though most of them were not yet of voting age, were backing Adlai Stevenson in the fall election.

"That isn't socialism, Lee. That's the Democratic Party."

Leonora explained that although it was correct that the Democratic Party had opposed people who were formally Communist, like Earl Browder, the policies of Roosevelt-Truman-Stevenson were welfarist, a form of socialism, "even though it is diluted."

Rachel listened, and remembered the intensity of her own and Leo's political opinions when they were seventeen years old. She had in times past described the life of the young Goldsteins in Poland, but Leonora was a better debater than her mother, who had less to say when Leonora insisted that the special privations her parents had suffered in Poland were because they were Jewish. "That burden prevailed," she argued. "But the burden in Poland now isn't just for Jews. It's for everybody, because the state is king. Socialism is taking over all of Europe. Remember, on my summer trip I was there when socialist governments were elected."

"Well, the same thing will certainly happen in America, if that's the case," Rachel observed.

As a high school junior, Lee had won two prizes, one for her studies, a second for the debate team. She began her comment oracularly, but when her mother looked over wistfully at the television set—she didn't like to miss the Ed Sullivan program—Leonora caught herself. Her humor usually rescued her from solemnity. "Momma, you shouldn't listen to Ed Sullivan."

"Is he a socialist?" Rachel looked up with alarm.

Leonora laughed and blew a kiss, aborting her lecture.

While her mother fiddled with the controls, Leonora sat on the kitchen stool and called Josiah. She had promised she'd take his advice. And of course she knew—Josiah didn't advertise it, but two or three students at Hunter knew it—that Josiah had met the author and philosopher Ayn Rand. Josiah had signed up for the new course in objectivism taught by Nathaniel Branden, and Miss Rand was often physically present, taking questions.

The very thought of laying eyes on Miss Rand caused Leonora to tighten her hands in excitement.

"Folks," Ed Sullivan came on, *"we're going to enjoy ourselves tonight, but there's sadness tonight, I'm telling you, because the Soviet army has struck out against the freedom people—the young people in Budapest—who were trying to give freedom and democracy a chance. So let's have a moment of silence, before we roll up our sleeves and welcome—well, I won't mention his name until after our moment of silence."*

Leonora, speaking on the phone, her voice lowered, could see over to the television screen in the living room. She said to Josiah that she would absolutely follow his advice and learn about Miss Rand's philosophy. "But right now I'm going to tune in on Elvis Presley."

"Me too. We didn't have much of a moment of silence, you and me, Lee."

"We'll do more than that to commemorate the Hungarian freedom fighters. Let's start right now, and make . . . a silent pledge."

5

Aᴙʏɴ Rᴀɴᴅ ᴛᴀᴘᴘᴇᴅ ᴛʜᴇ ᴀsʜ from her cigarette into the saucer. She sat, as usual, at the desk in her sparely deco-rated apartment at Thirty-sixth Street and Park Avenue. It would soon be the shortest day of the year. She looked forward to longer light, when spring and summer would let her read at her desk later into the day. But now she needed to turn on the overhead lamp. There were manuscripts on the desk to be read, awaiting her judg-ment on whether they were fit for publication in the Objectivist newsletter she contemplated.

She didn't *feel* lively. She closed her eyes and reminded herself that, by her canon, there had to be a reason for feeling under the weather, and that it was her responsibility to exercise her faculties to identify that reason. It would be immature and slovenly to put off such an inquiry inasmuch as, of course, a finding would explain her unusual torpor.

. . . A finding, not *the* finding. A finding would be true, the fruit of epistemological fidelity in reasoning. *The* finding could be what-ever nudged a public opinion poll or the jury in this way or that, toward popularity or unpopularity, guilt or innocence. A jury could of course reach the correct verdict—a true "finding"—*provided a jury could be got to think!*

And why should Americans not think correctly? They were per-fectly free to think. It wasn't, in America today, nearing 1958, the way it had been in Russia in 1921, when Alissa Rosenbaum had enrolled at the University of Leningrad. *Leningrad!* she snorted. She would think of it as *Petrograd*. That was better than "St. Petersburg," as the Anglo world had called the city of Peter the Great for 221 years until Lenin renamed it. To say "*Saint* Petersburg" you had to utter the word "Saint." She did not like words that paid implicit deference to religious convention. She had demonstrated in her teachings that religion was nothing more than the "mysticism of the mind."

Why do not Americans think rationally? Because they do not know how to think at all. This is not so about every American. It is so about most Americans. The girl in the objectivism class this morning had asked a stupid question. What do you do when asked a stupid question? You say it is a stupid question.

She thought of Barbara Branden, her assistant. *Dear Barbara.* Barbara was the wife of Nathaniel Branden, her closest associate, the true apostle of objectivism, *very nearly on a par with me in his mastery of the subject. I saw Barbara wince when I rebuked that stupid student. Will she reproach me tomorrow? I can tell when she is offended. She doesn't have to say so. My eyes are all-seeing, my ears all-hearing.*

Rand snuffed out her cigarette and let a half smile come to her face. *Only God could reproach Ayn Rand, and He does not exist. Aristotle might have tried it, but it would have been presumptuous, because Aristotle didn't get it all correct, wandering off into cosmology, inquiring into prime movers, etc., etc. Several members of my Collective were in attendance at class; they usually are. I think it was Nathaniel who first termed my inner circle the "Collective." I was amused at the use of one of the most despicable terms by which politics is corrupted brought into use in any association with my philosophy. In objectivism, there is no place—zero place!—for collectivism. My Collective is generally there, at my own classes especially, and at those classes that Nathaniel teaches when I am due to appear at the question period. Of course Nathan and dear Barbara are always there and, most of the time, Frank.* Her thoughts turned to her husband of thirty-eight years. *Nobody calls me Mrs. O'Connor. And nobody would call him Mr. Rand, though he doesn't mind people knowing who his wife is. The world will not gather to celebrate the work of Frank O'Connor, artist, though his paintings are pleasant and figurative. I must get back soon to my paper on the philosophical bases of art. But there are other things that take precedence. The whole world, Bennett tells me, wants me to appear to defend my novel. He doesn't put it that way, "defend" my novel. He was concerned, in the first few weeks after* Atlas *was published, because so many critics were negative—or so they told me: I don't read criticisms of my work. What on earth is to be gained from doing so? Reinforced knowledge of the arrant ignorance of so many reviewers? I don't need to do further epistemological work on that matter.*

Again she smiled, just a little, pulling out from her neat folder marked RANDOM HOUSE yesterday's letter from Bennett Cerf, the publisher. He told her that *Atlas Shrugged* would go into yet another printing, the third. Ayn Rand was not unaccustomed to success. *The Fountainhead,* published in 1943, had been an enormous success, and the movie based on it, featuring Gary Cooper, had made her the preeminent novelist celebrating the independent will. In the case of *The Fountainhead,* the will of the architect who, rather than accept unwelcome modifications on his new building, simply tore it down.

But it had been a decade and a half since her great success, and Bennett Cerf wanted to generate as much steam as possible to keep selling *Atlas.* It would help, his letter said, if she would accept just a few of the invitations to appear on television to talk about her book.

She would not reply to the letter. Bennett would know what that meant. It meant no.

Raising her head, she saw the silent girl standing just inside the open door. "Who are you?" Quickly she remembered. "Yes. You are"—she looked down at her memo pad—"Leonora Goldstein."

"Yes, ma'am. Barbara—Mrs. Branden—told me you said it would be all right to come by just to . . . meet you."

"Yes. I have it down here. You may sit down. Over there. Now. You have read *The Fountainhead,* and of course *Atlas Shrugged.* Have you read *We the Living?*"

"Yes, ma'am."

"*Anthem?*"

"Yes, ma'am."

"Where were you born?"

"Brooklyn, ma'am."

"When?"

"Nineteen thirty-nine."

"Where did your mother come from?"

"Poland."

"How did she get out of Poland?"

"My father's savings. They bought a ticket on a Polish liner."

"What did your father do?"

"He was a shipping clerk. He is dead. He died fighting the union Communists in 1940."

"What does your mother do?"

"She is a janitor. At the courthouse in Brooklyn."

"Barbara says you are attending college at Hunter. And that you want to work for us as a file clerk and assistant researcher. We have a very small budget."

"I know that. Mrs. Branden told me. I said I didn't care—"

"What do you *mean* you don't care! Does that mean that money is without meaning to you? Does that mean that the money that you pay to the store where you buy meat and potatoes and the store where you buy books and pencils and notepaper should *mean nothing* to the people who produce those things? The people who express their freedoms by choosing to produce for others and to live in a capitalist society that encourages trade and exchange and industry? Does all of that mean *nothing* to you?"

"Oh, yes it does, ma'am. It means a lot—individualism and capitalism and free exchange. I know because of what you have written on the subject—it's what makes me so eager to work for the Objectivist enterprise. I can't work for nothing, I didn't mean that, Miss Rand. I meant that I was willing to work for the least wages just to learn, to be in the company of Mr. Branden and Mrs. Branden, to hope to become a qualified Objectivist."

"There are only *two* Objectivists. Me and Nathaniel Branden. Others are called students of objectivism."

"Well, that is what I want to be."

Ayn Rand looked at the nineteen-year-old critically. The girl wore a wool skirt and a striped blue shirt and sweater over ample bosoms. Her dark brown hair was neatly tucked back behind her ears. She wore a trace of lipstick on full lips. Her brown eyes looked out directly, her nose and well-shaped cheeks were winter white. Her posture was that of an aspirant. Ayn Rand was familiar with the aspirant class.

"I will tell Barbara I have no objection to your taking the vacant position."

"Thank you, Miss Rand."

"You do not need to thank me for looking after my own interests as *I* see them. You have much to learn. To look after my own interests does not prohibit me from looking after yours. You should change your name."

"Change my... first name? Last name?"

"You can think about changing your first name, though there is no reason for it. Change Goldstein. You are aware that I was born Alissa Rosenbaum. Everybody is aware of it. Now, thirty years later, we have as common terms 'Randian,' 'Rand-like,' even 'Rand-worthy.'" She let out a mini-chuckle. "It would not have been convenient to speak of a 'Rosenbaumite.' You no doubt have seen somewhere that Nathaniel Branden was born Nathan Blumenthal? It is hardly accidental that his last name incorporates my own. B-*Rand*-en." She looked penetratingly at her visitor.

"I would not want to disguise that my father was Jewish."

"You need *disguise* nothing. And *I*—have nothing further to say to you. You may report to Barbara, as directed."

"Thank you—" Leonora corrected herself. "I am very pleased to be in the company of—to be a student of—your order."

Ayn Rand nodded and put a cigarette into her long holder.

6

"It's easy to remember how old I am," Robert Welch, tall, balding, animated, had begun his historic seminar in Indianapolis on December 8, 1958. "I was born minutes before the twentieth century came along." Welch liked to make his points expansively, as his listeners had abundantly discovered by the end of the second day, when he tied it all together and said that he was founding an organization which he would call the John Birch Society.

True to form, he didn't let it go with the simple "born minutes before the twentieth century." He tied it down exactly: the assembly learned that it had been on the first day of December, a Friday, "and when the century actually arrived, I was all of thirty days old." After that chronological fix, he proceeded with a little jollity, which appealed to Robert Welch and to most of his listeners.

But the levities were infrequent. Mostly there were long stretches of analysis and cadenzas of galvanizing, heroic rhetoric.

"I guess I was a prodigy of sorts." He guarded immediately against the peril of self-praise with a qualifier: "It was my mother, Lina, who chased after me. Maybe that's not the right word to use, chased after me. Because I was only two years old when she taught me to read. I could read at that age faster than I could walk or run!"

Twenty years ago—it was easy to do the arithmetic: in 1938, when he was thirty-eight—his pace, when he was addressing an assembly,

44

had been different. He had become accustomed to press briefings, which he gave regularly in Washington and occasionally in other cities. After he began his public career as chairman of the education committee of the National Association of Manufacturers, typically there would be press kits to hand out at press conferences. His answers were succinct, though not his expositions. When his designation as education chairman had been announced in Washington, a press conference had been called. Three reporters showed up. A weathery lady ("Miss Greer") had covered the NAM for the Associated Press for years and was renowned for her ability to take notes even as her eyes focused unremittingly on the speaker. She asked the first question. "Mr. Welch, what are your qualifications for serving as chairman of the NAM's education committee?"

Welch permitted himself a smile. A very brief smile—he would not wish to appear unctuous.

"I am a graduate of the University of North Carolina." He paused. "I was sixteen years old when I graduated."

That revelation got raised eyebrows and a nod of appreciation. And then the question, Was that the end of his academic training?

"Actually, no. At seventeen I entered the United States Naval Academy. I was seventeen in 1917." He used that mnemonic device every time he reasonably could.

"So you graduated from Annapolis?"

"Actually, no. In 1919, after two years, I pulled out."

"Mr. Welch, excuse me," the first questioner said, "but we have to ask these questions. Did you fall behind in your academic work?"

"I was number four in a class of about a thousand cadets."

"Why did you pull out?"

"The war was over. I decided to go to law school. The Harvard Law School."

The president of the National Association of Manufacturers, the silver-haired Eliot Parsons, smiled with satisfaction at the progressive display of the credentials of his education chairman.

"So you graduated from the law school. Did you go on to practice law?"

"No. I pulled out of law school halfway through my third year—"

"I guess I'm not going to ask you whether you pulled out for academic reasons." Louella Greer was in the inquisitorial mode.

Robert Welch took the bait. A little smile on his face, he said, "I wanted to start a company to sell fudge. I had a recipe."

Neither of the two reporters asked what the recipe was, though one contributed, mechanically, "Yes. Your candy company."

"No, my brother's, actually. I folded my firm and joined his. The James O. Welch Company."

"Successful?"

"Yes." This time Welch's smile was broad.

President Parsons raised his hand and said he thought it appropriate now for the new education chairman to say a word or two about what he hoped to do in the service of education.

Robert Welch started in. He spoke mostly from memory and with considerable fluency. His approach was didactic, but not pedantic. Welch had never taught school and hadn't picked up the habit of talking like teachers on duty. He was the businessman briefing business associates, merchandisers, colleagues. He wanted to tell a story, and this required that he hold the attention of those he was addressing. There was always a great deal on Welch's mind, and education was a foremost concern.

He had spoken twenty-one minutes on the shortcomings of public education when, slightly lowering her head to minimize disruption, Miss Greer gathered her notes, rose, and edged out of the room, leaving Welch talking to a dozen members of the staff of the NAM and the single remaining reporter.

He stressed his belief that education was the key to the success of the whole American proposition, that students needed not only to learn to read and write but to understand the historical basis of American ideals.

Robert Welch didn't reveal to the press that day, decades ago, the dark thoughts and premonitions that fermented in his mind. Although many businessmen affiliated with the National Association of Manufacturers were blunt in their privately expressed disapproval of the policies of President Franklin Delano Roosevelt, the rule at the NAM was that no official should take a partisan position at any public gathering. On legislation, yes, they were free to question, even to denounce, legislative initiatives or bills, but no adverse comments were to be made about government officials. The taboo on criticizing the president himself was especially stressed, with war in Europe threatening.

So Welch mostly kept it to himself, but what he didn't say to his education-minded audiences was written out on his typewriter vociferously, as he stayed home in Belmont, by Boston, with his wife and two children. He gave time to the pursuit of mathematics and the appreciation of poetry, and he persevered with his intensive general reading. He would, one day, have accumulated a personal library of five thousand books, every one of which he had read.

When war came, he went to an intelligence military unit in the U.S. theater. Soon after his discharge he traveled to Great Britain, specifically intending to survey the effects of two years of socialism under the postwar government of Prime Minister Clement Attlee. As he toured Britain his determination hardened: he would devote more of his time to antisocialist activity, now brilliantly menacing as the Communists tightened their grip on Eastern Europe. It was perhaps his addiction to mathematics and logic that prompted him, with increasing insistence, to search out the causes of current problems. *If A, then B* was a logical sequence. It meant that if Situation A exists, then derivative Situation B must also exist. If all men die, then Jones will one day die. Well then, if America is the land of the brave and the free, why doesn't America pursue policies that enhance freedom and reward bravery? How was it possible to account for the world he observed, in 1946? We had fought a great war to ensure sovereignty for Poland, and Poland was now a Soviet satellite. How was it possible that with the military advantages we enjoyed, the Soviet army should have been the first to reach Berlin? And having reached Berlin, the Soviet Union would, of course, make yet another satellite of the part of Germany over which its armies held sway.

His curiosity in the search of a cause-for-it-all continued, and his indignation and frustration increased. And then one day in June 1950, President Truman led us into war in Korea. A war, as Welch saw it, precipitated by the disastrous policies of Truman's secretary of state, Dean Gooderham Acheson. We engaged in the military contest against a Communist force under the command of an American general whose skills and tenacity were unequaled. So? President Truman proceeded to win the war? No. He proceeded to fire General MacArthur.

The cordite in Robert Welch's mind burst into flames. He collected his thoughts into a massive letter, which he distributed to friends. A copy of it was spotted by Henry Regnery, whose publishing firm in Chicago brought the letter out as a book in 1952, with the title *May God Forgive Us*. The closing paragraph was 200-proof Welch, the toughness, the unsparing postulation of cause and effect, the fire and the thunder of exhortation. People read the words, and now the little group in Indianapolis would hear him pronounce them:

> For the pusillanimous part that we have played in all this spreading horror; for our indifference to the grief of others; for our apathy to the crimes we saw and our blindness to those we should have seen; for our gullibility in the acceptance of veneered treason and our easy forgetfulness even when the veneer has been rubbed off; for all our witting and unwitting help to the vicious savages of the Kremlin and to their subordinate savages everywhere, may God—and our fellow men—some day forgive us!

7

W ELCH CAME ACROSS THE NAME in what became a near-
exhaustive study of documents pertaining to the broad
question of Communist activity at home and abroad. It was in the
Senate Office Building that he read the typed report on a singular
episode. It recorded a murder in Anhwei Province in China, near
Hsuwai, on August 25, 1945, ten days after the Japanese surrender.
The Senate committee report had been prompted by protests
against the relatively listless investigation of the death of a young
army captain. The report recorded the last words heard spoken by
the twenty-seven-year-old commander of the besieged U.S. Army
unit.

The report told of the small detachment (four American officers,
one Chinese liaison officer, five Chinese aides, and two Korean
noncoms) superintending a transfer of equipment dispatched by an
American army base. The mission had begun at an American airfield
near Fowyang, in northern Anhwei Province. It had been headed for
Tsingtao on the Shantung Peninsula and moved by a railroad car.
What exactly was in that car, and what exactly was the mission's purpose, Welch couldn't find out. He probed the report and then used
his own resources, unsuccessfully: the U.S. Army kept the relevant
orders sealed. Welch was tipped off, confidentially, by his friend Jack
McIntyre, who worked in the Pentagon and had personally examined the document, that its classification as "Secret" was unneces-
sary, inasmuch as there was nothing there the disclosure of which

could in any way damage American military or diplomatic interests. Welch was left to brood about it.

Although the war with Japan had officially ended ten days earlier, there were still three million Japanese in China. They were mostly disciplined soldiers and service personnel, a significant foreign presence whose peaceable repatriation was one of the huge postwar problems at hand. What proved especially threatening were scattered Chinese Communist guerrillas who had been mobilized to fight the Japanese under the Communist command of Yenan. They were undisciplined...or *were* they entirely undisciplined? Welch wondered about that.

There had been a break in the railroad line, so the U.S. mission had to settle for a self-propelled handrail, assembled at the near end of the break, in order to resume the tedious trek to Tsingtao. It was soon after they were under way that they were stopped. Armed Communist soldiers detached most members of the American complement to a village fifty yards away from the rail line, leaving only one U.S. captain and one Chinese liaison officer with the handrail. Lieutenant Tung had stepped forward to converse with the Communist commander, whose riflemen had trained their weapons on the U.S. convoy. After the conversation, Tung walked back to warn Captain John Birch that he sensed danger ahead. He advised Birch to make his way back to the village to which his men had retreated. The words later quoted by Tung as having been spoken by Captain Birch minutes before the guerrillas opened fire on him (and on Tung) were, "It doesn't make much difference what happens to me, but it is of utmost importance that my country learn now whether these people are friend or foe."

Robert Welch permitted himself to wonder why Captain John Birch had been left with any doubt, in 1945, that the Communist soldiers who had stopped him were foe, not friend. Yet what, exactly, had motivated the executioners to do what they did on August 25? Captain Birch was felled by a bullet to the leg. When his corpse was recovered the next day, a physical examination showed that he had been stabbed repeatedly by a bayonet, his body shoved into a ditch, left either dead or dying. Lieutenant Tung had been found alongside, barely alive.

Welch wondered: Why did these Communist soldiers kill an American soldier, an ally against Japan? He turned his dogged energies to the inquiry and eventually learned that complaints from comrade military officers and from Captain Birch's family had been insistent enough to reach, finally, the desk of Mao Tse-tung himself. Chairman Mao sent out the explanation that, regrettably, one of his soldiers—who, exactly, he did not know—had evidently mistaken John Birch for a militant Japanese soldier ignorant of the week-old surrender. Welch knew that this explanation was preposterous. For one thing, John Birch looked about as Asiatic as Jimmy Stewart.

What a remarkable man, John Birch, Welch thought. He was born in India, where his father served as a Protestant missionary. The family returned to Georgia when John was still a boy, and he later attended Mercer University in Macon. In 1940, at age twenty-two, Birch went to China to continue the missionary work of his father. When, in 1942, he left the mission to join the American army, he was placed in a special intelligence unit, where his knowledge of the Chinese language and culture proved especially useful. He was greatly valuable to General Claire Chennault, commander of the Flying Tigers, whose assignment it was to provision anti-Japanese resistance units in diverse areas of China. Welch could discern, from reports, letters, and interviews with Chinese and Americans who had worked with him, that Captain Birch was a magnetic presence, a young man who deeply affected those he worked with.

Surely it was no accident, then, that John Birch should have been singled out for special treatment by a Chinese Communist military unit? Those Communist soldiers were probably not as footloose as

American diplomats and army chiefs found it convenient to suppose, pursuing as they were doing *everywhere in the world* (Robert Welch underlined the words in his letter) coexistence with Communists. That amounted to giving in to them at every juncture—today that little village in Anhwei Province, yesterday Yalta and Potsdam, the capital cities of Western retreat.

Robert Welch made his decision.

He would write a book. *The Life of John Birch,* he would call it. It was only after the publisher, Henry Regnery, had the manuscript in hand that Welch thought to give it the subtitle *In the Story of One American Boy, the Ordeal of His Age.* Welch would tell the story and express his suspicions. He would not identify himself completely with John Birch, Christian. "Many of us today cannot share the simple and fundamental faith which moved John Birch to such a self-sacrificing life of service to his fellow men, but with his cause."

Welch, once the book was in print, would wait four years before promulgating the final, great memorial to the young Christian American martyr: the John Birch Society, a national society consecrated to mobilization against the worldwide Communist threat. That was four years off, but in the book, the necessary thinking and analysis were done.

In his book on Birch, Robert Welch reached back and told of the Communist infiltration of the New Deal. ("The time has certainly come to stop pussyfooting around with ambiguous language about important truths of our recent history.") He told it all. He wrote of Communist agents Lauchlin Currie and Harry Hopkins, Alger Hiss and David Niles, Alan Nunn May and Klaus Fuchs. He wrote of labor union chief Sidney Hillman and analyzed why President Roosevelt had solicited from Hillman approval of Harry Truman as vice president.

That was the politics of the accommodationists and the capitulators. And it was not therefore surprising that John Birch should be singled out as the first martyr of the Cold War. "Although determined on a career of ascetic dedication for himself, [Birch] had a fundamental American respect for the desire to own property" (the young John Birch had intended to acquire some farmland). Thus he was explained by Welch not only as a Christian missionary, but as a nascent capitalist. Birch's faith "was a dynamic faith, which pointed the way, through humility, brotherhood, and righteousness, to a better world composed of more noble human beings."

At his desk in Belmont, surrounded by his books and papers, Welch worked into the night devising a suitable peroration for his book. It was appropriate, he reflected, that the rest of the people in his house were asleep. The whole world was asleep. But now the memory of John Birch would no longer sleep.

He bent over his typewriter.

As John lay dying during that last hour or two of agony, after he had been shot and bayoneted and his body tossed aside, he must have realized that the rise of the anti-Christ, which he had foreseen, was already upon us. There is no way in which we can reach back, across the nine-year interval, and let him know that his death was not in vain. What really matters is whether his sacrifice does in fact help to awaken his countrymen to their danger and their duty. If we rediscover some of our sounder spiritual values in the example of his life, recharge our determination from the spark of his courage, and learn essential truths about our enemy from the lesson of his murder, then his death at twenty-seven ceases to be a tragedy, for in a full lifetime he could not have accomplished more.

8

ROBERT WELCH GAVE CONSIDERABLE thought to how to structure what he thought of as the high command of his prospective society. "High command" in terms of public recognition—in no other sense, commanders. His society would require central direction. He had learned from the Objectivist model and the Nathaniel Branden Institute. He had read and admired both *The Fountainhead* and *Atlas Shrugged*. The Ayn Rand movement implicitly acknowledged that she—Miss Rand—could not share with anyone authority for the development of objectivist thought, however complete her confidence in Nathaniel Branden. So Welch would not encourage any illusion of democratic leadership in a society whose animating epiphanies were, singularly, his own. A lot of people knew a lot of things about the Soviet conspiracy and the strength of its arm in the United States, but Robert Welch was the final interpreter of the scene. However modest the language he would use, he would in fact serve as sole director of the John Birch Society. He would give himself a title that sounded, well, paternalistic. As the founder of the John Birch Society he would call himself . . . The Founder.

Welch had crisscrossed the country many times for the Welch Candy Company, for the National Association of Manufacturers, and as author of the two Regnery books. He settled on Indianapolis to launch his society. Indianapolis was manifestly midwestern America, a center of industrial America, east of Chicago and Minneapolis, north of Cincinnati and Dallas.

He had a good sense of whom he might plausibly approach for his historic meeting. The invitees would be conservatives, wealthy, resourceful, and restive under the uncertain leadership of President Eisenhower.

Soviet advances worldwide had seemed relentless in the years of Eisenhower's presidency, as they had been under Truman. Welch knew why we were losing under Eisenhower—he had answered the key question for himself. But he did not propose to divulge this insight in Indianapolis. All that he needed to do to alert this group of people was to point out what *had happened* to U.S. interests when confronting Soviet interests.

What was there to point to, postwar? The Communist takeover of China; the atom bomb and then the hydrogen bomb tested in Russia; the heart-aching suppression of the Budapest revolution in 1956, just two years ago; Moscow's launch of the first satellite, in October of last year. At home, you could almost *feel* the listlessness of our foreign policy. The new president had authorized the surrender in Korea. He seemed helpless up against Soviet premier Nikita Khrushchev's repeated threat to make a separate alliance with East Germany, thus threatening the independence of Berlin.

And all of that, yes, under a Republican administration! An administration which—Welch would repeat and repeat—didn't even *begin* to think of repealing the New Deal's incursions on human freedom. Quite the contrary. Federal welfare continued to grow even as inflation ate away at the savings of the American people. And there, critically situated as chief justice, was Earl Warren. Appointed chief justice by. . . Dwight Eisenhower. Warren, the man in charge of the Supreme Court, quick to approve federal measures that curtailed freedom and to disallow as unconstitutional programs to bolster internal security.

Welch wrote out his historic letter.

Would you be able and willing to meet with about fifteen other men, all from different parts of the nation, in Indianapolis on Monday, December 8, and Tuesday, December 9?

Except for myself they are all men of well-recognized stature, unshakable integrity, proved ability, and fervent patriotism. The meeting will be completely "off the record." And since there is no way I can tell you of the idea which I hope to see thoroughly discussed there without writing volumes, you will have to take for granted that I would not ask such busy men to give up two whole days in this way unless I thought it would be worthwhile.

The letter was delivered to seventeen people. An astonishing eleven of them reported on December 8, so to speak, for duty. They had been given in Indianapolis the home address of a friend of Welch, a widow called Marguerite Dice, who lived in a substantial Tudor house in a suburb. One by one they came in, soon after eight in the morning. They were led to the living room, where comfortable chairs had been set up in a semicircle.

When the last of them was seated, Robert Welch, age fifty-eight (in 1958!), tall, conservatively dressed in a gray suit and dark blue tie, entered the room. He shook hands with his guests, one after another. He already knew the three guests who had served as presidents of the National Association of Manufacturers and one or two others. He hadn't before encountered Harry Bradley, the president of Allen-Bradley; or T. Coleman Andrews, President Eisenhower's commissioner of Internal Revenue in the first term; or Robert Stoddard, the world's largest manufacturer of metal forgings, and owner of two newspapers in Worcester, Massachusetts, and of the city's radio station.

Welch spoke without once referring to his sheaf of notes; spoke, in the two days, for a total of thirteen hours. His effect on these hugely successful men was catalytic. Ten of them agreed to serve on the national council of the John Birch Society.

By 1961, the Society would have thirty thousand members and forty-one full-time employees. Recruitment went on nationwide. Key Republicans felt the force of the burgeoning concern of a body of Americans awaking to the need to give special attention to the wayward drift of national affairs. At the GOP convention in July of 1960, the delegates in Chicago, after nominating Nixon for president, rejected first Barry Goldwater for vice president, then Walter Judd. Those rejections of conservative figures were the successor blow to the rejection of conservative icon Senator Robert A. Taft on that other fateful day in Chicago eight years earlier.

Welch drove his points home in his monthly magazine, *American Opinion,* and in the bulletins sent out every few weeks. The Society encouraged collateral ideological activity, including anti-Communist documentaries. These were shown at chapter meetings and at meetings of veterans' organizations, rotary clubs, and associations of concerned and civic-minded women. At Belmont, reviewing plans for a documentary on the crushing of the student rebels in Budapest in 1956, Jesse Andrews drew Welch's attention to Woodroe Raynor, the JBS student member at Princeton.

"My card file pays off, Bob. In his membership application he said he was in Austria in 1956 when Hungary was invaded."

Welch moved quickly.

"When does the kid graduate?"

Andrews looked back at the card. "In June."

"Let's get him up here. I'll invite him to the spring seminar."

9

THE DISCIPLES CONVENED at her apartment every Saturday evening, arriving after dinner and staying on sometimes until two or three in the morning. Calling them "The Collective" was rather like calling members of a war cabinet "The Doves"—that name, given to the most passionate concentration of anticollectivists in America.

They sat comfortably in her studio living room at 36 East Thirty-sixth Street, from which the skyline of the city's Murray Hill district was visible. Frank O'Connor, her husband, arrived late and was met at the door by his wife.

"Hello, Fluff," he said, leaning forward to kiss her on the forehead.

"Hello, Cubbyhole," she responded.

Frank O'Connor, in recent years diligently engaged in oil painting, would usually come to gatherings of the Collective, but he did not pretend to be schooled in the intricacies of the philosophy that bound them together. He always listened worshipfully, though if it got late, sometimes he would snooze a bit.

Worship was an important part of the communal exercise. Yet it was in part social, in major part of course instructive. These were young men and women of extraordinary intellect, and Ayn Rand was their lodestar. If there was any deviation, however unintentional, the errant compass was fine-tuned by her word. By her afflatus, though that term would never be used, suggesting, as it does, divine inspiration.

Although most of the Collective were ethnically Jewish, they scorned the Torah as they did Christianity, if not so comprehensively, Judaism being focused more on life on earth than on afterlife. But Judaism, like all religions in objectivist terminology, was nothing more than superstition. A first axiom of objectivism was the nonobjective nature of religion.

Traces of a religious legacy were there in the Collectivist Room, even if hardly integral. When Alissa Rosenbaum changed her name, soon after her arrival in Chicago from Russia at age twenty-one, she selected as her new first name "Ayn," which, one biographer has noted, derives from the Russian *Ayin* ("eye"), her father's not-uncommon Hebrew pet name for her as a child. The diminutive "Ayneleh" implies "bright eyes," perfectly singling out the most conspicuous feature of Ayn Rand's face, her lustrous, riveting eyes. And then the adopted surname—Rand—was the word everywhere associated with the currency of South Africa. It was the resource of the (mostly Jewish) entrepreneurs in South Africa who mined gold, gold becoming, in the literature of the author, something in the nature of a sublime substance, the fruit of reason and productivity and egoism. Her father's little business in St. Petersburg was nationalized when the Communists took over, the family apartment expropriated. Even so, the young Alissa did a year's academic program at the University of Leningrad before making her way, through family friends, to America in 1926.

There in the room, seated at her side, was her twenty-seven-year-old successor-designate, the brilliant Nathaniel Branden (born Nathan Blumenthal), named coadjutor in 1955. There was a haze in the room. Only Joan Mitchell resisted smoking. Encouraged by the leader to do so, even Leonard Peikoff, philosophy student at New York University, had begun to smoke cigarettes at age twenty. He, like Branden and his wife, Barbara, was Canadian, as was Elayne Blumenthal, sister of Nathan and wife of Harry Kalberman, account executive at Merrill Lynch. Allan Blumenthal, a cousin of Nathaniel, was a psychiatrist and physician, if a disappointed scientist, having labored to succeed as a concert pianist. Alan Greenspan was the professionally trained economist. The non-Jews were Mary Ann Rukavina and Joan Mitchell, graduates of NYU's Institute of Fine Arts, now engrossed in Randian objectivism and at work studying philosophy at NYU.

The year 1958 was high season for the Collective: *Atlas Shrugged*, the much-heralded novel of the prophet, successor to the great *Fountainhead* of 1943, had been published the previous October. This was a work of genius, manifestly, but also of stupendous importance to the movement, culminating in a torrential display of the objectivist epiphany.

Ayn Rand had devoted thirteen years to its creation. Two whole years had been given to a single episode in it, the speech by its protagonist, John Galt, wherein he vouchsafed the objectivist code of thought and of social and political organization.

Two years to compose that speech! The mere recitation of it, done in the closing pages of the novel (it played the role of scriptural revelation), took three hours. Members of the Collective had been permitted to read prepublication excerpts of the book, but Nathaniel Branden alone had read it all. He would discover, soon before the publication date, that Ayn Rand had dedicated the book to two people, to her husband, Frank O'Connor—and to Nathaniel Branden. His gratitude, pride, and jubilation overwhelmed him in the heady days after the book's appearance. In the weeks and months following publication, the members of the Collective passed about among themselves news of its commercial progress and reports on its critical reception. The massive, 1,168-page book had had an initial run of 100,000 copies. Almost every day, enthusiastic publisher Bennett Cerf passed on to Ayn, or if she was away, to Frank, or Nathaniel, news of sales. "He has told me that there will assuredly be a third printing," Ayn reported to the Collective. Ayn was seated at one end of a large sofa, wearing a cotton print day dress with short sleeves and single-button trim.

"Before *Atlas Shrugged* stops selling there will be a hundred printings," Branden proclaimed. There were excited murmurs of approbation.

"Read out the review by Ruth Alexander," Leonard Peikoff said, addressing Rand.

"You read it, Leonard." She pointed to the folder on the desk. Peikoff went over to pull it out.

"Read the last sentence first," Frank O'Connor said.

Peikoff turned the page. "'*Ayn Rand is destined to rank in history as the outstanding novelist and profoundest philosopher of the twentieth century.*'" He turned back to the beginning of the review and read the whole of it out loud.

Frank had finished his second glass of whiskey, and he put down his foot in dangerous territory. "It's a pity about Whittaker Chambers."

There was silence.

Then he said, simply, "To hell with Whittaker Chambers."

Barbara Branden said, "I'll see you and raise you one: To hell with *National Review.*"

"And I'll raise *you*, Barbara. To hell with Bill Buckley," Nathaniel said.

Ayn Rand turned to her husband. "As you know, I have not read the review by Whittaker Chambers and I will never do so. The very idea of sending *Atlas Shrugged* out for review to an ex-Communist religious fanatic!"

"Ayn, I want to read you the letter I sent to *National Review* when I got the copy on Monday with that review."

Ayn raised her hand for silence. "Yes. Go ahead, Alan. I would like to hear it."

Alan Greenspan took his letter-to-the-editor from his pocket. "'*I have just read Whittaker Chambers's review of Ayn Rand's* Atlas Shrugged. *I am shocked, though perhaps I shouldn't have been. This man is beneath contempt and I would not honor his "review" of Ayn Rand's magnificent masterpiece by even commenting on it. But you who consider yourself a defender of free enterprise should feel shame. Someone has finally defined the rational morality underlying capitalism and you treat it in such a vulgar manner.'"*

Ayn drew deeply on her cigarette. "That is probably appropriate. The magazine does great harm. It poses as the conservative voice, but its editor is wholly ignorant of the implications of freedom. And I know this not just from reading him. He was here one time, so I tested his ignorance personally. Let me now make one ruling on the general subject: Under no circumstances will the review by Whittaker Chambers be mentioned again in my presence, and I reiterate my pledge never to read it.

"Now," she turned to Branden, "let us speak for a moment on a confusion I have detected on the question of ego and self-fulfillment. A proper functioning of the mind in search of reason will lead to—notice, I did not say *will divine*—the constituents of self-fulfillment."

One hour later, Nathaniel was still developing the subject. It was gratifying to see Ayn nodding her head as he proceeded to disclose the arrangement of the text of the lecture he was preparing for the Objectivist series.

BOOK
TWO

10

THE TIME HAD COME to pass resolutions. Bob Schuchman reminded the assembly—it was a full house, ninety-three delegates—that special importance attached to these resolutions. "They'll be the first ever adopted by the Young Americans for Freedom." The delegates had settled on this organizational name to succeed the provisional "Interim Committee for the Founding of a National Conservative Youth Organization."

"That means our resolutions will be historic!" Carol Dawson, acting as secretary, took notes and smiled a pert smile.

"Of course, Madam Secretary," the chairman said, turning his head to the twenty-year-old college junior. "History is in our hands!" Schuchman, a broad smile on his face, called for attention.

"But we've already got the Sharon Statement." Leonora Goldstein spoke up in the high, confident voice the delegates had got used to in the two days they had deliberated together. Goldstein, a commanding presence, though just turned twenty-one, was seated five or six rows back from the speaker, who stood by the tiled fountain pool in the large sheltered patio between two wings of their hosts' residence.

"Leonora, that's different." Schuchman could go into the pedantic mode with just a little prodding. He had made his way through college by tutoring students younger than himself, when he could find them. "The Sharon Statement is our *constitution*. We're through with that. That's done. Over and out. We're talking now about resolutions on immediate public questions like"—Schuchman grinned—"do we go along with electing Richard Nixon president?"

There was a titter of applause followed by playful booing, and some not-so-playful. Dick Cowan spoke for the hard-liners. "Nixon hasn't done *anything* for the cause since nabbing Alger Hiss, and that was...what?"—he started to count out loud—"1948, 1949, 1950...this is *1960*—twelve years ago. He sits around in Washington approving everything our great President Eisenhower does—*doesn't* do—*almost* does—*thinks about* doing."

Carol Dawson turned from her seat in the front row. "So you want Senator Kennedy to be president?"

Cowan said nothing, returning to his writing pad. Woodroe Raynor, seated next to him, heard him mutter, "What's the difference? They're both socialists." Raynor accosted the dissenter in a voice everyone could hear clearly. "That's *the* question, Dick. Do we want to elect Kennedy president?" Woodroe had special standing in the group. He alone, of the students present, had experienced firsthand the workings of Soviet repression.

"Let's vote, get that resolution out of the way." Schuchman gaveled. He liked to use his gavel, even when there was no special need for it. The patio was large, rising to the third story. Etched windows protected the patio from rain. They tilted up to let in the air. Voices were easily heard from one end of the room to the other; the gavel sound was muted by the foliage, so Schuchman struck it down more heavily.

The vote was 55–26 in favor of endorsing the GOP national ticket in November.

"Next?" Chairman Schuchman recognized Jim Kolbe.

"This resolution is offered on behalf of the enlightened Young Republicans of Northwestern University," Kolbe said, "all six of us." He bent his head to his writing pad to make sure he would recite exactly the text he had prepared. "Resolved, The House Committee on Un-American Activities should investigate the record, the sponsors, and the finances of the Bulletin of the Atomic Scientists."

Schuchman moved his head thoughtfully, left to right. "I don't know, Jim. We don't want a congressional investigating committee poking around looking into every outfit we disapprove of—"

Jim's face colored. He brushed back his hair and looked up from his notes. "It *is* the government's business if the organization is run by Communists or pro-Communists. J. B. Matthews said that the sponsors of the Bulletin of the Atomic Scientists have between them—among them—"

"'Between them' is okay," Alice Sulzer, the parliamentarian, volunteered. "You can say 'between' even when it's more than two people."

"—between them. The Bulletin's sponsors, which include Professor Albert Sechuan from Ithaca, have a cumulative record of backing forty-eight Communist fronts, according to Matthews."

J. B. Matthews was the acknowledged national curator of U.S. pro-Communist activity. His renowned files were said to have in them the names of every American who had ever participated in an official capacity in any Communist-front organization.

"Look," Schuchman said, "we're a libertarian organization—"

"Libertarian-conservative," Stan Evans, the young editor of the *Indianapolis News,* corrected.

"Yes. But as libertarians we don't want to get the reputation of— we don't want to encourage government prying into private activities."

Woodroe Raynor felt challenged. "Mr. Chairman—" He stood up to address the entire assembly. Moving back, he brushed his head on one of the vines that hung down from the second-story balcony. "Okay, yes, Senator McCarthy is gone, and okay, he didn't uncover a dark plot in government, so he is discredited—"

"Not so fast," Evans shot back. "What happened wasn't that Joe McCarthy was discredited. What happened was that the bad guys won."

There was a smattering of applause.

"I understand your point, Stan. But what I want to say is that it is legitimate congressional activity to pursue organizations being run at the direction of the Communist Party, and we ought to go on record on that point. People can't defend any longer, thanks to the McCarran Committee, the Institute of Pacific Relations, for example. Thanks to an investigating committee, we know that it has been, the exact words used in the McCarran Committee report—signed by Republicans *and* Democrats—'a conscious, articulate instrument of the Soviet conspiracy.' My point is that we ought to come up with a resolution that encourages the continuation of that kind of congressional investigation."

"I see your point," Schuchman said. "But the resolution shouldn't single out any one organization, like the Bulletin of the Atomic Scientists. We should just encourage the investigation of subversive activity—"

"Why not?" Raynor said. "What we have from that atomic scientists' group is at no point—*never*—anything different from what Moscow wants. Those . . . scientists . . . don't want further nuclear tests, they don't want any development of an antinuclear missile, they don't want civil defense activity, they're criticizing the ruling on Oppenheimer that denied him security clearance. We have to ask ourselves, a young people's conservative political organization—have to ask ourselves, What is the responsibility of democratic government when there's seditious activity out there taking advantage of civil liberties?"

"Again, I see your point, Woody, but I say no to singling out any one organization to go after."

"Vote."

"*Vote!*" a tier of delegates chimed in.

It was—by acclamation—time to vote.

It had been a long day, following the long working night on Friday. And it was getting late, edging toward evening at summer's end.

Cocktails had been scheduled for six, the buffet supper would be at seven. Schuchman was anxious not to disrupt the schedule made by sixty-five-year-old widow Mrs. Buckley. She had kept well away from the proceedings themselves, but she exercised a firm supervisory role over the catering staff, assembled in her large kitchen awaiting word to activate the bar in the living room adjacent to the patio.

The young men all wore ties and jackets, most of the women, skirts. Jewelry is a spice of life, and the young ladies affirmed the point with earrings and costume diamonds. And then, as on the two preceding evenings, there was the splash of Miss Aztec, as Katherine Harter of Arizona, laden down with turquoise and silver Indian-ware from Goldwater country, had been dubbed. Soon after 6:30, drinks having been served, the voice level rose. The excitement and self-satisfaction of the founding delegates became palpable. Word buzzed about that a *New York Times* reporter had called in to do a story on the founding convention.

Bob Schuchman, standing busily by the double-door entrance to the patio, didn't turn on the microphone to welcome an august guest. John Dos Passos, always self-effacing, had said he didn't want "any fuss" made about his being there. But everyone knew of the high reputation of the writer, a prize-winning novelist and journalist, author of the acclaimed *U.S.A.* trilogy. Dos Passos had made his opening to the American Right in *National Review* four years before, writing, in his trademark medley of news-style reporting and lyricism, an account of presidential campaign events. His article in 1956 was called "Patrician on a Mission." The essay spoke inquisitively of Adlai Stevenson's distinctive campaign style.

Dos Passos, sometime socialist, had mingled with great contemporary U.S. literary figures, here and abroad—Pound, Hemingway, Fitzgerald, Steinbeck. He had lived in their company in Paris and had traveled with George Orwell to Spain during the civil war. Gradually, late in the 1930s, skepticism set in and his critical attention turned to America's burgeoning centralized government, to the expansionism of the Soviet Union, and to the arrant and mischievous claims of the fellow travelers. The Communists, standing by the Marxist-Leninist canon, spoke through official channels in Moscow and Peking, Prague and Bucharest, Warsaw and Budapest, encouraging in Europe and America visionaries and nihilists, ideological swashbucklers and housebound sectarians. They kept aflame in many in the West a fugitive hope for the fruition of the Communist ideal. And then there was the blend of fear of world war and fatigue with the apparent endlessness of the Cold War. Dos Passos, a distillate of native American idealism and Yankee common sense, would no longer have any part of it.

"I read *U.S.A.* last year," Alicia Ellsworth said to him, a smile from ear to ear. "I can't believe it, going back and telling my professor—American Studies at Wellesley, Mr. Dos Passos—tell her I actually *talked* to John Dos Passos!"

"Tell her thanks for getting my book around, and tell her I've just finished another."

"What's it called?"

"It's called *Midcentury.* It's about...Well—" He smiled, and yielded the floor to *National Review* senior editor Frank Meyer, his crew-cut hair gray, his left hand gripping his scotch on the rocks, two fingers clutching the lit cigarette.

"How're you doing, Dos?" Meyer's hoarse voice told the story of a lifetime with cigarettes. "This is a great development here, don't you think? A *conservative* political youth organization!"

"Yes, Frank." Dos smiled his shy smile, his face slightly tilted to turn his good eye to Frank. "We know a lot about young political organizations. Well, that's not quite right. I wrote about them, you organized them."

Frank Meyer, when a young Communist studying in London, had become a prominent Party organizer. Soon after the 1945 Potsdam Conference, which effectively ceded great European territories to Moscow, he rejected the Communist faith. Meyer immersed himself in the conservative canon, which he was soon undertaking to refine. He served now as book editor of *National Review*, a portfolio he discharged from his country home, a hundred miles north of New York City in Catskill country, and as unofficial ideologue-in-chief of the conservative movement.

He lived with his wife and two boys, rose from his bed in mid-afternoon, drew deep on his first cigarette, drank coffee, read the *New York Times*, and began then his scheduled reading, his book-review assignments, and his own writing. Late in the afternoon he would put all else aside and devote himself, with his wife, Elsie, to coaching the two boys, ages twelve and eight, in their schoolwork. It was illegal, under the laws of the State of New York, to fail to send one's school-age children to public school (or to a licensed private school). It delighted Frank Meyer to defy that law, and as many other laws as, in his dogged search for antistatist expression, he could put his hands on. He declined on principle to declare in Customs his regularly imported English cigarettes. He would read and write until ten or eleven at night and then go to the telephone, through which he exercised his glossolalia—though, over the telephone, he preached less to the heathen than to those young and old already persuaded by the conservative faith, or nibbling at it. His expansive and avuncular good nature and his anxiety to give aid and counsel meant continuous phone calls, narrowing, sometime after one or two in the morning, to others who kept such hours—students, mostly, or Californians who hadn't gone to bed, or Englishmen who had already risen. One constant companion on the telephone was a fellow *National Review* senior editor, Brent Bozell, brother-in-law of Buckley. Bozell, law graduate, had written speeches for Joe McCarthy and wrote now— he was responsible for the book *The Conscience of a Conservative*— for Senator Barry Goldwater. The wisecrack at *National Review* was, "How do you describe a telephone call from Frank Meyer to Brent Bozell?" Answer: "A telephone call that interrupts their regular telephone call."

Meyer laughed his hoarse laugh at Dos Passos's gibe. "Yes, Dos, I had a hand in this kind of macho thing while you were out there writing great literature."

"What was the big difference between our group—this group—and the kind you had a hand in, ten, fifteen years ago?" Bob Schuchman put the question to Frank Meyer. He added, "I guess back then we were mostly Jews, right, Frank?" Schuchman was only twenty-two years old, freshly matriculated at Yale Law School, but already he was addressing the senior and venerable figure by his first name. This surprised no one, because Meyer, operating from his eyrie in Woodstock, New York, smelled out up-and-coming young conservatives wherever they gestated. He would spot their writing in student journals, getting word of them from cross-references in his network. He cultivated them over the telephone and formed enduring disciples and friends.

Meyer laughed at Schuchman's point. "Yes, quite right, Bob. A lot of them were Jews. Like me."

"And like me," Bob said.

"And here you are, first president of the Young Freedom Americans."

"Young Americans for Freedom."

"Yes, sorry." Meyer drew on his cigarette and swallowed his drink. "Well, you watch, Bob. You watch, Dos. And you"—a courtly nod to Alicia Ellsworth, whose name, extraordinarily, he hadn't caught—"you watch too, young lady. We Jews are so smart, just give us five or ten years and the most prominent American conservatives will be Jewish!"

Dos Passos said, "Well, we've got a pretty good start with Barry Goldwater."

"He's only half Jewish." Bob recounted animatedly the Goldwater story about being denied access to the golf club in Phoenix because he was Jewish and asking whether, since he was only one-half Jewish, he could be allowed to play nine holes.

Bill Buckley approached them with his diminutive mother, wearing her pearls, the tidy lace across the divide on her breasts, her brocaded light-blue dress stretching down to regulation height above her very high heels. She smiled her all-encompassing smile. She had already greeted Dos Passos and Frank Meyer. Indeed, she had shaken hands with all the delegates on their arrival two days before, and more than once with many as she came across them during the weekend, wandering about in the salons and playrooms of the large house where she had raised ten children. She never missed a chance to welcome with her smile anyone who might be lifted by her greeting or encouragement.

Buckley addressed Schuchman. "Mother says it's time to start supper. Would you do something? Get the word around?"

Bob Schuchman was direct in all matters. He took Frank's highball glass and banged on it with his own glass, eventually engaging attention.

"Chow time, gang. I mean, chow time, *Young Americans for Freedom!*"

The tables were set in two parallel living rooms, the buffet in the connecting section. An hour or so after they had sat down—after the pumpkin pie, the apple cider, and the red wine—Schuchman situated the microphone within view of one set of diners. Others, leaving their tables, stood about.

He began by giving thanks to Mrs. Buckley ("who, among other things, educated Bill"). Hearty applause. Welcome was extended to distinguished guests: Dos Passos and Meyer; John Chamberlain, author and literary reviewer; James Burnham, *National Review* senior editor, strategist, author of *The Managerial Revolution*; Frank Chodorov, editor of *The Freeman*; Marvin Liebman from the Committee of One Million Against the Admission of Communist China to the United Nations. They each had applause. "We also welcome someone from the enemy camp. Murray Kempton is—well, you all know—Murray Kempton is Murray Kempton. When he called up and said he wanted to do a column about us, he asked, Did we have any room tonight for a middle-aged American for socialism?" Laughter. "Anyway—welcome, Murray. We conservatives make way for late vocations."

Schuchman then announced that he had had a very informative telephone call. "I have a spy at the *New York Times*." Laughter and applause. "I know, I know, I'm kidding. But what I'm *not* kidding about is I got from my spy the lead paragraph of the story that will run tomorrow! In the Sunday *Times!*" Applause. "You want to hear it?" Applause. One voice rang out, "YAF doesn't care *what* the *New York Times* says, right, gang?" Applause, laughter. "Okay, then I won't read it." Boos, laughter.

"Come on, Bob," Bill Buckley said. "They're the enemy, but we want to know what the enemy is saying, don't we?" Applause, laughter.

"Okay, okay. So, here it is:

"'A convention of students met over the weekend at Sharon, Connecticut, at the home of Mrs. William F. Buckley, mother of the editor, to form an association called Young Americans for Freedom.'" Cheers. "'Ninety-three student delegates from seventeen states resolved to launch a national organization that would give voice to the views of young conservatives, some of whom demonstrated at the Republican convention in Chicago in July urging the nomination of Senator Barry Goldwater for president. When that move failed, they sought Congressman Walter Judd for vice president. The organization's manifesto declares, "The United States should stress victory over, rather than coexistence with, the Communist world."

"'The delegates elected"—Schuchman clasped both hands over his head in the victory pose of the prizefighter, to much laughter and a smattering of applause—"'Robert Schuchman of Chicago as its first president.'" He paused.

"The news story goes on at some length to record my accomplishments, but we can skip that." Applause and laughter.

Schuchman dropped the *Times* report and went on to give out administrative details. He said that all delegates would receive within a week or ten days notice about YAF activities. "Make sure that in the registry in the main hall, you have down your address at college, not just your home address."

He took his wineglass to his lips.

"So, the conference is adjourned. We have music on the patio, and Mrs. Buckley says to stay, and dance if we want to. The bar is open. The mini-bar. The maxi-bar is reserved for Frank Meyer and his closest friends. He is on the telephone with them right now. The bus and cars will leave Great Elm"—the name of the Buckley residence—"at 11 P.M. to take us to where we've been staying. You've all made your own arrangements about getting back tomorrow to New York and other foreign capitals. Some of us call this the diaspora. *And we too will thrive!*" There was general applause.

Woodroe Raynor asked Leonora Goldstein if she wanted to dance. "Not really," she said with a smile. "But let's anyway. The decision to dance is the reasoned exercise of my free will."

"What else would it be?" Woodroe asked, putting his hand behind her back.

As they danced in the dim patio light to recorded music of Frank Sinatra and Johnny Mercer, Leonora said, "I want to talk to you, Woody, about what you said in the resolution sessions."

"About Communist organizations?"

"Yes. About investigating Communist activity."

"Right. But why not wait until we get back to the Coleys'?"

She nodded her assent. "But we don't have to hurry off the dance floor."

Friends and neighbors had volunteered to put up some of the guests, the remainder lodging at the Bartram Inn on Sharon's elm-lined quadrangle. At eleven, Mrs. Coley was there with her station wagon to pick up her boarders. Woodroe shared a guest room above the garage with Henry Mandelbaum, but Henry had left after dinner, getting a ride to New Haven from a Coley son who came and went to Sharon, unconcerned with the goings-on of the Young Americans for Freedom. Leonora's roommate was Alicia Ellsworth. They bade good night and thanked Mrs. Coley, who before leaving for her own room said, "You know where the kitchen is, if you want anything." Alicia said she too was going upstairs to bed, leaving Woodroe and Leonora to sit together at the kitchen table.

"You sleepy?" Leonora asked Woodroe.

"No. Not a bit."

She got up and opened the refrigerator door. "I'm going to have some of this"—she gripped a gallon jug of apple cider. "Want any?"

Woodroe nodded. "On the rocks."

Seated, Leonora said that from her "perspective," the word *sedition,* which Woody had used that afternoon to define the activity of the congressional committees, was simply not useful anymore.

"Why?"

"Because *all* collectivist thought is seditious."

"Well, I think I know what you're getting at, Lee. Ayn Randites consider all collective activity—I suppose the fire department would be included?—'seditious.' But there's a difference. I mean, you can say that Norman Thomas, running for president on the Socialist Party ticket, is preaching a seditious doctrine—he wants programs that would limit the freedom of Americans. Granted, we think that's seditious, like when George III did it. But that's not the same as Earl Browder, president of the American Communist Party, running for president. He's an agent of a foreign power. And he's prepared to use every weapon he can put his hands on, including the use of agents, to give the enemy information on American security arrangements. And what Browder wants is the same thing those scientists want, though a lot of them probably don't know who's calling the signals in their organization. But if they prevailed, hell, they'd tie up our entire defense system, if they could put their hands on it."

"I knew you'd say that kind of thing." Leonora reached back into the refrigerator for more cider. "But my point is that you're really talking about gradations of assault on our freedoms. And sure, I'm perfectly willing to endorse the security laws, the whole apparatus— J. Edgar Hoover, Pat McCarran, Joe McCarthy, the Smith Act. But our basic understanding of the enemy—the *generic* enemy—isn't really illuminated. Woody, have you read *Atlas Shrugged?*"

"Ayn Rand's novel?"

She nodded.

"It's very long."

"I've read it three times."

"Whoa! Reading something that long that many times? That gets in the way of other things, doesn't it? Like, oh, *Gone With the Wind?*"

"I'm being serious, Woody."

"Well, okay. Let me be serious too, then. I think the difference between the liberals and the Communists isn't slight, like what you think. I say it's critical. And our trouble isn't that we fail to identify the central similarity between them, both determined to reduce freedom, whether in Russia through regimentation or in Washington through taxes and regulations. The central problem is that we are accepting the sincerity of critically situated people who are—who are, actually, on the other side. Who we think of as simply, well, Left liberals, but who are, *really,* people who are *affecting* to be Left liberals but are *actually* Communist sympathizers. Some of us call them 'Comsymps.'"

"You say some of *us.* Who is 'us'?"

Woodroe paused. If he lit a cigarette, he'd gain a moment's time. He did, and exhaled the smoke, and with it his fleeting temptation to hide his affiliation. "'Us' is the John Birch Society."

She stared at him. "I'll be damned. I've never read much on Robert Welch and the Birchers. I do know they want to impeach Earl Warren. You can't drive five miles in California—I know, I was there in July—without running into 'Impeach Earl Warren' signs or stickers or whatever."

"They're strong in California. *We're* strong in California."

"So you're actually a member of their society?"

"Yes. It's not expensive, the dues are nothing, if you're under twenty-five."

"Well, I want to hear a lot more about it. I hope you're not going to tell me you think Earl Warren, dopey though he is, is a secret Communist?"

"You'd have to give that a lot of thought."

"I don't mind doing that. Giving things a lot of *thought* is what we objectivists specialize in."

"Now *you're* telling *me* about an organization *you* belong to—"

"Oh, no." Leonora drew back. "We don't have an organization. And I'm not 'an objectivist.' Only two people are authorized to call themselves that. Miss Rand, of course. And Nathaniel Branden."

"Who's he?"

"Her primary assistant. And head of the Nathaniel Branden Institute. He teaches courses. In New York. And more and more, he's touring the country and lecturing about objectivism."

"How do you know all that?"

Leonora looked down at her glass and twiddled with it. "I have been doing work for Miss Rand. I suppose you have been doing work for Robert Welch?"

"In a way, yes, though of course it isn't work being done for him directly, it's work being done to . . . spread the word."

"About how everybody is a Communist?"

"Aw, shit, Lee. Cut that stuff out. But to say not everybody is a Communist doesn't justify saying *nobody* is a Communist."

"Okay." She smiled, and her eyes joined in. She got up. "Okay, okay, okay. We've got a little crossbreeding ahead of us."

"I hope so," Woodroe said cheerfully, touching his lips to her forehead.

11

ONE AFTERNOON, AFTER READING from the material he had been sent by the John Birch Society and admiring the clarity of the exposition on U.S. foreign policy, Woodroe wrote a letter to the *Princetonian,* the student newspaper, calling attention to the biblical *Blue Book* of the John Birch Society. The next morning, opening the door of his room at Blair Hall, he retrieved the daily paper and opened it to the letters page.

But his letter was not there. On the fourth day, he walked to the offices of the paper. He asked to see the editor in charge of letters and was motioned to the desk of a junior whose feet were on the desk, a clipboard on his lap with an assortment of papers. Woodroe asked about his letter. The editor took his feet off the desk and said that the *Princetonian* didn't make room for letters "simply endorsing a product. There has to be an angle. What's yours?"

Woodroe said he was concerned to get out the word on the Communist menace.

"So's Ike," the young editor said.

Woodroe was flushed. He had not spoken, except to family and close friends, about his experience in Austria, but now he told the editor that with his own eyes he had seen refugees from Hungary "and tried to help a couple of them out."

"Well, put *that* in your letter and we'll run it."

Woodroe thought to tell the story of his letter to Professor Romney, whom he had befriended in his junior year. Theocritus Romney,

79

a fellow Mormon from Utah, had retired from lecturing, but helped out in the overcrowded postwar scene at Princeton by teaching one seminar, "The Rise of the American West," the same title he had given to his best-known book. He was now in Princeton winter and summer, having sold his summerhouse in Utah soon after his wife died, in 1952 (on election day). He lived a bachelor life in his comfortable apartment off Nassau Street.

The quarters were everything he needed. Students who came in for his seminar, or went to him during office hours, were initially distracted by Mr. Romney's pursuit of his hobby. Theo Romney was a historian of nineteenth-century America and loved best the snow-capped mountains he had been all but surrounded by when young, attending school in Provo. His major book had given the history of the Mormon Church. A later book, a handbook of sorts on the Rocky Mountains, he had illustrated with his own charcoal sketches, carefully collected in his days as a mountaineer and skier.

He had resolved, as soon as his wife permitted it, to fulfill the ambition of painting the view of the Rockies as seen from the window of his parents' house. Lucy never did authorize him to proceed, so he put it off until his retirement as lecturer in 1954. Setting up the platform on which, for two hours every day, he would lie on his back, palette and brushes in hand, was a delicate business, but he was pleased by his sketch, and then the dark blue-gray that rose to the snow level, and the first of the eleven peaks he had framed in memory. The painting would stretch over the entire ceiling. When moving from one mountain peak to another, he had to move his platform. Though the movements were not more than six or eight inches, this required, from time to time, moving the whole of the wooden scaffolding, which had to be done in such a way as to accommodate the sofas and chairs on which the twelve seminar students sat. Students who came in during office hours quickly got used to arrangements, and found they could easily converse with Romney while he lay on the platform above their heads.

Professor Romney was the only member of the faculty to whom Woodroe had told the story of his missionary duty at Andau. Romney divulged his own passion on the subject of life under Communist rule. He revealed that when a very young man, he had broken with his Christian faith, joining the Young Communist League. In the 1930s, he had experienced the disillusion of so many others after the starvation of the kulaks, followed soon by the Moscow trials. But he had tried to make up for his delinquency, actively supporting anti-Communist political candidates and calling important books to the attention of his students. When Senator Joseph McCarthy died, Romney had worn a discreet black sliver on the lapel of his jacket.

It had become routine, while Woodroe was enrolled in the seminar, for him to stay on after the Tuesday and Thursday 4 P.M. meetings to have a glass of sherry with Mr. Romney. When the semester was over, Romney had suggested that Woodroe continue with the late-afternoon conversation-with-sherry, never mind that he was no longer studying with him. Woodroe gladly agreed, and their friendship continued. In the fall of 1960, Romney had been very pleased to learn from his favorite student about the founding of the national student conservative organization, the Young Americans for Freedom, in Sharon, Connecticut.

This afternoon they spoke of the rejected letter to the *Princetonian*. "I would counsel you to go ahead in the new draft of your letter. Tell the story of Austria and Andau—"

"You don't mean—not the whole of it?"

Romney himself did not know the whole of it, but he knew about Woodroe's wound, and about his hospitalization in Vienna.

"No, I don't think it's necessary, to make your point, to say that you were visited in a hospital bed by Vice President Richard Nixon. But I see no reason to hide that you were hit by a Hungarian Communist bullet aimed at someone trying to get away from Communist tyranny."

Woodroe agreed. "I'll make that part very brief. Otherwise it might look as though I was, well . . . exhibiting my Purple Heart."

Romney looked up at his beloved ceiling. "All we're looking at here—everything we grew up with in Utah—would be red in our eyes, if we lived where those poor people live. And what did we manage to learn from the massacre of the freedom fighters in Budapest?"

He drew breath, and looked up at his ceiling. "We have an obligation to remind the community of the—the ordeal of Eastern Europe, never mind what it's like living within the Soviet Union."

Woodroe wrote the letter, and it was published. And he took other opportunities to call attention to the work of the John Birch Society. As a member, he received the full range of the Society's publications. He was astonished by the prodigious output—the monthly magazine, *American Opinion,* with its opening letter from Mr. Welch, and then the bulletins, some of them thirty and forty pages long. Impetuously, he one day wrote personally to Mr. Welch, acclaiming his work. Welch answered in a long, friendly letter, inviting Woodroe to write an article for *American Opinion.*

A second letter, unexpectedly personal, made mention of occasional intensive seminars conducted by Mr. Welch himself, inviting Woodroe to attend one. In the Easter vacation of his senior year, Woodroe traveled to Boston to attend the special two-day seminar. He was flattered on being told that he was the youngest person ever to be admitted to the august meeting, which was patterned after the historic seminar Robert Welch had held just over two years before in Indianapolis, where he had launched the John Birch Society. That seminar was ongoingly repeated, here and there in major cities, but not more often than once a month.

Woodroe Raynor had then, in late March of 1961, the full measure of Mr. Welch's extraordinary recall, organizational skill, and dedication. The seminar was nonstop. There had been a break for lunch on both days, and cocktails were given at the end of the second day for sixteen men and four women exhausted by the impact of two days' analysis and exposition of the tightening threat to American freedom and sovereignty.

One month later he was offered employment by the Society at the head office in Belmont, Massachusetts, to begin as soon as convenient after graduation from Princeton.

12

BELMONT, MASS.
OCTOBER 22, 1961

Dear Lee:

Maybe I really do love you, because today I actually finished reading *Atlas Shrugged*. You'll hit me over the head for saying this, but it took *great effort*. I can hear you saying, *If it's that bad, how do you account for . . .* is it one million sales? You're right, it doesn't work to be condescending about it. So okay, it's a hell of a yarn. It *has* to be, I guess, to eat up 1,168 pages. Lee, were you having me on in Sharon when you told me you had read it *three times?* That means you haven't had time to read, oh, Sophocles, or *The Making of the President, 1960*. Or to practice your scales on the piano.

But let's get back to the point we've been arguing on and off since Sharon. We both think the Communists are edging us out in the Cold War. We agreed on that at Sharon. Since then, the Soviets have forged ahead in space exploration, they've put up the Berlin Wall and outmaneuvered us in Cuba.

Americans Mr. Welch calls "Comsymps" gloat over what they did to Joe McCarthy, hounding him to death, and they make fun of any suggestion that there are actually people in the United States who pretend to be on our side but are actually on *their* side.

Now, who contributes most seriously to the rectification of *that* problem? Your John Galt? Admit this about the big figure in *Atlas Shrugged*. He is . . . bear with me, Lee . . . *the most improbable figure since King Kong*. And what does John Galt do to rescue the entire country from paralysis? He goes to a radio station and delivers a *three-hour speech*.

Does Ayn Rand think she's really getting away with it? Stop the Communists by objectivist thought? What does she tell her gang, when she has her hair down and is sitting around with her Collective? She is so full of *reason*—she's up to her arse in reason—so what's *reasonable* about a situation in which 175 million Americans in her novel are at hell's door until John Galt goes to the radio station and tells them what to do. In a speech that lasts sixty-five pages!

I'm up on *Atlas Shrugged*, Lee, now that I've worked my way through it. But I have a hard time taking it seriously as a countermeasure to the Cold War we're fighting, or trying to fight. We at the Birch Society are concerned about the survival of the United States in the last half of the twentieth century. Rand's people are concerned only about . . . *themselves*. I give you what's-his-name. I'll be polite and come up with— Here it is, his full name. . . . What did Ayn Rand *have in mind* calling somebody "Francisco Domingo Carlos Andres Sebastian d'Anconia"? Why didn't she add "Jr."? We bump into him early in the novel, he's still a kid, really, college-age. And we get this, Miss Rand's cock-of-the-walk paean to youthful objectivism:

> *"Don't you ever think of anything but d'Anconia Copper?" Jim Larkin asked him once.*
> *"No."*
> *"It seems to me that there are other things in the world."*
> *"Let others think about them."*
> *"Isn't that a very selfish attitude?"*
> *"It is."*

"What are you after?"

"Money."

"Don't you have enough?"

"In his lifetime, every one of my ancestors raised the pro-
duction of d'Anconia Copper by about 10%. I intend to raise
it by one hundred."

And this is not just Ayn Rand passing wind. Anybody who thinks
anything different is presented as caricature. Here that young
prick—I mean, that young pr-ck—is being lectured by his friend
Jim, a senior in college, who's made to sound like a socialist vanilla
malted. Listen:

"I think that now that you've reached college age, you ought
to learn something about ideals. It's time to forget your self-
ish breed, and give some thought to your social responsibili-
ties, because I think that all those millions you're going to
inherit are not for your personal pleasure, they are a trust for
the benefit of the underprivileged and the poor, because I
think that the person who doesn't realize this is the most
depraved type of human being."

I mean, cut it out. This is Ayn Rand making like St. Francis of
Assisi.

My concern is: What do we have going to hold the Communists
back? For instance, we've got to get Castro out of Cuba. How're we
going to do that? Send John Galt over there? *Yo soy John Galt. Yo*
explico todo. . . . We need an air force and a military and a CIA. We
have to pay the cost of encounters in Berlin and Taiwan, in Cuba
and—in Hungary; I know firsthand about that. And now we've got
China in the hands of the Communists, and what do you know, *they*
have an atom bomb. Are we prepared for sacrifice to contend with all
that? Not according to objectivist dogma, we aren't. "This country is

the product of reason and could not survive on the morality of sacrifice," *Atlas Shrugged* preaches.

Well, nobody loathes socialism more than Robert Welch. Nobody. But he thinks it has to be fought by something more than a heady philosophy which begins by explaining that—in her language—"existence exists." That's the trouble, Lee. Existence *does* exist. Ask the 150 million people behind the Iron Curtain. They can *feel* its existence.

Love,
Woody

P.S. I really look forward to the weekend you're coming up for. You can *reason* your way to the incontestable conclusion that Princeton will beat Harvard.

———————————

NYC
OCTOBER 28, 1961

Dear Woodroe:

I don't know why I take the trouble. You are in love with your ignorance. The exact words were found by Miss Rand to express my thoughts about your letter. Rearden was thinking about the despicable Larkin and what his presence provoked in him. Listen to Rand on the subject of hatred:

> It was not a thought, it was like the punch of a fist inside his skull. Then when he could think again, Rearden knew what the boy he had been would have felt: a desire to step on the obscene thing which was Larkin and grind every wet bit of it out of existence. He had never experienced an emotion of this

87

kind. It took him a few moments to realize that this was what men called hatred.

Which is pretty much what I felt after reading your desiccation of *Atlas* and your treatment of that genius woman I work for. Why didn't you select, to ponder over, one of the mature, glowingly thoughtful passages? For instance, where Miss Rand describes her philosophy of the sexual experience:

They had moved by the power of the thought that one remakes the earth for one's enjoyment, that man's spirit gives meaning to insentient matter by molding it to serve one's chosen goal. The course led them to the moment when, in answer to the highest of one's values, in an admiration not to be expressed by any other form of tribute, one's spirit makes one's body become the tribute, recasting it—as proof, as sanction, as reward—into a single sensation of such intensity of joy that no other sanction of one's existence is necessary. He heard the moan of her breath, she felt the shudder of his body, in the same instant.

Disgustedly,
Lee

BELMONT, MASS.
NOVEMBER 2, 1961

Lee:

I'm sorry you took what I had to say the way you did. Let's adjourn the quarrel. We're looking at two phalanxes, and how they serve in the anti-Communist struggle. There is the objectivist philosophy, which seeks to teach us how to reason the case for freedom. Then there is the JBS, which is trying to mobilize the national will to confound the enemy, *"foreign and domestic,"* in the quaint words of the presidential oath of office.

I have to concede it about your Miss Rand. When she isn't engaging in caricature, she can draw beautiful pictures. *Atlas Shrugged* is a work of ideological fabulism. My favorite passage (though it's hard to beat the sex scene you quote) is when she and lover-boy set out on the train ride to test whether his new steel alloy really works. Miss Rand was obviously swept away. Well, I was too: I am typing it out, as an oblation. I especially liked *"the glass panes of their vault."* My boss has something called Xerox which makes copies. So I will make an extra copy of this and send it along and you can thumbtack it over your desk and remind yourself of . . . the other Ayn Rand.

It was a succession of minutes, but it hit them as a single whole. First, they saw the lone shapes, which were factories, rolling across their windowpanes—then the shapes fused into the blur of streets—then a delta of rails spread out before them, like the mouth of a funnel sucking them into the Taggart station, with nothing to protect them but the small green beads of light that scattered over the ground—from the height of the cab, they saw boxcars on sidings streak past as flat ribbons of rooftops—the black hole of the train-shed flew at their faces—they hurtled through an explosion of sound, the beating of wheels against the glass panes of their vault, and the screams of cheering from a mass that swayed like a liquid in the darkness among steel columns—they flew toward a glowing arch and the green lights hanging in the open sky beyond, the green lights that were like the doorknobs of space, throwing door after door open before them. Then, vanishing behind them, went the streets, clotted with traffic, the open windows bulging with human figures, the screaming sirens, and—from the top of a distant skyscraper—a cloud of paper snowflakes shimmering on the air, flung by someone who saw the passage of a silver bullet across a city stopped still to watch it.

Unless you plan to cancel, I will be at the railroad station in Boston at 11:22 on Saturday.

XXX
Woodroe

13

THE HEAD OFFICE of the John Birch Society was just a few blocks from the home of Robert Welch. Visitors to the Belmont, Massachusetts, office entered into a large, bright room lined with bookcases.

Woodroe's main responsibility was to proofread the copious communications from Mr. Welch to the Society's subscribers, sent out in *American Opinion* and in supplementary bulletins as often as twice a month.

It was after he had been in Belmont more than a year that he was summoned to the office of principal Welch aide Jesse Andrews.

"You understand, Woodroe, Mr. Welch has the highest opinion of General Walker. We've made the case for him ever since he was fired—"

"That was in April 1961."

"Good for you. Of course, he wasn't *fired*. He was *silenced*. That disreputable paper in Germany said that General Walker was calling some American leaders Communists. That's wrong, and anyway, it's ill-advised. We call them Comsymps."

"But General Walker wasn't quoted exactly, I don't think—"

"No, but the Comsymp press does that kind of thing," Andrews said. "Exaggerates and defames patriotic Americans. Like Ed Walker. What General Walker did was launch an educational program for the Twenty-fourth Infantry over there in Germany. It was no accident, by the way, that he—a superior combat commander—

was put in charge of the Twenty-fourth, since that would be the front-line U.S. force in Europe if the Communists decided to move. Not that they'll need to, at the rate we're going. Easier just to wait for an American surrender.

"Anyway, you and I know that what General Walker undertook, plain and simple, was to teach the fundamentals of pro-Americanism, the ABCs of anti-Communism to American servicemen. And we're proud that some of the material he was using was generated by the John Birch Society. Now he's back home for a while and he's a national figure, and an important arm of the cause—"

The phone on the desk rang.

Woodroe waited, his eyes straying to the framed picture of General Douglas MacArthur shaking hands with Robert Welch, and to another of Senator Joe McCarthy's coffin, lying in state in the Capitol, surrounded by mourners.

Andrews, meanwhile, on the phone, was talking to somebody about a rally planned for Los Angeles, where one-quarter of the members of the John Birch Society lived. He pulled out what was apparently a roster of sorts and checked off names as they were dictated to him over the telephone. Woodroe mused on the special difficulty Andrews now had in keeping his cigarette lit while holding the telephone to his ear and taking notes. Jesse frowned with indecision over the three priorities, but then made his election: "Hold on just one minute, Al." He dropped the pencil and balanced the cigarette on the lid of the ashtray. He took the pencil in hand again and resumed the phone project. "Asworth, yes; here. Blatchford, yes. No, no Blake. . . . This is October's list, maybe he came in since then. . . ."

Woodroe waited, his curiosity keen over the reason for the summons to Mr. Andrews's office.

Andrews was finally off the phone.

"Yes. On the matter of General Walker, Woody. We were talking about General Walker's plan to go to Oxford, Mississippi, to protest the federal troops that are likely to be sent there to reinforce integration. The Warren Court is closing in on our liberties, and the attempt to dictate admissions policy at the University of Mississippi is just one more example of our diminished liberties. Still, Bob—Mr. Welch—thinks we have to guard against precipitate action, technically subversive: the troops, if they're sent to Oxford, will be there to enforce a court order. Just like in Little Rock! And who was there to enforce the law in Little Rock? General Edwin Walker!"

"But the general offered to resign, back at Little Rock."

"Yes, but that story didn't come out until later—after the situation in Germany exploded and everybody started talking about General Walker. But never mind that, it's this simple: Mr. Welch wants you to go down to Texas and to act as liaison between the John Birch Society and General Walker. That way we can keep an eye on what he's doing and . . . take precautions, if necessary."

"Yes. But why me?"

"We gave that some thought. General Walker is used to young people. He led them in action in France and Korea and he's trained young men ever since. If we sent someone older, he might, well, not quite understand, he might think we're interfering. It is a delicate job but we are convinced you are up to it, and the needs of the Society need to take precedence in all matters. If you are willing to take on the assignment, you will be briefed by Mr. Welch."

"Sure," Woodroe said. "General Walker is a great hero. And Texas is—halfway to Utah. I can buzz off and visit my family!"

14

WOODROE THOUGHT IT WOULD be interesting, and even entertaining, so he accepted right away Lee's invitation. ("By the way, Woody, I am now Leonora *Pound*. Not Goldstein. And I don't really want to talk about it.") He had set aside the weekend to spend in New York, en route to Texas. He would take her on Saturday to Princeton to watch the football game, this time with Cornell. A few parties ("By the way, Lee, I now drink spirits. And I don't really want to talk about it"), then back to New York, a day of city sightseeing, dinner at the restaurant Leonora had twice mentioned in her letters, and then, on Monday morning, the Eastern Airlines DC-7 to Dallas. So Friday afternoon was now reserved: he would hear a lecture by Nathaniel Branden. And, Lee told him, "There is a high probability that Miss Rand will be there, to take questions after Nathaniel's lecture."

He arrived at Grand Central just after noon. She said she would be waiting for him at the Oyster Bar and it wouldn't matter to her if the train was late. "It receives federal subsidies, so you can't expect first-rate service."

The *Boston Globe* he had read en route gave disturbing news. He noticed especially the statement by Dr. Edward Teller, made at a San Francisco meeting of UPI editors and publishers. In his judgment, the Soviet Union was now "ahead of the United States in the nuclear race." And then on the next page notice that Soviet official Leonid Brezhnev had journeyed to Belgrade to visit with Tito, an obvious attempt to reintegrate Yugoslavia into the Soviet orbit. On the other hand, Robert Welch preached that Tito's break with Stalin was not genuine—Welch judged it one more attempt by the Communists at strategic deception.

Woodroe carried the two bags and briefcase with difficulty, but he got them to the checking station and then eagerly went down the stairs to the Oyster Bar.

My, but Leonora . . . Pound was ravishing. "You know, you look like Barbara Stanwyck," Dick Cowan had said to her at cocktail time two years ago at Sharon. Woodroe, standing by, had sort of nodded agreement. He'd have nodded enthusiastically today, looking at her bright face framed by the blue cotton suit and the wood paneling of the venerable eating spot.

They sat down. He waved at the waiter to bring the menu, and Lee gave him some background.

The Nathaniel Branden Institute (NBI) lectures were held at the Sheraton Russell Hotel at Thirty-seventh Street and Park, a mere five blocks from where they were having lunch. For that reason she had reserved him a room in the hotel. "If you want a success story, hear this. Nathaniel Branden—he is like God Junior at our place—came up in 1958 with the idea of a lecture course on objectivism—"

"Did he begin his lectures on December 8?"

"Why?"

Woodroe broke into a wide smile. "That's the day—December 8, 1958—that Bob Welch launched the John Birch Society."

"Oh, come on. I mean, objectivism is serious stuff."

"So is the Communist threat."

"I know, I know. But listen. I don't remember the exact date, but it was in the fall of 1958. The idea was to initiate a lecture course called 'Basic Principles of Objectivism.' It would amount to a systematic presentation of Miss Rand's philosophy. How to launch something like that?

"Well, what he did was write letters to a hundred people who had written to Ayn Rand complimenting her on *Atlas Shrugged*. He and Barbara—you'll meet her. They married in 1953. She's beautiful. But Nathaniel is even *more* beautiful—"

Woodroe gave off an exaggerated wince of jealousy.

"That's all right. You're beautiful too."

"I was voted the most beautiful boy in Princeton at graduation."

"Oh, come on. Anyway, so he wrote letters to the fans announcing the course, and twenty-eight people subscribed to it."

"You mean, actually *paid* to hear the lectures?"

"*Absolutely.* Objectivism doesn't believe that anything should be free. And that was clear up front. The dollar sign, remember, was John Galt's symbol for free exchange—for freedom, really. Eat your oysters. Anyway, that was 1958. The class we'll be going to now has 160 subscribers. They pay seventy dollars for twenty lectures."

"Which is the one I'm coming in for?"

"He's lately been going in the direction of 'Critical Analysis of Contemporary Psychology.' There are other lecture series. Barbara is offering a course called 'Basic Principles of Efficient Thinking.'"

Lee pulled a printed NBI card from her purse to remind herself of all that was going on within the Rand world. "Leonard Peikoff—he's our brilliant young philosophy student—is teaching 'A Critical History of Philosophy.' Mary Ann—that's Mary Ann Rukavina—is doing 'The Aesthetics of the Visual Arts,' and Alan Greenspan, of course, is doing 'The Economics of a Free Society.'"

"So what will happen when we show up? I'll have to pay to get in, I take it."

"Actually, you won't. I'm staff, and staff can bring people in—a maximum of two free lecture invitations for any one guest—who might be interested in subscribing for the next series. Nathaniel does two sets of lectures every year."

"So all I have to do is sit and listen?"

"Yes. And try to learn something. You know, objectivism tells you how to reason and how to acquire knowledge, including knowledge of yourself. If you learn the nature of your power, you also learn about your possibilities."

Woodroe was tempted to make a wisecrack but wisely didn't. Instead he said, "Well, let's wait and see. The lecture's at four, right? So we have plenty of time. Lee, maybe we shouldn't discuss world affairs."

"Okay. We can discuss *Atlas Shrugged*."

They both laughed.

A few hours later Woodroe was seated at one side of the hall. Fifteen rows of ten folding chairs had been set up, all but a few of them now occupied by the students of objectivism. They ranged in age, Woodroe estimated, from eighteen to seventy. At four exactly, dressed in a dark blue suit, thirty-two-year-old Nathaniel Branden walked out from a side door to the lectern. There was a hint of applause. But when, a moment later from the door opposite, Ayn Rand herself emerged, the applause was sustained. She too wore a suit, gray wool, a white shirt with wide collars, her hair set in the legendary pageboy style. She sat down with pencil, pad, and ashtray on a special, upholstered chair to the speaker's right, an upright bookstand next to it. She did not smile, but slightly nodded her head in acknowledgment of the applause.

Branden spoke from notes. The thoughts were orderly, the presentation systematic. His voice was sure, his scholarly enthusiasm beguiling. Almost everyone took notes. After his hour, the great moment arrived.

When Ayn Rand was present, questions from the floor were automatically directed to her. Woodroe had been warned that "Ayn's manner is . . . direct." Lee's point was quickly demonstrated. The young woman whose hand had shot up was acknowledged. "It is obvious from Mr. Branden's talk that moral judgments must be passed, but aren't there *any* circumstances in which you might advise discretion?"

Ayn Rand answered: "No."

There was silence. But she continued seated, taking a puff from her cigarette. Nathaniel Branden knew to act quickly, not to divert attention from her rebuff. He called for the next question.

"Miss Rand, what in society today do you personally find *most* threatening to the idea of objectivism?"

To that question she devoted more than merely a single word. "All things threatening should be pointed out, but it is the pervasive collectivist thought which is most dangerous. This failure of men to realize the necessity of self-interest, and the freedom that flows from it, is quite frightening and at times downright depressing—" Lee leaned over and whispered into Woodroe's ear, *"She herself has been depressed a long time. I'll tell you about it."*

The questioner persisted. "Then you advocate complete self-interest at any cost?"

Rand: "If you practice complete self-interest, there will be no cost. The greater danger is *altruism* at any cost. I don't know how much more clearly I can state this."

A young man asked, "Miss Rand, I've read various interviews with you, and as a philosophy major it seems to me that perhaps you are being too hard on Plato. He was, after all, Aristotle's mentor and—"

Rand cut him off. "Am I to suppose that my kindergarten teacher deserves high praise for my successes?" Laughter. "I think not. Plato was anything *but* honest, and everything *but* rational. We should be thankful that Aristotle didn't fall into that mystical hole in which Plato resided."

There was a titter of applause.

Another questioner said, "Miss Rand, I stumbled upon *Atlas Shrugged* in a reading list I was given for a class at school and was greatly taken with it. Is it safe to assume you have another novel in the works?"

"She doesn't like talk of future work," Lee whispered.

"My books are not written merely for enjoyment." Miss Rand adopted a professorial tone. "They are catalysts for societal change. What *is* safe to say is that if you do not feel called to action by *Atlas Shrugged,* I do not think that another book will be of any service to you."

Societal change? So what to do, of a practical sort—the next questioner wanted to know—in order to help bring about this change?

Her answer: "You must *think.* Actually use your head. That thing on top of your shoulders is not a bowling ball, it is your greatest asset. Use it. Use all of it. Fearlessly strive for success, and, in turn, encourage others to do so as well."

Nathaniel Branden thanked her and the students applauded. Branden then said that looking forward to the month of December, he noted that the sixteenth scheduled lecture would happen to fall on Christmas Day, and although the Nathaniel Branden Institute hardly felt any obligation to pay special attention to Christmas, except to smile at its presumptions, considerations of staff and hotel and transport and vacations argued the case for postponing that particular session for two weeks, to one week after New Year's Day.

It was almost six o'clock. Lee had told Woodroe she would need to do postlecture catch-up at the NBI office, one block away. She retrieved her scarf from the hook in the lecture hall and they walked together to the lobby. She would come back to meet him at the hotel at 7:30.

Woodroe was glad for the respite. The whole thing was creepy. Or was it that he just didn't get it? But he had read *Atlas Shrugged.* And he shared her opposition to the growth of the state; after all, no one was more opposed to the growing state than Bob Welch. Was his background as a Mormon a structural block?

Then there was the exposure to Herself. That primal source of ideas. That brilliant, resourceful, imaginative novelist. Creepy.

Leonora had begged off the expedition to Princeton for the football game, not having enjoyed the Princeton-Harvard game which Woodroe had taken her to in Boston. "I don't much like football, and it's part of my objectivist training not to do anything I don't much like."

"Have you left off defecating?"

"Don't be vulgar. I'll see you Sunday. Go ahead and root for the Tigers."

Woodroe did that, though not bracingly enough to lift the Princeton team to victory. He found, some tedious minutes after halftime, that what he was really looking forward to postgame was not so much the serial cocktail parties as the visit to Theo Romney. He'd go to Nassau Street right after the game, and carouse later.

It was all just as the last time Woodroe had visited, in May. There was only Mount Timpanogos to go on his ceiling canvas, and the eight peaks completed now lit up the entire lofty room. Romney greeted Woodroe warmly, sat him down, and went off for the sherry ("Rather special. Harvested during the civil war, 1935. Amazing there was anybody left in Spain who could do the vineyards. Probably grandparents and little girls").

It was as if Woodroe were once again there on his weekly visits as a student, though there was a perceptible difference in tone from the undergraduate days. Woody didn't know whether this was because he had graduated or because he was doing front-line patriotic duty with the John Birch Society. He caught his old professor up on his new assignment to Dallas, doing a nice imitation of Robert Welch giving him his orders to keep an eye on Edwin Walker.

"Interesting," Romney said. "I have great sympathy for General Walker, and of course you know about his war record. But I heard him answering questions on television a few months ago, and I have to admit to having had some difficulty in following him. Following him exactly. He was of course right on the main points.

"Still, General Walker is an imposing figure. He turned his aggressive instincts against the Communists. Which means we'll have to be careful. So will you, Woodroe."

"I promise I will be," Woody said, nodding his head.

Careful of what? he asked himself. But before he could dwell on the question, the professor had moved on to talk of the upcoming congressional elections. They also spoke of threatening developments in Cuba, where Fidel Castro continued to get shiploads of aid from the Soviet Union.

Woodroe kept his eye on his watch, having promised to meet up with his old roommate at his club. "I wanted to tell you something about the Objectivist clan. I was there yesterday for a seminar by Nathaniel Branden. He's Number Two in the order."

"Was she there?"

"Oh yes. Sitting on the stage. Smoking. She was turned on after the lecture, to answer questions from the students."

"What did she say? Anything I should know?"

Woodroe laughed. "She said lots of things, but nothing you need to know. That you don't already know."

"The Objectivists pose a special challenge. Because if they succeed in implanting their creed on the Republican Party, it becomes a vessel for . . . a kind of misanthropic anarchy. The GOP has to beat a path to a wholesome conservatism, and that isn't helped by anything I've read by Ayn Rand."

"Have you read *Atlas Shrugged*, Theo?"

"Well, no. If by reading it I could help liberate the captive nations, I'd do it. As a matter of fact, I'd do it if I thought I could talk to somebody in the Kennedy administration about sound economic policy."

Romney noticed the empty glass and filled it.

"The Kennedy people are getting it wrong on all fronts. Those people at the White House are so concerned to look peaceful and affable to Europe and the Third World, they're even arguing for the demilitarization of space. They'll go for demilitarizing the Pentagon, at this pace. And now Mr. Kennedy has his trade bill. They call it a free trade bill." Romney's face brightened. He walked over to the magazine rack. "The current issue of *National Review* has great sport with the items that the government can, under the new law, find some means of protecting from foreign competition." He laughed mischievously. "Want to hear the list?"

"Sure."

Romney tilted his glasses over his nose and moved closer to the lamp.

"It says here that under the new law there is to be special care taken for: 'watches, figs, linen towels, thermometers, stainless steel flatware, carpets, rugs, sheet glass, fur-pelt hats, garlic, smoking pipes, printed silk scarves, scissors, ground fish fillets, cover seed, bicycles, lighter flints, velveteen fabrics, violins, umbrella frames, tartaric acid, baseball gloves, ceramic tiles, straight pins, safety pins, clothespins.'" Romney roared, put down the magazine, and walked over to sit down again opposite his friend. His old, twenty-five-year-old friend, he now thought Woodroe to be. Fellow Mormon. Fellow conservative. Fellow soldier in the anti-Communist struggle.

Romney led Woody out to the door. "Wait a minute."

He turned a light switch on, a second one off. "Look up at the ceiling."

The room dark, Woodroe gazed up proudly at the illuminated surface, at the peaks of the Rocky Mountain range he knew so well, and loved so deeply.

15

J OHN F. KENNEDY WAS in a deliberative mood. He sat up suddenly from his seat behind the imposing desk presidents had used since 1880. He pressed a button on his telephone. "Tell Salinger to come in."

A moment later he interrupted his thought and buzzed again. "Cancel Salinger. Tell Mr. Bundy to come see me."

McGeorge Bundy had a singular capacity for organizing thought and for suggesting an appealing line to draw through scattered events. Kennedy wanted to feel his way through the reports of renewed Soviet testing of their intermediate-range ballistic missiles. He fretted over the relative torpor of U.S. progress in the missile field. *Yes, always, always something to think about, to worry over, that had to do with the Cold War.*

But then, JFK was good at handling crises. He had learned very early from the disaster—a mere three months after he took office— of the military operation at the Bay of Pigs in Cuba. He had acted quickly, appearing on television and addressing the nation. He hadn't exactly taken personal responsibility for the fiasco of the armed attempt by Cuban exiles to displace Fidel Castro. But he knew to make the one point that proved psychologically critical. He had looked beyond the bungled invasion of the Bay of Pigs, beyond the residual problem of one thousand Cuban prisoners held by Castro, beyond the angry stirrings of Congress.

What blame there is to be assigned is mine, as president.

That had been very successful; his ratings had soared.

But the Cuban setback had been exactly that—a setback. A solid entry in the ledger more and more people were keeping: *good news/bad news* for the Communists, *good news/bad news* for the United States. His popularity had held through the breath-catching construction of the Berlin Wall four months later, in August. And then, in January, the Soviet defense minister, Malinovsky, informed the world in *Pravda* that Soviet missiles could now destroy all the industrial centers of the United States and also those of any country that allied itself with the United States.

Fuck. That's Soviet bully-talk. He knew well the sound of it. It was something *else* that was bugging him. His father had once told him that, back in the days when he, the Founding Father, was busy accumulating the family fortune, he had met time after time with business figures. "My eye was pretty good, Jack. In meetings like that, one guy would say something. Something a lot of people wouldn't even notice. But I caught it. Sometimes I didn't realize it—realize that something had been said I wanted to pay attention to—until later. Sometimes until maybe a week later. But then it grew. And other things that were said, well, took a seat further and further back in the room. Good trick that, assigning importance to things that *prove* to be important. They won't teach you how to do that at Harvard, but think about it. It might prove more useful, when coping with a professor, to know that he likes Cole Porter than all the stuff he's telling you about Aristotle. It's the perspectives that matter *to you* that count. Everything else is shit."

President Kennedy reminded himself that in the two hours since he had seen that morning's *New York Times* and read about one more critical political speech by a Republican, his mind had turned to the story of that one speech, by *that* Republican, given under *those* auspices.

He buzzed again. "Cancel Bundy. Get Bobby. Attorney General Kennedy. Get him on the phone."

A sold-out meeting in New York's Madison Square Garden! Sponsored by a right-wing youth organization. Young Americans. Young Americans for Freedom, they called themselves. Their principal speaker was Barry Goldwater. *Sold out! Twenty thousand people!* How the hell did that happen? There'd be congressional elections in November. It would be two years before the Republicans would be shaking out a presidential candidate to oppose him. Was there any other Republican who could fill Madison Square Garden? Tricky Dick? Rockefeller? Scranton? Not likely.

The telephone buzzed.

"Yeah, Bobby. Did you see about Goldwater at the young people's, the young Americans' meeting in New York?"

The attorney general, alone in his office after shooing out two aides, said yes, he had seen the item.

"Well, what's the right wing up to?" the president continued. "That man Welch discovered last year that Ike was really a secret Communist. What are they on to now? Is God a Communist?"

Bobby laughed.

"...Well, that's good news," the president said. "I want to talk about that whole scene, Goldwater especially. And the General Walker business. Has anybody put him away yet? That lunatic. Somebody's going to shoot him someday—wish I could."

The attorney general said Walker was a pretty big figure.

"Big where? In Texas? Everything's big in Texas. I suppose even General Walker can be big in Texas, but nobody gets to be bigger than your big brother in Texas in 1964. These guys got any IRS problems?...Yeah, that's an important date, your lunch speech. I won't hang you up. But we should keep our eyes on the right wing.... Malinovsky? Malinovsky you want to talk about? Well, he's shown us his, one day we'll show him ours. Get to that speech, Bobby. Talk to you later."

16

GENERAL WALKER HAD BEEN TOLD by letter from Bob Welch that Woodroe Raynor, a very promising second-year employee, was being sent to Dallas to work out of the John Birch Society office there, in close quarters with Helena Crowder. "But it's also my idea that he should maintain close liaison with you. You are a great asset of the anti-Communist movement in America," the Founder wrote, "and we want to continue to be in touch and to be helpful and, as required, to coordinate plans."

Woodroe, who had been coached on reading between the lines, groped for its full meaning. He knew that he was to look in closely on the general's activities and report back to the Belmont office, his first loyalty.

The past year had been very active for Edwin Anderson Walker. First the Pentagon had removed him from his post in Germany, protesting that he was indoctrinating U.S. troops with Birchite literature. Six months later, his professional career ended when he resigned from the army, by doing so forfeiting a considerable pension. And then, in January of 1962, he had announced his candidacy for the Democratic nomination for governor of Texas.

The six-foot-three general was by now a familiar figure. "Texas is my home state," he reminded the reporters who came to the crowded announcement at the Driskill Hotel in Austin. "I was born in Central

Point, an' Texas always figured, in my mind, as the heart of the real America. And that's the America I hope to represent, the America I was taught about at West Point. I did my best to represent the real America in Korea and I got in trouble for doin' just that in Germany. But whatever it is that's infected the United States Army and the State Department—an' the White House—can't have infected the State of Texas."

The local headlines focused mostly on General Walker's charge that a former Mexican president, the left-wing Lázaro Cárdenas, was secretly acquiring arms. The scene in Mexico, Walker said, was comparable to the scene in Cuba that had culminated in Fidel Castro's takeover.

Political analysts doubted Walker had the clout to win the nomination, or finances sufficient to make a big showing. But then, in April, General Walker was called to testify before the Senate Preparedness Investigating Subcommittee. In a prepared text he charged that "high-ranking U.S. government officials" were members of a "hidden control apparatus" that was bending the army and other organs of the United States government to the will of the international Communist conspiracy.

That statement—that language—gave rise to press surmise that the John Birch Society had coached the general for the meeting with the Senate committee. This was correct—the statement had been written by Medford Evans, a Society scholarly associate and an editor of *American Opinion*. On the matter of his removal from command, General Walker said that it was saddening that the commander in chief, President Kennedy, had acted as "both prosecutor and judge" against him.

The Senate chamber, crowded with General Walker's supporters, several times broke into applause, especially when friendly Republican senator William Jenner trained attention on the history of the general's heroic exploits in years gone by. This the senator managed to do by coming up with devices by which to return to the biographical point. "Would you have thought, General Walker, when you made a surprise landing on the Hyères Islands—that's H-Y-E-R-E-S Islands, Mr. Chairman—killing or capturing a strong German garrison and clearing the way for Seventh Army landings on the mainland—would you have thought, General, that the government you then served would have protested your teaching what it is that the enemy in Germany believed in, or the enemy in Korea believed in?"

No, the general had responded, he would not have guessed that possible. There was applause. Senator Stuart Symington, the Democratic chairman of the Senate subcommittee, held down the applause and warned against its repetition. The purpose of the investigation, he reminded the witness, was precisely to inquire whether, in the opinion of that committee, the general had been mistreated.

At a ten-minute break, General Walker was informed by an aide that soon after the general had been sworn in, demonstrators had assembled outside, headed by George Lincoln Rockwell. The troop of twenty-odd American Nazis had displayed banners and placards supporting Walker and denouncing "SENATE TRAITORS." Two of the Nazis, including Commander Rockwell, had actually come into the chamber, prepared to listen to the testimony. "They were asked to remove the Nazi buttons on their lapels," Walker's aide reported. "They refused, and were taken out." Walker nodded his head in sober understanding.

The succeeding hour was spent accumulating information on exactly what it was that General Walker had done in his education program and what literature he had distributed. He described that material at some length, but was not precise on just what the books and pamphlets said, or implied, about the loyalty or disloyalty of government officials, or on where, exactly, and under whose auspices, the information had been garnered.

The committee concluded its session and adjourned at noon. Walker was led to the press room. The first questions were to be expected, having to do with the general's charge that a hidden control apparatus had taken control of U.S. affairs. General Walker, his presence imposing, his manners impeccable, took on the questions volubly, but it was hard for reporters to make out exactly what he said. The general's confusion was in part syntactical, but it was not knowable what exactly he had intended to say.

After a few minutes, *Washington Daily News* reporter Tom Kelly, seated in the front row, asked, "How do you account, General, for the fact that the American Nazi Party is outside, giving you its support?"

General Walker accosted that question by striding forward, lifting Mr. Kelly up by his lapels, and punching him in the face.

The uproar was eventually contained, but the press conference was certainly over. General Walker, a security guard at either side prepared to subdue him if necessary, turned to a veteran reporter from the *Washington Post* and bit out his thoughts: "Does that son of a bitch know that I led a parachute drop raid against the Nazis in 1945?" The press scurried away with their stories and their photographs.

General Walker returned to Texas and gave campaign speeches, attempting to generate support for his candidacy. In Abilene, he said that the Communist conspirators didn't observe No Trespassing signs on American soil; and anyway, as Senator McCarthy had proved and as the John Birch Society was busy day and night documenting, "Our people don't really want to just post No Trespassing signs anymore." In Austin he vowed to continue the fight whatever happened on primary day. What did happen on May 5 was that General Walker came in sixth in a race of six candidates.

The postmortem the next day at Belmont was, initially, despondent. "General Walker is through," Jesse Andrews, putting down the AP wire ticker, said to Robert Welch at their ten o'clock coffee. But Welch emphatically refused to agree. Andrews pressed his point: The primary vote was only the most recent thing. There was the physical brawl at the Senate, "and, Bob, the general's problem is getting things said right about our movement."

"The election meant nothing. Elections don't ever mean anything."

"Yeah, but the general doesn't, well, doesn't have much self-control and can't really defend our position very well. You notice, the Young Americans for Freedom put off giving him an award at their Madison Square Garden rally? In fact, the Young Americans for Freedom are evenly split over whether to go through with a scheduled award for him at their fall meeting."

"So? We're going to start taking lessons from the Opportunist Right? What are you advising, Jess, that we wait to hear whether *National Review* okays a continued relationship with General Walker?"

"I know what you mean."

"Well, the *NR* people tried to do it to Ayn Rand and *she's* still around. And we have more chapters and more subscribers than a year ago."

Robert Welch always had the last word, and he said simply that the Society would keep its eyes on the general, while supporting him fully.

But a critical point had arrived.

The George S. Patton John Birch Society Chapter in Dallas was headed by Helena Crowder. And Helena Crowder was a formidable member—wealthy, resourceful, active, and enterprising. She wrote to Welch. She had a great idea, she said. Organize a statewide political rally for Thanksgiving Day and announce at that rally that the George S. Patton Chapter would change its name to the Edwin A. Walker Chapter. "We'll have the affair in the football stadium. We'll get the right people in Hollywood to come. It will be the biggest rally of the year, just two weeks after the congressional election."

Helena Crowder wanted Bob's reaction.

That was when Welch decided to send Woodroe Raynor, his top young aide, to Texas. To deal with General Walker. And with Helena Crowder.

17

ARRIVED IN DALLAS, WOODROE soon learned that the activist conservative community acknowledged Helena Crowder—blond, heavyset, imperious—as its leader. More than that, she was den mother, hostess, financier, coach, cheerleader, and chairman of the board. It required an active curiosity to establish that there was a Mr. Crowder. Jerry Crowder was in the oil business, successful, quiet, laconic, amused and amusing. He was not always wholly amused by his wife's frenetic political activity. Soon after she was elected head of the George S. Patton Birch Chapter, he told her she would need to have a separate telephone line at home. Helena saw Jerry, and raised him: she would have a separate telephone line, yes, but she would also occupy, on the first floor, *an office in separate quarters.*

Jerry Crowder retreated, spending more and more time at the Dallas Petroleum Club. He amused himself and some fellow club members, though not by any means all of them, when he posted on the bulletin board a form asking members to sign their names if they were members of the Communist Party. Everybody finally got the joke, but when Helena heard about it she announced that she would not speak to him, nor expect him to speak to her, for twenty-four hours, "not one word." Even so, she twice broke her quarantine, for the purpose of reminding Jerry that she was *independently* wealthy. "You may not be as concerned as others think you should be about the Communist threat to your oil and gas wells, but that doesn't mean I shouldn't be concerned about what a Communist government would do to my father's trust. To say nothing of the Bill of Rights." Jerry nodded, clasped his throat with his left hand, and scrawled in block letters on a piece of paper, "I'd comment, but can't speak." Helena left the room and slammed the door shut. At lunch with Sam Eustace, her personal lawyer and childhood friend, she was reminded that Jerry was a staunch conservative who contributed generously and had had an active hand in supporting John Tower, Texas's first Republican senator, at the special election a year ago.

The Dallas office of the John Birch Society had two full-time employees: a secretary and a file clerk. But a battery of volunteers, seated at the thirty-foot counter with its telephones and writing pads, did regular duty, telephoning members and potential members, distributing literature sent down from Belmont, and calling attention to special events. In another room there was the special project of Helena Crowder. It had begun in February, when General Walker announced his race for governor. Mrs. Crowder announced her intention of taping every one of the general's speeches and making them available to other John Birch Society chapters. To this end she had procured four Phillips tape recorders. They were efficient, but not speedy: you could run a tape of a human voice at approximately twice the speed spoken, copying it onto a second reel, but nothing speedier than that. Since the general's speeches ran usually about fifty minutes (counting the applause), she could reduce to twenty-five minutes the playing time of a tape for the purposes of duplication. But Unit A linking to Unit B while Unit C linked to Unit D meant only two tapes per hour. Sending one to each of the 260 chapters was a prodigious undertaking, especially when General Walker was giving a fresh speech every day. Perhaps the young Raynor could figure out a way to expedite that operation.

Before setting off for another engagement, Helena gave instructions to the day's volunteers. Jody, the secretary, who kept her earphones on while working on her typewriter, thereby serving two purposes, took notes. Mr. Raynor was to call Mrs. Crowder as soon as he checked in to his office. Helena had rearranged the office so that the young man from Belmont could have a telephone and desk of his own. She took one of the larger poster-photographs of General Walker and thumbtacked it on the wall behind the desk Raynor would be using. Her bridge date was at two, so she would not be reachable until later in the afternoon. But Raynor could leave a message on her phone and she would pick it up from the answering service.

Woodroe arrived just after lunch, after checking in at the board-inghouse where he would have a room and breakfast. In the JBS office, on Churchill Way, he introduced himself to Jody and Sonny, the file clerk, and to the volunteers, who were hard at work. He familiarized himself with the layout of this nerve center for the third-largest JBS community in the country, outnumbered only in Los Angeles and Phoenix. Seated behind his desk, he called Mrs. Crowder's number and left a message. He devoted himself to reading office files, checking budgets, and passing an eye over the inventory of political material. Sometime after four, Jody signaled him to pick up on 117, his phone connection.

Helena Crowder was on the phone. She said how happy she was to know that he had arrived and how anxious she was to spend some time with him, to be debriefed about everything going on in Belmont, and to brief *him* on everything going on "and planned"—her voice had a tone of mystery now—by the George S. Patton Chapter in Dallas. "Why not come to my place for a drink? I have complete privacy in my part of the house. Do you have a car yet? . . . Well, I will send for you. It's 4:30 now. Where will you be at six?" Woodrow said he would still be at the office at six.

"Perfect. And welcome to Dallas, Mr. Raynor."

She lived in a large Georgian house in Highland Park. Nacho, the Mexican driver, escorted Woodroe across a large lawn to an entrance in one wing. The driver touched the bell, then opened the door for his passenger. Woodroe entered a living room luxuriously appointed. It served the owner—that great, tall, resplendent figure who greeted him—clearly as more than a living room. It was also an office. At the corner was Mrs. Crowder's polished wooden desk with stacks of papers and clippings on it. Behind were signed photographs. She gave him a little tour. There was General MacArthur, in a large frame. Then Senator Taft, and Admiral Nimitz, and General Walker. "General Walton Walker. No relation. But before he went to Korea, where he was killed in an accident, he was in Dallas, head of the Eighth Army Group. He came to this house several times. That's me and Senator McCarthy, before he died." She stopped herself, and suppressed a giggle, shaking her head. "Obviously it was before he died, since he is alive in the picture. What I meant was, taken *soon* before he died—he died a year later. Of a broken heart. Senator McCarthy, you must realize, was really *the first Bircher,* though the Society didn't exist when he died. What did him in was that he voiced the same suspicions as Bob Welch.

"On that other wall"—she pointed—"are the intellectuals. That's Eugene Lyons, then Ludwig von Mises—you know, the great economist?" Woodroe nodded. "And that's Ayn Rand. Have you read *Atlas Shrugged*?" Again Woodroe nodded. "Inspiring. If we could get every pro-Communist in the world to read that book, they'd all understand, understand the *whole story.*"

They sat down and she rang for a maid. "What can I give you to drink, Mr. Raynor?"

"I wish you would call me Woodroe."

"Yes, of course. Though I'm old enough to be your mother"—she paused—"if only barely. We have no children. Twins died at birth. Yes, you must call me Helena. Everybody does. Your drink?"

"I would like a gin and tonic."

"That's my favorite too. With just the right slice of lime. Not lemon."

Woodroe sat in an armchair, his hostess on the sofa. She said she wanted to hear more about his background. "I have Bob's letter, of course, and he says you saw the Communists at work in Austria."

"In Hungary, actually."

"Yes, in Hungary. What were you doing? Oh yes, you are Mormon and were doing missionary work. Did you have actual contact with the Hungarians?"

"Yes." He paused. "I saw the refugees. They flowed into Austria across a little bridge, over a canal. They call it the Einserkanal. The bridge, about forty yards long, took them across to Austria. They call it the Andau Bridge because the nearest town is Andau, about forty-five miles southeast of Vienna." Woodroe had discovered long ago that any mention of Andau required geographical orientation.

"And then Princeton?"

"Yes. In senior year I went to Sharon. I was one of the founders of Young Americans for Freedom."

She bridled. "I am not so hot on YAF. They were going to give General Walker an award last spring, and there were votes against him."

"Yes, I knew about that."

Helena Crowder got up, walked over to her desk, and picked up and displayed the photograph of Edwin Walker. "Did you know that General Walker, as a colonel, commanded the paratrooper commando Canadian-American First Special Service Force? They fought in France, Germany, and Italy. He went to Korea then, and never got over having to pull away. It was after that that he was named commander of the Twenty-fourth Infantry in Germany. He joined our Society in 1959." Helena laughed. "I've counted up his special dislikes. They are Eleanor Roosevelt, Adlai Stevenson, *Mad* magazine, Edward R. Murrow, and Harvard University."

"That's . . . eclectic."

"Can you make out the inscription? His handwriting is not very clear. It reads, 'To Helena Crowder, a princess of freedom!'" She paused and lowered her eyelids for a second.

Seated then with her drink, she said, "I want you, of course, to meet General Walker. He has a suite of offices on the seventeenth floor downtown, courtesy of the American National Oil Company, so he doesn't have far to go to the Adolphus Hotel, where I've booked a private dining room for lunch tomorrow, so we can talk with complete confidence and security. And now I want to tell you what my idea is for Thanksgiving. Or did Bob tell you?"

"Yes, he did. It sounds very exciting."

"Well, keep it *completely* confidential. When we announce it, we want a total surprise. I'm thinking of a big splash the first week of November. I've already discreetly inquired. The football stadium is free on Thanksgiving Day."

They talked and chatted for an hour and shared their concerns over the Soviet government's declaration, the day before, that any attack by the United States on Cuba or on Soviet ships bound for Cuba would bring a nuclear war.

"It was all very well," said Helena, "for Secretary Rusk to say that the United States wasn't nervous or afraid. *Nervous or afraid!*" She repeated the words with contempt. "The same secretary of state who was too nervous or afraid to help the Cuban freedom fighters at the Bay of Pigs or to resist the partition of Berlin. . . . Well, you know all that. Thank God for our Senator Tower."

Woodroe told her he hadn't read what Senator Tower had said.

"He said that U.S. policy on Cuba and the Soviet Union was, I quote, 'one of massive appeasement.'"

Woodroe looked again at Helena's photograph of Ayn Rand. Warmed by the drink and by the personal allure of his hostess, he ventured, "I know somebody who works for Ayn Rand."

"Lucky man."

"He's a she."

"Lucky girl."

"She is very enthusiastic about the Nathaniel Branden Institute."

"We're thinking of helping out the people who want to sponsor some lectures here in Dallas. What do you call what they call themselves?"

"Objectivists."

"What does that mean, exactly?"

Woodroe smiled and swallowed a large draft of his gin and tonic. "It takes Branden twenty lectures to spell that out. And *Atlas Shrugged* was—"

"—One thousand one hundred and sixty-eight pages."

"Right. Well, the important thing, I guess, is that objectivism absolutely rejects any increase in government power."

"We have to have an army and an air force."

"Yes, but what they say is that only volunteers should serve. Never conscription. In fact, everything that is done by anybody should be voluntary, and volunteers shouldn't be guided by anything more than self-interest. And the mind must be free to recognize what a person wants and can reason for himself—herself—what they want, and why they want it. That kind of thing."

"Well, I know she's a great writer and a great champion of freedom. That's why I have her picture up there."

Her house phone rang. "Yes. Yes, Jerry. I'm coming. I'm just having a nice chat with the very nice young man taking over the JBS office. . . . Yes, Jerry. He's taking over the JBS *subject to my direction.*" She smiled broadly, a splendid figure of a woman. Her face was expressive, the lips full, the makeup highlighting the blond hair, the pin on her jacket displaying the American flag in rubies, diamonds, and sapphires.

"Nacho will take you wherever you want. Then tomorrow I will meet you at 12:03 P.M." She laughed. "General Walker is *very* insistent on punctuality, so he never makes an engagement using round numbers."

"See you at 12:03, Helena. Many thanks."

Nacho was waiting for him outside the door.

18

I T WAS TOWARD THE END of the lunch that General Walker
confided his plans to Helena and Woodroe. He had put off
disclosing them until he had moved well beyond the perfunctory
handshake with the young man Helena had brought in. Woodroe
Raynor's membership in the John Birch Society was a pretty fair
warrant of his reliability. But after all, it was the responsibility of the
Society to be skeptical about presumptive credentials, and to pene-
trate disguises. Accordingly, General Walker waited until after
dessert had been served. He was impressed by Woodroe's account
of the Hungarian refugees' fleeing their country in 1956. But he
instructed Woodroe that the *apparent* revolt by the *apparent* freedom
fighters in Hungary had been exposed in one of Robert Welch's
communications as having been, in fact, an elaborate ruse. The
Communists had staged the entire thing—

"Why, General?"

General Walker smiled. There was a hint of condescension
toward the young man. "Because, Raynor, the Communists' idea was
to expose the *real* anti-Communists, find out who they were, then
lug them off to prison and execution. There were 13,890 people
shot and 2,492 students hanged."

Woodroe drew breath. "Gee. Where did you get those figures? I
never saw *them* before."

"I had my sources of information when I was in Germany. In
fact, I still do. You don't believe it about Hungarian treachery?"

"Oh yes, General. Yes, I do believe what you say about . . . Hungarian treachery."

The general looked Woodroe square in the eye. "I trust you, young man." And then to Helena. "Draw your chair up a little closer. I'll keep my voice down."

He divulged that he was going to go to Oxford, Mississippi. "The time has come for a showdown with the federal government. They— the Kennedy people—haven't said it, but I *know* it: they're going to send federal forces, maybe the army, to force Ole Miss to admit a Negro." He lowered his voice still further. "Helena, you know this— maybe *you* don't, Raynor. I was the commander on the field in Little Rock just five years ago when General Eisenhower—"

"President Eisenhower," Helena corrected him.

"I always think of him as a *general*. And"—turning to Helena— "we both know what Bob Welch says about the general. I'm not sure I'm on board on that one—I'm not yet prepared to say that Ike was a Communist agent—but it would explain a lot of things."

"Like Little Rock?" Woodroe asked.

"Yes, like Little Rock. Here was the Supreme Court ordering the integration of the local schools, which the people in Little Rock just didn't want to do. It wasn't for the federal government to decide these things. What the government did was tear up the country by sending troops into Little Rock. And tearing up the whole country is *exactly* what the Communists want, like Bob Welch says. I tried to resign—that was later published in all the papers—"

"Yes, I read about that."

"But they wouldn't allow that, wouldn't allow me to pull out. That was tough, me following orders on *that* assignment. But I'm out of the army now. And you know, they're going to try, you watch, to do the same thing in Oxford."

"What's the legal situation there, General?"

"Yes," Helena said. "Explain that to Woodroe. Call him Woodroe, Ed."

The general leaned back in his chair. "Well, you know, I'm not a lawyer. But this is how it is, pretty much. I might be getting the courts a little crossed up, but the colored outfit, that . . . National Committee of Colored People, or whatever they call it, they lined up this young feller, he's twenty-nine years old—already married and has a kid—and he's got no more interest in going to the University of Mississippi than I've got, oh . . . in enrolling in the navy.

"So what happens? So the colored people line him up and look at him and tell him where to dot the i's and cross the t's in his application form. Then they go to court. Court in Mississippi, I believe, they began with. And the court said no, there's state law against mixing the races, and the governor, he said right away he was going to enforce that law. So what do the colored people do? I shouldn't say the colored people, because my impression of it is that they have only one or two they bring out for parades. What they have up there is mostly white Jews.

"So they appeal to *another* court. That'd be a federal court, right?" Helena nodded.

"And *that* court says the Supreme Court, back in that ruling— the *Brown* ruling—ruled that separate schools were unconstitutional. So the federal court ruled—not unanimous, like maybe . . . 3–2, something like that. They said the colored student had to be admitted."

"His name is Meredith," Woodroe contributed.

"Well, of course there was an appeal, and the governor—Governor Ross Barnett—he backs the appeal to the hilt, says either state governments have control over their schools or some foreigner, some foreign body, has control."

Helena turned her head slightly toward Woodroe. "They pleaded the doctrine of 'interposition.'"

"Yes, something like that. So the Mississippi court says that Mississippi police and troopers have to take orders from the governor. So"—he raised both arms in a gesture of despair—"the colored society goes to a federal court in New Orleans, the same one that had, you know, that split decision, and this time the court splits in favor of states' rights, but not by a big margin. So? Back to the next higher federal court."

"The Court of Appeals."

"That's the one, Helena. And the good news was, the Court of Appeals upheld, granted it was a close vote, the New Orleans court. You following me, son?"

"Yes, sir."

"But that means the colored people are going to appeal *both* of those court decisions. That's been done, and now it goes over to the Supreme Court. The Warren Court. *Impeach Earl Warren*, the John Birch Society says. Yes. You might as well say, *Free Cuba*. You can bet on it, the Commie-dominated court is going to rule that socialism wins. When it's states' rights versus socialism, socialism wins."

He took a gulp of his iced tea.

"So the Supreme Court is going to vote with the integrationists. Then Kennedy will have to *enforce* that decision. And there's a congressional election coming up, four or five weeks down the road, and I don't reckon the other Kennedy, Bobby, is going to hurry up to advise his brother to send troops down to Mississippi a few days before an election."

Woodroe permitted himself to look at the carpet. The general had been taking him in with concentrated attention. The fixity of the general's eyes had disconcerted him. When Woodroe raised his head again, he affected a cough. But the general was undistracted.

"When you see the enemy getting ready, that's the time for *you* to get ready. Maybe I told you that once, Helena?"

"I think you did, Ed. I think it was in one of your speeches."

"I like to think you'll find it in *all* of my speeches. So? That's the job I've assigned myself. Be up there with the Mississippi troops. The freedom fighters. If the feds come down, the freedom fighters will need professional help."

Woodroe worked to control his breathing. He eased his eyes over to Helena.

There was silence. The first silence since they had come into the room.

The general took a sip of water. "I wanted you to know my plans, Helena." And to Woodroe, "You are sworn to secrecy."

"Yes, sir."

"Well, it's time to get to work."

"Yes," said Helena. "And you've got the speech tonight at Fort Worth. You're great to take everything on the way you do."

The general rose. He was a commanding presence in his double-breasted blue suit, standing taller even than Helena Crowder. The general turned to Woodroe. He winked broadly. "You know what I call her, Woodroe? I call her a princess of freedom."

Helena smiled and led the way out of the dining room.

19

O N FRIDAY MORNING, September 28, Helena Crowder went directly to her office at the Birch Society and used the intercom. "Woodroe, dear, come in. I want to talk to you about something important."

He picked up his steno pad and walked by the volunteer section, past the library, to the office of the chairman. The six newspapers she required to see every day waited for her on the desk. A basket of mail rested at one corner.

"Now here is what has happened." Her blouse was trimly cut. Except for the pearls, the only jewelry she wore was the little American flag on the lapel. She spoke now in the executive mode, pencil in hand, her own notebook open.

"This is very confidential." She looked to the door, reassuring herself that it was closed. "I had a telephone call last night, just before dinner, from General Walker. He said that since the Supreme Court had acted, he was going to live up to his commitment to go to Oxford. Then he read me the public statement he will issue on Sunday. The big rally is scheduled for that night. I asked him for a copy of his prepared statement but he didn't want to send it over. What he did want, and asked me for, was a public endorsement by the John Birch Society of what he was doing. Preferably the JBS nationally. If not, at least the George S. Patton Chapter here in Dallas."

"I'm not sure individual chapters have the authority to do that, do they?" Woodroe asked.

"Good point. And as I'm about to tell you, I got hold of Bob Welch. That took a little jumping around. He was giving a seminar in Peoria and I finally got him in Urbana. He was staying at the home of Revilo Oliver. You know him?"

"I've seen his name in *American Opinion*. And back a while, some of his short book reviews in *National Review*."

"Well, I've met him. Striking man, taller even than General Walker. A classics professor. Anyway, when I called, the Olivers were giving a reception for him, so Bob said he'd have to call me back from Professor Oliver's study as soon as he could get away from the party people. *Sooo,* it wasn't until eleven that his call came in. I told him about General Walker's plans to go to Oxford and to make a public statement. Then I repeated as much of it as I could remember."

"Will the general encourage outright defiance?"

"It's a very emphatic statement. He even has Christ involved, but I can't exactly remember just how."

"What about the declaration of support he asked for?"

"Bob said no-go on a national declaration but said it would be okay for the Dallas Chapter to support the general. *But,* Bob said, we should do that in general language, not sort of attaching ourselves directly to his declaration. Woody, I want you to put something together for me."

"Is the something I put together going to acknowledge that he's going off to Mississippi?"

Helena paused. "Well, I'm not sure." She doodled on the paper and bit her lip. She looked up suddenly. "What do *you* think?"

"We've got to have a reason for issuing a statement, going out suddenly, on September 28, so . . . Hang on. Helena, let me go to my typewriter and come back. What I'm thinking of I can get done in three minutes."

"Take as long as you need. But that statement is top priority. I have a lot on my desk and I'll be here all morning."

Woodroe was quickly back. He handed her a sheet of paper.

The George S. Patton Chapter of the John Birch Society today joined with other chapters in deploring the Supreme Court's decision setting aside the lower courts' validation of Mississippi law respecting admissions policy at the University of Mississippi. Dallas's own General Walker has publicly called on the federal government to abide by state law and the tradition of the separation of powers. We will welcome reports from him after his planned visit to Oxford.

"That's . . . perfect." She looked up, a smile on her face. Then, "Now I've had another thought. This may require one more call to Bob Welch, though he'll be hard to get for a while—he was leaving Urbana early to fly back to Boston." She looked out the window. "But maybe we can figure this out on our own. My idea is: *You* should go to Oxford and keep your eye on the general. Maybe even help him out, if it's the kind of situation you can help with. If you're willing to go, we don't really need Belmont's okay. We can finance your trip from our own funds."

"I couldn't very well do that without checking with the general, could I?"

"That's a problem. He's already en route. I can find out where he's staying. Jody would know that."

"I'd guess, Helena, that the whole world will know about ten minutes after General Walker lands where General Walker's staying."

"Yes, I see your point. But do you agree to go? I'll tell Bob we couldn't get hold of Walker, that he was traveling, and that I thought it would be a good idea and we had to decide quickly."

There was no seat on the Memphis flight until Sunday. Woodroe went to his Royal portable typewriter. First, a letter to his mother, though with only the sparest description of his new assignment, and no mention at all of what he sensed was coming up at Oxford. Then a letter, overdue, to Theo Romney.

"Our man is bound for Oxford, if you're watching the evening news and the Mississippi scene. I'm going there myself. I'm in kind of an ambiguous position—I'm really going there for the JBS. We're supposedly all on the same team, but I'm just not sure about telling the students to block the enrollment of that Negro student. Theo, us folks from Utah aren't . . . racists. I never even felt the urge, but I assume there's got to be an urge to do it, to look down on Jews and Negroes. So many people do. I can't remember if in your course you commented on how the Chinese railroad workers were treated when they crossed God's country. That's *our God,* Theo. I haven't forgotten. Other Christians get it almost right. We get it *all* right.

"You'll certainly be reading about the general in Mississippi. I hope you won't be reading about your old pal."

He signed off, as always, "With gratitude, Woodroe."

He added a P.S. "If I get back before the world ends, I'll shoot down, say hello. Save some sherry for me and don't put too much sun on Provo Peak."

At the Memphis airport, Woodroe took the airport limo and traveled downtown to the bus terminal. He boarded the packed bus for Oxford just before it pulled out. He had to stand up the whole of the ninety-minute trip. There were mostly young people, of college age. They were excited and talkative. A few minutes into the trip, a blue-eyed blond girl launched a song, and others quickly joined in. The songsters were especially robust in their rendering of "Dixie," which they sang militantly soon after the bus pulled away from Memphis, and again just before it pulled into the station in Oxford.

Another girl, probably nineteen or twenty, was seated by the window, to one side of Woodroe. Her red hair was in braids and she was busy with a heavy black crayon. Standing in the aisle, clinging to the overhead strap, Woodroe, looking down, could see what she was writing on the cardboard placards her companion handed her, one after another, from the pile on his lap. When she had finished one, she would hand it back to her supplier, who would place it on the bottom of the pile.

Woodroe watched as the block letters were written out. "HANG WARREN." She did three or four of these. There was "GIVE US LIBERTY OR DEATH." She did "NIGGER GO HOME," but after sketching it she paused and deliberated. She had a conversation with her companion. He called back to a student called Ray, who got up from his seat, four rows back, and walked up the aisle to where the artist-activist sat. Woodroe couldn't hear what the three said, but after Ray returned to his seat, the girl tore that placard in half and resumed with others.

The students were met by a delegation from Ole Miss and walked off excitedly, preparing for the big evening ahead. Helena had said she'd ask Jody to make reservations for him at the same hotel as the general, which was the Hilton-South. Woodroe spotted a taxi and told the driver to take him to the Hilton Hotel.

"Who's stayin' at the Hilton Hotel is General Walker. Did you know that?" The driver, wearing a baseball cap and sunglasses, had the radio on.

"No," Woodroe said. "I'm in town to sell books, schoolbooks for the students."

"The students ain't reading books tonight, mister. They're fixin' to demonstrate against the federals. The president's going to *talk about it* tonight."

"President Kennedy's doing a television talk?"

"Yes, sir. Ten-thirty P.M. And it's all about what's goin' on here in Oxford, Mississippi."

Signing in at the hotel, Woodroe spotted the typewritten notice posted on the desk. "GENERAL EDWIN A. WALKER WILL MEET WITH THE PRESS AT THE HILTON-SOUTH CONFERENCE ROOM AT 7:30." It was just after seven. Woodroe took his bag to his room, looked over at the bedside telephone, and thought suddenly, *Why not?*

"I'd like to speak with General Walker."... No, he didn't have the general's room number.

There was a pause. Then, wide-eyed, Woodroe was staring into the phone after hearing the familiar voice.

"General, this is Woodroe Raynor. Helena Crowder suggested I come to town and...you know, in case you need any help."

"Thanks, son. I'm all set up, doing a press conference downstairs in just a few minutes. Then some students are coming for me and I'll go on campus for a rally. I suppose you can come, too. Why not? That's the idea, rally the freedom fighters. So I'll see you later, Raynor."

Woodroe, impatient with the laggard elevator, walked down the four floors to the lobby and over to the entrance to the conference room. He could see into the crowded room, floodlit by camera lights. A hotel attendant at the door thrust out his arm to keep him out. "We're full, sir."

He pulled out his Birch Society card marked STAFF and said, "I'm with the general."

Once admitted, he edged himself along the wall and found a spot alongside others who couldn't get a seat.

At exactly 7:30, General Walker, preceded by two hotel men doing duty as security, strode in.

There was a considerable stir. The television cameras began turning.

The general walked to the lectern and raised his hand. "I have a statement—"

"*Louder. Loud-ehhrrr.*"

General Walker knew all about microphones and loudspeakers and electrical defects. He pulled out a heavy blue pen and tapped the head of the microphone, turning it clockwise, then counter-clockwise.

"How's that, men?"

There was a murmur of assent.

"I have a statement to make, after which I'll take questions."

He leaned just an inch or two closer to the typewritten sheet on the lectern and began:

"This is Edwin A. Walker. I am in Mississippi beside Governor Ross Barnett. I call for a national protest against the conspiracy from within."

Woodroe looked about. The reporters were taking notes. There were spectators from the Oxford community, he guessed, but mostly he was in a room full of students dressed in jeans and sports shirts. Everyone was keenly attentive.

"Rally to the cause of freedom," the general continued reading, "in righteous indignation, violent vocal protest, and bitter silence under the flag of Mississippi at the coming use of federal troops."

He paused and looked up from his text for a moment.

"This today is a disgrace to the nation in dire peril, a disgrace beyond the capacity of anyone except its enemies. This"—the general's voice rose—"is the conspiracy of the crucifixion by anti-Christ conspirators of the Supreme Court in their denial of prayer and their betrayal of a nation."

There was silence, except for the whirring of the cameras. After a bit there was applause at the back of the room. Tentative applause, Woodroe thought. Not the kind you expect after a great call to action from a great American war hero. Perhaps they were waiting for more? But the general had put down his notes. He had finished his statement and was ready for questions.

Walker raised his hand. "Before we take questions, somebody is smoking a cigarette back there. Please put it out."

Again, silence. Then, from the floor, "General, I think I have your statement down pretty well. You said it was time for... 'violent vocal protest.' What do you mean by 'violent'?"

"'Give me liberty or give me death.' We Texans were brought up on that." Again there was silence. Elaboration was expected.

The same voice came back. "General, I know about that...great statement by Patrick Henry. But what I'm askin' is, Are you recommending to the students that they resist by force what the federal troops are called in to do?"

"I'm not going to try to improve on the language of Patrick Henry."

The questioner gave way to a young woman standing by a television camera. "General, I'm here for Station WMCT. Is it true you're going from here to the campus to address a student rally?"

"I am here to do what I can for my country."

"Yes, but what are you going to urge the students to do?"

"I will urge them to do their duty."

Woodroe could hear the reporter seated at knee distance from the questioner mutter to his colleague, "Oh, shit. We'll just have to *see* what he does. What he says to the kids."

General Walker said it was time for him to meet with the student leaders.

He walked out of the room. There was, again, a smattering of applause.

20

THE STATES' RIGHTS COMMITTEE leader, law student Roy Atkinson, lanky, earnest, highly motivated, had labored since his arrival that afternoon from Memphis to put together something that could serve the protesters as center stage. Of course it would have to be at the Circle, the central green in the academic quarter of the university. He knew he wouldn't be able to set up anything like what he had done junior year, for his boyhood friend from Tupelo, Elvis Presley. Back then he had made provision for twelve thousand students who, seated on the grass, exulted over Elvis-sound on the eve of Elvis's departure for the army. Acting then as Ole Miss coordinator, Roy had had the help of two sound technicians who wired in loudspeakers at the quadrant corners of the Circle. Today he'd have to settle for a single microphone with loudspeakers placed at either end of the Confederate monument standing at the head of the Circle, in front of the Lyceum.

Ole Miss was officially on the governor's side. It was the admissions policy of the university, defended by Governor Ross Barnett, that kept Negro students away. Still, the frenzied administrators at Bryant Hall were not about to expedite Roy Atkinson's return to campus for the purpose of galvanizing a student protest that might well get out of hand.

At 8 P.M., Ole Miss chancellor John Davis Williams and two aides looked out through the broad windows in his office to the expanse of the Circle the students were rapidly filling. It would be a long night, John Williams sensed.

As arranged, a squadron of U.S. marshals would escort James Meredith to his dormitory room—the first black in history to set foot on the university campus as a student. General Walker was in town and would be a speaker at the monument site. At 10:30, President Kennedy would speak from the White House, presumably to urge submission to the law. Muriel Stetson, the forever-blond television news personality from Memphis's WMCT, was already on campus. She had set up at one end of the monument and was interviewing students as they passed by.

"She's been talkin' here nonstop for nearly two hours," the chancellor commented, turning dejectedly from the window to the television on his desk, from which Muriel's voice, it seemed, issued endlessly.

The chancellor's aide commented, "Every time she talks about protests, she makes it sound like anybody who protests is a Confederate survivor. Notice how she points over at the monument every couple of minutes?"

"Yeah," said the chancellor. "I'm surprised WMCT isn't handing out free bullets. . . . Oh, *here we go.*"

General Walker had arrived and there was great shouting and revelry. The WMCT camera dollied to the nest of student organizers. Roy Atkinson was talking excitedly with the general. The camera looked out over a crowd getting denser by the minute. Placards were cropping up. Many called for the impeachment of Chief Justice Earl Warren. One double placard said, "JFK GO HOME," and on the tier-placard directly under it, "AND TAKE JIM-BOY WITH YOU."

The camera showed a student grabbing Roy's shoulder and saying something to him. Roy, arrested by what he had heard, turned to the general and pounded his right fist into the palm of his left hand. Muriel Stetson came back on screen.

"We have news here from our field contact that the Negro student James Meredith has entered Ventress Hall protected by twenty U.S. marshals—correction, that's *eighteen* U.S. marshals. We'll see if we can get a comment on that from student leader Roy Atkinson. Roy? Roy? . . . Well, we'll have to wait on that." The camera focused on Atkinson, who was talking again with the general and pointing his finger at the lectern. "I guess they're getting ready to hear from General Walker. Let's tune in."

Roy was now tapping on the microphone. The noise from student demonstrators posed an apparently impossible obstacle to getting heard. Hoping that the presence of the general himself, in the spotlight, would silence the students, Roy could be heard only by those close by as he introduced *"the greatest general since Douglas MacArthur, who"*—but even the television mike lost the ensuing words, then picked up *". . . will now. . . ."* Again words were lost.

But now the microphone was in the hands of former major general Edwin A. Walker. When young Captain Walker had been assigned in 1943 to lead a parachute raid, the colonel serving as military coordinator discovered to his dismay that Walker had never before used a parachute, let alone qualified as a paratrooper. This discovery was less than one hour before the mission was due to lift off from the airfield for a practice run. He was scanning the roster desperately for a replacement leader when Walker rose from the briefing room and said, "Just tell me how to put it on, Colonel." Walker was oblivious to surrounding disturbances.

Ten thousand students who could not make out the words being spoken from the lectern were simply today's problem for Ed Walker to overcome. He roared into the microphone, but only the TV viewers and a few students immediately in front could hear what he was saying. Those immediately beside him could make out his call to resist federal movements to trample down on local authority, the greatness of the southern tradition of holding on to ideas, and the great Confederate standard of liberty above all—

"What the shit's he saying?" the chancellor said, looking at the screen.

"Doesn't much matter *what* he's sayin'," his aide said. "Those people out there, John, they're not gonna listen to *anybody.*"

They certainly were not listening, two hours later, to the president of the United States. Speaking from the Oval Office, John Kennedy was telling the American people, "Our nation is founded on the principle that observance of the law is the eternal safeguard of liberty, and defiance of the law is the surest road to tyranny. Americans are free to disagree with the law, but not to disobey it."

But things were out of control at Ole Miss.

Thirty thousand students and townspeople were in the streets protesting. There were stringy bands of people on the other side—supporters of civil rights, James Meredith, the Supreme Court, JFK—but they served primarily the purpose of augmenting the intensity of the majority. The turbulence grew, on campus and off campus. Nationalized state guardsmen were contending with billy clubs in what seemed a losing battle. Here and there shots were heard. One U.S. marshal was brought to a first-aid station, a shotgun blast in the neck. A nickelodeon repairman from Jackson was killed, shot in the head with a bullet designed for who-knew-whom. A correspondent for Agence France-Presse was found dead, a bullet fired at close range into his back. The protesters gave no quarter, rioting through the night in what Muriel Stetson, yielding now to NBC's Chet Huntley in New York, had labeled "the most massive state/federal confrontation since the Civil War." Sometime after midnight, army scouts from Jackson's army base brought word that three thousand federal troops and four hundred more U.S. marshals would arrive on campus by midmorning.

In Washington, at the White House command center, Attorney General Robert Kennedy was on the phone to the marshals' detachment at the Oxford airport. His voice was strong. "Tell you what, Marshal. Arrest General Walker."

Bobby Kennedy looked up at his brother for approval.

The president said, "What's his crime?"

"Inciting to riot."

The president paused, then nodded his head.

The attorney general spoke on the phone again to the marshal. "We'll get a court order. You'll have it in hand by the time the troops get to him."

It was shortly before dawn that General Walker was accosted by a single U.S. marshal. Two others had slipped behind him, and in an instant the general was manacled. The driver of the army transport standing by picked up the radio message and drove through the stragglers to where the general was held.

Walker was advised, in the transport, that he was charged with assault of, or opposing, federal officers; preventing a federal officer from discharging his duties; inciting or engaging in an insurrection against the United States; and conspiring to overthrow or oppose by force the execution of U.S. laws.

He was arraigned before a U.S. commissioner and bail was set at $100,000. He was driven then to the Oxford airport, which had been transformed into a brightly lit army base, placed in an army transport, and flown to Springfield, Missouri, where he was taken to the unit designated Federal Bureau of Prisons. There, pursuant to the order of District Judge Claude Clayton of Oxford, General Walker was informed that he would receive a psychiatric examination.

The federal troops arrived throughout the night and into the morning of October 1. They set up roadblocks, and by 11 A.M. they had quelled most of the rioting, arresting 150 protesters. Late that morning, James

Meredith was escorted to class. Governor Barnett made a show of attempting to block his entry into the classroom building but was quietly turned to one side. General Walker watched that scene on television, through the bars of his cell.

21

I T HADN'T BEEN EASY for Woodroe in Oxford that night to move about and maintain any sense of direction. There was simply no way to make one's way resolutely through the student mobs. Woodroe had quickly lost any idea of where General Walker was. He ducked into the student union, thinking to get a TV view of the local scene, but there were too many people crowded about the set and too much noise. Emerging, he decided to pursue a U.S. marshal platoon that appeared to be trying to work its way southbound across the Circle. There were six marshals. Their leader was talking on a radio held close to his ear. Perhaps the platoon leader knew where General Walker was and would lead Woodroe to him.

Moments later, the little column stopped, at the signal of its leader, who listened for instructions, radio to his ear. When the leader put the radio down, he noticed Woodroe standing by and called out, asking him what he was doing.

"I work for the John Birch Society in Dallas. They thought General Walker might need help."

"You guessed right on that score. But we're here about restoring order and we don't need any out-of-towners on the campus. You're staying where? Hilton? Well, get your ass back there. Go back that way, other side of the Lyceum." He pointed. "Turn right and you'll see a sign. And don't let us catch you again on campus."

Woodroe wondered whether it was wrong—dumb, maybe—to have told them he was with the John Birch Society. But then *why the hell not?* The Society was a perfectly legal body. On the other hand, it wouldn't make sense to find himself in jail as a JBS rioter.

So he made his way toward his hotel. He'd be better off watching the scene on television in his room. It took forty minutes to make the fifteen-minute walk, but he got there, and found a security agent at the entrance, who satisfied himself that Woodroe was a guest of the hotel. Woodroe wouldn't mind a beer, maybe two, take them up to his room. He stepped toward the bar. It was closed. Order of the police, they told him at the desk. "All bars are closed, citywide."

In his room he turned on the television. For the next two hours the cameras took him to scenes of student rioting, of looters detected and sometimes arrested, of snatches of exhortations from speakers on both sides. He got the report of the dead French correspondent and the technician-repairman, but nothing about General Walker.

Sometime after three in the morning, Woodroe closed his eyes. He dreamt of an interrogation at which what he struggled to say was not being heard. The interrogator's dream voice blended into the voice of a reporter broadcasting from Cape Canaveral. Woodroe woke with a start. Astronaut Walter Schirra was being prepared to attempt a six-cycle orbit around the earth, scheduled for October 3.

Woodroe was relieved that TV was carrying news other than from Oxford. But just then Barbara Walters was back on the subject. She said that General Walker had been arrested. That he was charged with inciting a riot and had been taken off to a federal prison. "There are a total of four charges filed against General Walker. He is a member of the John Birch Society, but it isn't known if the general was in Oxford yesterday representing the Society. He made a statement to the press before his campus speech last night. It called for 'violent vocal protest' and charged that the order to integrate Ole Miss was 'the conspiracy of the crucifixion by anti-Christ conspirators.' Questions from a reporter didn't elucidate exactly what the general meant by that. At last count, over 150 protesters have been jailed. There is still riotous action, though it has calmed down. In a matter of hours, the 2nd Infantry 2nd Battle Group will be in Oxford and also an armored cavalry regiment and federal forces of the 1st Infantry Regiment, from Fort Benning, Georgia, with 3,500 paratroopers of the 101st Airborne Division. There are roadblocks on the street and public transportation is suspended."

Woodroe kept his eyes on the screen as other accounts came through, including, and this came as a surprise to him, a report that the United States was resuming its atmospheric nuclear test series in the Pacific. He shut off the television.

He had to decide what to do next. He had better call Helena. He grabbed his address book and got the operator: he wanted to place a call to Dallas.

"No long-distance telephone calls are going out."

"Any idea for how long?"

"Sir, I don't know whether things will *ever* be normal in Oxford."

He closed his eyes for a moment. *I've got to get out of here.*

He was ready to use up his cash reserves. He would approach the desk. . . . No. Better one service echelon down. "Is room service operating?" he asked on the telephone.

Yes, what did he want?

"What have you got that's ready?"

"Well, sir, we have juice and coffee and rolls and—"

"Bring that. Please. Is there a morning paper?"

"No, sir, no papers today."

He shaved, showered, and dressed. He answered the knock on the door. The waiter was an elderly black man holding a tray.

"What's your name?" Woodroe asked quietly as the waiter carried the tray to the table.

"My name is Henry."

"Henry, I've got to get to Memphis and the buses aren't running. If you know somebody could take me in a car, I'd be willing to pay fifty dollars."

The old man hesitated before saying, "I'll take you. But not until eleven. I go off duty at eleven."

Woodroe would wait two hours.

It was twenty-six hours later that he finally arrived in Dallas. His first call was to Lee. He explained that he hadn't been able to get through to her from Oxford, had spent a long night in a car, and now had urgent business in Dallas and would call her later in the day. He rang Helena and got through to her at home.

"I'm sure glad to hear from you, Woodroe. It's terrible what they've done to General Walker."

"I need to catch up. You coming to the office?"

"Yes, I sure am. I have a date there with the *Dallas News* reporter and with the AP reporter."

"Have you gotten through to Bob Welch?"

"I did. I spoke with him last night. He said the right thing. We've got to raise unshirted hell about the way they treated the general."

It was five days before General Walker was released from federal detention. Arrived in Dallas, he conferred with his lawyers, and they fanned out to seek reparations. Lawsuits were filed against the federal marshal who had arrested him, against the judge who had ordered a psychiatric examination, against the superintendent of the facility in Missouri who had kept him confined, against the doctor in Oxford who had affirmed the need for a psychiatric examination, against the Associated Press, which had broadcast news of his alleged psychological illness, and against newspapers in Memphis and New Orleans that had spoken of the general's alleged illness.

Helena Crowder was cheered the next day by the telegram from Welch quoting the editorial in *National Review.* The magazine had been critical of the Society in past issues. This editorial should be given wide circulation in Dallas, Welch said. "Its summary is good and well put." General Walker, the editorial read, had been in Oxford nonviolently protesting government action. "Whereupon (1) he was whisked off to a local judge, who (2) ordered him to submit to psychiatric treatment in a federal prison on the recommendation of a government psychiatrist who had not even seen General Walker; and thereupon (3) was spirited off to Missouri and detained on $100,000 bail; which bail (4) was refused, when it was finally raised, pending the completion of compulsory psychiatric examinations. If that is not a judicial horror story," the editorial concluded, "we hope we never hear one."

The editors, whose magazine had gone to press while Walker was still confined, ended with a broad reference to the famous telephone call by presidential contender John Kennedy to Mrs. Martin Luther King when her husband was jailed in Atlanta. "One can only hope that all civil libertarians in the United States will take on the General Walker case, and that President Kennedy will telephone his condolences to him in jail, that being his habit when people involved in racial entanglements are abused by local courts, proving that Mr. Kennedy is willing to intercede on behalf of the victimized, irrespective of race, color, or creed."

Another week went by. The general's primary lawyer, Robert Morris, who served also as president of the fledgling University of Dallas, a Catholic institution, stayed in close touch with Helena Crowder. He confided to her his recommendation that General Walker not give *any* speeches or hold *any* press conferences until after the post-Oxford scene settled down. He confessed a hope that, under pressure, the attorney general would drop the charges against Walker. "He could make up, a little, for the way he treated Ed in Oxford. I know Bobby Kennedy. He did work for Senator McCarran when I was first counsel for the Senate committee. And he did work also for Senator McCarthy. Bobby can be mean and determined, but he doesn't like losing, and we've got enough due process objections on the Walker case to stop the prosecution dead, I mean stop it dead."

On October 22, there was another speech by President Kennedy. He revealed that the Soviet Union had emplaced medium-range nuclear missiles in Cuba and that he had ordered the United States Navy to block any Soviet ships heading for Cuba.

The blockade of Cuba was challenged by the U.S.S.R. the following morning. Premier Nikita Khrushchev warned that Soviet ships would not submit to search, and that U.S. aggression could lead to thermonuclear war.

Woodroe, breathless on hearing the TV report in his room, meditated on what appeared a nuclear deadlock. *But how could this be?* John Birch doctrine didn't allow for a showdown—the Soviet Union was effectively in charge of U.S. responses, wasn't it? How would Bob Welch analyze *that* development? Why wage nuclear war against a country already under Communist control? Meanwhile, the United States of America was under threat of nuclear devastation from missiles that could be launched from an island ninety miles away from the state of Florida.

In 1949 the Communists reached seven thousand miles to New Mexico to ferret out the secrets of the nuclear bomb; in 1962 they have thirty-eight nuclear missiles a rowboat's ride away from the United States. Some foreign policy, Woodroe thought, *a U.S. foreign policy that permits that to happen in thirteen years.*

Unaccountably, his thoughts turned to Leonora. He could imagine almost anything in a nuclear age. But he couldn't imagine life without Lee. He put in a call to her.

BOOK
THREE

22

I T HAD BEEN ONLY THE ONE month in Texas, but it had been full, and Woodroe's mind was grudgingly at work trying to assimilate everything that had happened. He was discomfited when, for his weekend visit to Salt Lake, he learned that his mother had arranged for him to be a guest at a meeting of the local John Birch Society. Inevitably he'd be asked to speak, and Woodroe wasn't confident about how to frame his narrative. Ezra Taft Benson, a Mormon elder, had been a cabinet member with the Eisenhower administration and would probably be there—ironically, since Mr. Benson had to have read what Welch had written about Eisenhower in *The Politician.* The three-hundred-page book detailing reasons for believing Ike to be a Communist agent was not an official publication of the John Birch Society, but it had been widely circulated. It was not conceivable that Mr. Benson was unaware of it.

Mrs. Raynor was proud of the attention being paid to her son. He had had such a *"harrowing"* experience in Oxford with General Walker, "who really relied on Woodroe, you know," she explained to Mrs. Chafee, at whose house the members would meet. It rather annoyed Mrs. Raynor that her daughter, Ellie, had said she did not want to go with them, much as she loved Woody. Woodroe didn't find this out until time came to get out to the 6 P.M. meeting and he learned that his sister, a sophomore at the University of Salt Lake, wasn't accompanying them to the car. He thought to ask her why, but stopped himself. Perhaps Ellie didn't want to have to answer questions, at college, about her brother and the John Birch Society. Woodroe was understanding, but sad. One more datum to reckon with in the swirl of things.

No alcohol in Mormonland. Woodroe had concealed from his mother his defection, but he had to acknowledge to himself that he missed the drink he'd have been offered almost anywhere else, at 6 P.M., before being called on to speak.

He spoke well, carefully avoiding any evaluation of General Walker's deportment, in particular at his Oxford press conference. Woodroe spoke only about the abuse of the general's civil liberties and the probable complicity of the attorney general. Asked his opinion of the conclusion of the missile crisis, he said only that he thought it unconscionable that the president should have assured the leader of the Soviet Union that the United States would never mount an invasion against the same Cuban leader who had harbored destructive missiles with which to threaten the United States. That criticism was met with applause, including by Ezra Benson, Mrs. Raynor noticed, recounting this proudly to Woodroe on their drive home.

That night, back in his bedroom, he read his book and waited until he knew his mother had gone up to bed. Ellie's room was at the end of the hall, and she would probably not be coming down. Woodroe wanted to talk with Theo Romney and it wasn't the kind of conversation he'd wish to share with others in the family, and there was only the one phone, in the living room.

It would be nearly midnight in Princeton, but Romney stayed up late and welcomed telephone calls well past midnight. "I just finished speaking with Frank Meyer," he told Woodroe. "I'm doing a book review for him. Where are you?"

"Home. Salt Lake. I spoke to the JBS chapter on the Mississippi scene and on the missile crisis. Ezra Benson was there. I tried to call you from Oxford—"

"I was hoping to hear from you."

"The phones weren't working. Then when I called after Kennedy's Cuba speech there wasn't any answer."

"I was in New York for a few days. I went to a seminar, Ludwig von Mises. He has it right about the state, the enemy of liberty. I call on a lady in New York."

"Well, that's nice, Theo."

"I know what you're thinking. I'm rather old for that. Well, I'm only seventy-two. Your Ezra Taft Benson is what, a hundred and seven?"

"That's great, Theo. Do I get to meet her? When?"

"Before the next Soviet ultimatum, I hope."

"That's what I wanted your views on. Here, of course—I mean, at JBS—it's simple. *The U.S. was told to do it.*"

"Well, of course, that isn't what happened. JFK was just scared. What we need now is to wait for the Republicans to be heard from. Nothing much yet from them. Nixon is busy trying to become governor of California, Rockefeller trying for another term in New York, Scranton trying for Pennsylvania. Everybody drawing huge breaths of relief that we aren't at war. That's good, we aren't at war. But we should never be threatened by war, not with the right leadership. So look at the status quo ante. The Soviets have pulled back their missiles. Well, they weren't there before. And *we've* promised not to invade Cuba—that's a fresh promise. And also to remove our missiles from Turkey—that's a fresh promise. So the Communists are net ahead, one more step."

Woodroe asked what in Princeton had been the reaction to the crisis. There had been angry talk among some students, he learned. "The faculty didn't have much to say. They're remarkably docile, you know, Woody. If there's a Democratic administration supervising things, they tend to just sit and take it."

The conversation went on another ten minutes.

Woodroe promised to visit soon.

"Maybe you'll see me in New York."

"I hope so. I'll be back in a couple of days. I'll call. How're the Rocky Mountains doing?"

"I'm having a problem with Mount Olympus."

"I'll snap a picture of it tomorrow and send it to you. Thanks, Theo. Good night."

Woodroe had a happy time those three days. His mother asked whether he would like it if she invited to dinner, that last night, Hester Adams. He laughed. "Mom, I took Hester to the senior prom in *1956!* That was like a million years ago."

"No, darling. It's been only six years."

Ellie disposed of the issue. "Hester Adams is engaged, Mom. The announcement was made a couple of weeks ago."

His mother invited, instead, two old friends—a classmate, and a teacher Woodroe had especially liked. In the two and a half hours, the John Birch Society was not once mentioned. He thought that faintly odd. But he wasn't going to bring it up himself. Besides, his mind was on the next evening meal he'd be having. With Leonora Pound, in New York.

In his hotel room at the Sherry Netherlands he waited for the phone to ring. She had said she would call his room from the lobby at seven o'clock. At 7:15 the telephone finally rang. He heard her out, nodding his head as she spoke, as if signaling acquiescence at every point.

She had suddenly decided, she said—late in the afternoon—that it would be more pleasant to eat "at home." She had brought together everything they would need, now cooking in her own oven. But if he wished, he could bring around an extra bottle of wine. "I don't have a big cellar."

He knew the address. He had used it—1012 Sixth Avenue—in writing to Leonora from Texas. She had gotten her own apartment after signing up to work full-time with the Nathaniel Branden Institute. He arrived with two bottles of wine, one of them a sauterne, and with the cake that had caught his eye at the corner bakery.

Did he wish anything written on the cake? the lady had asked. "It's compliments of the house."

Woodroe paused. "Well, yes. Write two words, 'Altruism'—that's A-L-T-R-U-I-S-M"—he spoke the letters slowly while the woman, wielding the tube, squeezed out the frosted lettering. "Yes," the woman said, "and the next word?" Woodroe didn't look into her face to see if she smiled: "S-U-C-K-S." The cake was boxed, and he walked down the block and into 1012. At the elevator he rang the eleventh floor, then walked down the hall to 11E. The door opened and she was radiantly there. The measuring cup in her left hand didn't hinder their embrace. With one hand, Woodroe held the straps of his two packages. He let them down to the floor and renewed his embrace, touching his lips to hers, diffidently, then with a trace of passion.

"Let me check the stove," she managed to say. "Put your coat in the closet. Give me the wine. What's that?"

"A cake."

"Oh, I had some ice cream. Well, we'll have ice cream first, and if the election returns are good, we'll have the cake."

Two hours later they sat on the sofa, the wine and demitasses on the coffee table. They had touched on every subject in their excited, happy talk—on General Walker and Barbara Branden, Helena Crowder and Robert Kennedy, Salt Lake City and the NBI lectures.

"Hey," she said, "let's have a look at the elections. After all, they only happen every other year. And it was the last election—no, it was the Republican *convention* of 1960, not the *election* of 1960, that brought us to Sharon. That was a . . . happy event for me, Woody."

He took her hand. "Well, the national election, post-Sharon, gave us President Kennedy. That was *some* choice, it turned out. It gave us the Bay of Pigs, the Berlin Wall, and the missile crisis."

"Oh yes. On the other hand"—she spoke in an even, academic tone of voice—"it got that Communist Eisenhower out of the White House." She broke into laughter.

So did he. Maybe his complete surrender into laughter was a little . . . disloyal to his employer? He'd think about it. He could only retaliate in their running mockery, Birch vs. Objectivism, by saying he'd like a piece of cake. She bounded up and brought the box over from the kitchen with two forks and a knife. She opened it and the ensuing laughter was, once again, mutual.

They drank from the dessert wine and then he told her, his throat dry, that he would like to take her to bed. Wordlessly, she led the way. He didn't want to think about his night with Teresa in 1956, but as his excitement mounted, he was taken back to that exhilarating rapture, and tried now to pass it on to Lee, to his lovely Lee, and he knew the extra measure of his elation. Now they whispered to each other. It was midnight when she said, "Let's go see what happened. No. No. Don't put any clothes back on." She preceded him to the living room and they made do with only the light from the television screen. It was as it had been in Kapuvar.

The Democrats had scored big gains in House and Senate races. The dramatic personal news was California: Richard Nixon, former vice president, had been soundly defeated by the Democrat Pat Brown.

She turned the sound not off, but down, and they lay on the sofa, remarking on the news as the items cropped up on the screen. Other GOP presidential aspirants had scored. Nelson Rockefeller in New York, George Romney in Michigan, William Scranton in Pennsylvania.

"Guess that means something," Leonora said.

"Nothing *we* care about, Lee. Right?"

"Right, Woody."

"We care about other things." He leaned over and brought his lips to hers.

23

THERE HAD BEEN AN INKLING of it a month earlier. Ayn Rand had not left her Park Avenue apartment in weeks. Nathaniel and Barbara Branden worked night and day, it seemed, on the concerns of the Nathaniel Branden Institute. Ayn said at a gathering of the Collective on Saturday that she thought there was a little pallor in the handsome face of Nathaniel. Her eyes searched the room and touched down on the faces of the seven Collective members in attendance. Only Leonard Peikoff was absent—he was in California and had served notice he would not be there. The deliberated passage of Miss Rand's questioning eyes gave the impression that this was a forum, and that the views of everyone there were being consulted in a probe for consensus.

But of course it wasn't that way with Ayn Rand. If she detected a pallor, there *was* a pallor; and if others did not espy it, the explanation was as simple as that they were blind. Even so, her eyes looked about inquisitively as if seeking confirmation of what needed no confirmation.

Alan Greenspan attempted to contribute to the question being explored. He said, "Yes. Nathaniel, perhaps you and Barbara should get away for a day or two? As an economist, I know something about the allocation of effort. It is economically profligate to deploy high skills that are not required for the undertaking at hand. You may say that there is an inelastic demand for work of a clerical nature being done to promote the fortunes of the Nathaniel Branden Institute, and I would acknowledge that—but without acknowledging that the allocation of your special skills to such work is the reasonable way to proceed."

Ayn liked the direction in which the talk was proceeding. She elucidated with manifest pleasure.

"As Alan says, there are demands which, because they are inelastic, by definition need to be met, and it is in the nature of social accommodation that these are often—note, I am not saying *necessarily*—undertaken by persons whose time, measured by their resources, is not reasonably used in such activity.

"Consider me—" She pointed to Barbara, seated to her left, next to Frank, and traced one of her habitual finger arcs over the heads of all the members of the Collective, reaching finally Nathaniel, seated at her right hand. "I spent thirteen years composing *Atlas Shrugged*. With my fingers depressing *exactly* the right keys on that typewriter"—she pointed to the hallowed object on the desk in the corner. "I was fully allocating my mind to the work in hand. As most of you know because of the frequent readings I did here with the Collective, the words—the language, the images, the ideas—were the product of intense thought and—"

"A brilliant imagination," her husband interposed.

Ayn Rand nodded her head slightly and produced a faint smile. She resumed: "And the end product could not have been effected except by the allocation of my entire attention. Now. . . ." She paused dramatically, leaning over to light a cigarette. There was silence. "*Sometimes,* working alone at, say, two in the morning, I would need or desire sustenance. And then? Are you following me, Joan?"

Joan Mitchell, who had been married briefly to Alan Greenspan, nodded her head and volunteered, "You made your own tea."

"*Exactly,*" Miss Rand said. "You have here the actualization of the economic conundrum. Aristotle and I both boiled water, which is work that does not tax the resources even of an illiterate slave boy. The point, as applicable to Nathaniel and Barbara, is that they should give more thought to the distribution of the work of the Institute so that they do not need to spend so much time, so to speak, boiling water."

Mary Ann Rukavina asked, "Ayn, might it be contended that the use of one's mind in such activity as is unrelated to that which requires the full application of the mind could be understood as nature's means of exacting rest? I mean, when you were writing at two in the morning, there had to come a point when you had to stop in order to rest. And, clearly, when sleeping, one is, in a sense, just going one step beyond the boiling of water—"

Ayn stopped her. "We are hardly discussing the natural biological requirements of the human body, which engages in activities— the use of the mouth to eat, of the alimentary canal to process, the anus to excrete—necessary to the cyclical demands of organic life. If you are saying that a pause in order to boil water is a means of resting the mind, giving it surcease from the level of exertion required for hard rational application, the answer is: No. Alan is correct. It is a misallocation of economic energy."

After most of the Collective dispersed, at about one in the morning, Ayn tilted her head back and blew smoke up toward the ceiling.

"We have established, Nathaniel, that the pallor I spoke of is there. You and Barbara must go on a few days' vacation."

24

W HAT MADE IT ALL PERFECT was that Ayn, two days later, said that she would consider Nathaniel's invitation to travel with him and Barbara to Toronto.

Joseph Blumenthal, Nathan's father, had a men's clothing store in Toronto. He and his wife were very proud of their son and of his national recognition as the right hand of Miss Rand's Objectivist movement. Dinah Blumenthal had told Miss Rand nine years earlier, at the wedding of Nathaniel and Barbara in 1953, that she had read *The Fountainhead* with great enjoyment. Actually, she hadn't read it, but Joe Blumenthal had done so with especial curiosity after fourteen-year-old Nathan announced to the household that *The Fountainhead* was the most important book he had ever read. A few years later, Nathan departed for Los Angeles. Once there, he wrote to Ayn Rand, imploring her to give him just one hour of her time. He was desperate to meet the illuminating genius who had changed his life with a single book.

The invitation extended, Nathan Blumenthal arrived at the ranch house at eight in the evening. He left at five o'clock the next morning.

At Nathaniel's wedding in 1953, Ayn Rand served as matron of honor, Frank O'Connor as best man. The bridal party was held in White Plains, New York. Joseph Blumenthal had risen to his feet to give what proved to be an extended toast. He said he had wanted friends and family present to hear something of the nature of the letters he had received after Nathan met Miss Rand. Unfortunately, the packet of letters from his beloved, brilliant son had been lost in the fire at his establishment—"the fire that burned up enough men's clothes to equip the Canadian army!"

But he remembered much from them. How Ayn Rand had received Nathan at the Chatsworth home in Los Angeles. How she had told him, after an hour or two, to stay on and have dinner with her and her husband—"that lovely man, Frank O'Connor. If anybody here doesn't know it, Mr. O'Connor is embarking on his own career as an artist. He will be a *renowned* artist, you take my word for it. I have seen pictures of several of his oil paintings, and my knowledge is not limited to evaluating the quality of men's clothes!" There was polite applause.

He told of Nathan's stupefaction when Miss Rand kept him at her ranch *until five o'clock in the morning.* They had discussed, young Nathan had written home, "everything in the world, and all of the ideas that were...generated by her *Fountainhead* book."

That nine-hour session—Mr. Blumenthal had extended both arms, raising his eyes skyward—had been the birth of a wonderful association, following which Nathan came to New York to live and study and Miss Rand and Frank also moved to New York from California.

Pressing his invitation to join them on the trip to Toronto, nine years after the wedding, Nathaniel reminded Ayn and Frank that they had not traveled out of the city in months. Ayn pondered the invitation, puffing deliberately on her cigarette. She would decide that night, she said.

Nathaniel and Barbara learned of her decision at six the next morning. The telephone rang, waking them up with the good news. Ayn would accompany them on their vacation.

Nathaniel had intended to fly to Toronto, but Ayn had never been on an airplane. Although she didn't say so, Nathaniel detected the problem immediately: She was afraid to fly.

"We can always drive, Ayn."

And so they did, breaking up the long trip with a night at a motel in Syracuse. Arrived in Toronto, Ayn was respectfully and warmly received. She in turn was civil to the Blumenthals.

It had been suggested that on the third and last day of the visit, Ayn and Nathaniel might offer an informal seminar at his parents' home. After Nathaniel had said on the telephone in New York that Ayn had okayed the idea, the Blumenthals invited a dozen friends. A reporter from the *Toronto Star,* getting wind of Rand's visit, rang the Blumenthal house to ask if he might make mention of the seminar the next day in the "Goings-on About Town" section of the paper. Nathaniel placed his hand over the phone and relayed the request to Ayn. Getting the signal from her, he went back to the phone. The answer was no. But the reporter did not hang up. He asked if he might himself attend. "Not professionally. I am just a fan." Again Nathan covered the phone with his hand and relayed the request.

"How many times has he read *Atlas?*"

Nathaniel smiled and put the question to the caller. After getting the satisfactory answer, he said, "Okay, you can come."

Nathaniel was nervous about how Ayn would behave before an audience untutored in objectivism, half of them personal friends of his parents, the rest, friends of friends. He took Barbara aside and consulted with her.

"The thing to do, Nat, is not to permit questions. If nobody asks a question, she can't be rude to anybody."

That gave rise to an idea.

After Nathaniel's talk, Barbara would be introduced and would advise the assembly that she would now put to Miss Rand the five questions most often asked at her seminars. Barbara was well qualified to do this, she'd say, having attended, with her assistant, Leonora Pound, *all* of Nathaniel's lectures that had been followed by Miss Rand's Q & A.

Ayn agreed to the format.

Nathaniel and Barbara devoted a half hour to devising the five questions. They must be questions that did not presuppose specific knowledge of the Objectivist movement, let alone familiarity with the lectures that had gone before. But they must exploit the natural talent of Ayn Rand for exposition. They resolved to ask:

1. *Is it true that objectivists can't believe in God?*
2. *What is the difference between objectivism and libertarianism?*
3. *What is it about objectivism that is unique?*
4. *What are the political prospects of success in the movement you are leading?*

The final question would bring an answer very pleasing to their hosts. Barbara would ask, in Joe Blumenthal's house:

5. *Who is equipped to lead the Objectivist movement after you have retired?*

An hour later Ayn announced that she wished to dine alone with Nathaniel the night before the seminar. She would wish to consult with him about their appearance. They would go to a restaurant, one that a friend had recommended, L'Esprit du Nord.

Upstairs, an hour later, there were three exchanges. In their own bedroom, Dinah Blumenthal said to her husband that she was rather surprised by Miss Rand's decision about dinner the next day, since Dinah had prepared a good dinner at home for all four of their visitors. Joseph told his wife that they were dealing with a very great lady, and that people of genius had to be expected to act—differently.

In the guest room, Frank O'Connor told his wife that her decision to go out alone with Nathaniel might upset their hosts, who undoubtedly had made preparations for them all. "Cubbyhole," Ayn said, "I need to make my own decisions in these matters. You know that."

In the children's room where they were staying, Barbara Branden made something of a scene, keeping her voice down only with effort. "What do you think you're doing, leaving your parents' house on the first visit with them in *five years* to have dinner with Ayn, who you see in New York *every day of the week?*" Nathaniel said that he had been a little put out by the suggestion, but what was he to do? Ayn was their guest, and the primacy of guests' desires was how the world worked.

"Besides," he said, "Ayn is Ayn. The whole world revolves around her. Why would it be different in Toronto?"

Barbara thought to say that it was certainly clear that *Nathaniel's* world revolved around Ayn.

But she stopped when she reflected that this was so also of her own world. That world too revolved around Ayn.

25

O N THE DRIVE BACK in the rented car, Frank was at the wheel, as he had been ever since setting out for Canada. Barbara Branden sat at his side, but her mind was not on the discursive patter Frank now and then engaged in. She trained her mind on the scene in the back seat. Ayn and Nathaniel were speaking to each other endlessly, in a high pitch of exuberance. They spoke about everything, about the seminar the night before, about the philosophical innocence of his parents, about Nathaniel's boyhood memories, about Ayn as a girl, about her confidence in him as eventual successor and leader in the Objectivist crusade, about the high hopes he had for the success of her forthcoming public lectures, about the great ambitions they both had for the Nathaniel Branden Institute, which owed everything to her thought and her patronage.

Barbara slightly adjusted the rearview mirror and brought a lipstick to her lips to feign the need for the mirror angled to her use. She left it in place, giving her a view of the back seat whenever her indignation sought it out. Ayn and Nathaniel were holding hands.

They stopped for lunch on the outskirts of Syracuse. The conversation between the Numero Uno Objectivist and the Number Two Objectivist continued unchecked. Barbara bought a copy of the Sunday *New York Times*. She shared it, and some fried chicken, with Frank. Across from them in the booth, Ayn and Nathaniel ate and talked. After lunch they made their way back to the car. Nathaniel volunteered to take the wheel, but Frank said he rather enjoyed driving, which he had scarcely had a chance to do since leaving California. An hour or so later, there was silence in the back. Once more, Barbara adjusted the mirror. Ayn was asleep, her head on Nathaniel's shoulder, his arm around her neck.

They reached the outskirts of Albany and found the recommended motel just off the highway. They entered the restaurant for a light evening meal. Ayn and Nathaniel were suddenly silent, but Frank and Barbara could both see the bewitchment in her eyes. They agreed to start out for New York at eight in the morning.

In the bedroom, Barbara wheeled on her husband. She hissed out the words. *"She's in love with you. And you're in love with her."*

Nathaniel usually liked to talk and to explicate, to argue and to expound, to analyze and to opine. But tonight he thought only to say, "Barbara, I'm tired. We'll talk tomorrow."

"Don't you want to make love with me? Why not just pretend I'm Ayn Rand?"

His face flushed, he marched in his shorts into the bathroom and slammed the door shut. Seconds later he opened it, walked to the end of the room, thrust his hand into the briefcase, and pulled out a volume. He reentered the bathroom, shut the door, and locked it.

Two weeks later, toward the end of the afternoon, Ayn waited for Nathaniel in her studio. He had lecture notes he was to go over with her.

She sat in the living room, a book on her lap, at the same end of the sofa from which she presided at meetings of the Collective. Opening the door, following the usual, perfunctory ring of the bell, Nathaniel headed for her desk, where he and Ayn usually sat when they had work to look over together. But today she beckoned him to the sofa. She said she was ready to talk over with him the "private subject" he had told her, on the way back from Canada, he wanted to discuss.

Nathaniel Branden had actually phrased in his mind exactly what he wanted to say. He came out with it.

He could no longer go on as things were between them. He loved his wife, Barbara, and was in many ways happily married, but he felt in his loins an urging that Barbara did not satisfy. "It could only be satisfied, Ayn, by you."

He was not John Galt, he said, referring to the fabulist hero of *Atlas Shrugged*, a man handsome beyond description, intelligent beyond peer, dominant beyond comparison. But in years of association with her, he said, inexorably he knew that the union they had accomplished intellectually cried out for enhancement. In his thought, Nathaniel had deployed the perfect word to describe what he did *not* want.

"I don't want a Platonic relationship."

Ayn looked with her great eyes at her enchanted, enchanting, virile junior by twenty-five years. She stood, walked to the door, locked it, and then pulled down the shade.

She took his hand and drew him down on the sofa.

26

I N PLANNING HIS RETURN to Belmont and the meeting with
Bob Welch, Woodroe called Jesse Andrews. They chatted for
a bit about the national election results and the missile crisis in
Cuba: "Bob's bulletin analyzing that scandal will be in the mail in a
couple of days. It is very long—thirty-six pages."

"Are we still on for tomorrow afternoon, a conference with you
and Bob?"

"Yes. We want to talk to you about General Walker and other
things. But you shouldn't plan to go back to Dallas. The Walker
operation is on hold, pending the lawsuits and all that business. But
Bob has an idea, and I fully endorse it: We need a presence in the
pro-Communist, cultural capital of the United States. And you
know I got to mean New York City. So come in about three o'clock,
but plan to return to New York in a day or two. We'll go over the
whole Dallas business."

Bob Welch looked older than he had even two months ago. He was,
as ever, civil and courteous. He tried to make his asseverations in
soft-spoken tones. He said almost parenthetically that the arrest of
General Walker and "the attempt to pronounce him insane" was a
straightforward strike by the Communist arm within the government
but this time they had really overdone it, what with the flagrant
denial of civil liberties. "They will face the consequences."

Woodroe listened. He waited for Welch to go on to discuss the future of Edwin Walker. Welch said nothing further about Walker, so Woodroe prompted him. "Bob, the general's problems with the U.S. marshals in Oxford came *after* he made his press statement and the Q & A that followed. There was something . . . not quite right there in that statement."

"The general was rattled."

"Bob, in the first place, *nothing* rattles Edwin A. Walker. He wouldn't have been rattled at Hiroshima. In the second place, he prepared that statement for the press *in Dallas,* two days before he delivered it. He even tried it out on Helena."

Robert Welch gave the smile Woodroe had seen before, seen several times in the fourteen months he had spent in Belmont. It meant: I have heard your position, now let us move on.

"General Walker is an American hero and he is a dedicated anti-Communist and that means he will be misrepresented and persecuted. *That,* really, is all we need to know in order to proceed with our plans concerning him."

Jesse broke in. "But that doesn't mean, Woody, that we're saying you need to go back to Dallas—"

"Right," Welch amplified. "What we needed you for there needs . . . no further attention, at this point. Helena Crowder is topflight. And she has a young man in tow, Jonathan Summers, a graduate of Southwest Texas recommended by Senator Tower. He can do some of the work you were prepared to do.

"No. Where I want *you,* Woodroe Raynor, is in New York City. Largest city in the United States and, after Washington, the most corrupt ideologically—the most pro-Communist–oriented—and our membership there is very low. . . . We need in New York a—if you will excuse it, Woodroe—a nice, bright, presentable young man who can go to meetings, speeches, forums, and identify himself as a representative of the John Birch Society. And have the chance to get into the public forum on the subject of the Communist movement and the subversive failure of the United States government to contend with it."

"Yes, Bob, and I like the idea. Jesse tipped me off to it on the phone yesterday, so I've had a chance to think about it. And I've checked in New York at your office. You have at this point exactly one paid secretary in New York and enough office space for a handful of volunteers. Do I go in there with a budget to expand that operation?"

"We're not thinking so much of increased membership in New York as we are of heightened presence. Most anti-Communist activity in New York is, well, free—free admission, I mean. People are welcome to come in. The key character in New York is Marvin Liebman. He raises the money and organizes letterheads—the whole thing—for most of the anti-Communist organizations in New York. The key outfit of the Liebman operations is the Committee of One Million Against the Admission of Red China to the United Nations. He also runs Young Americans for Freedom—your old outfit—and a half dozen other fronts. You need to get to know him."

"I met Liebman at the Sharon conference."

"Good. Cultivate him."

"And what about a budget?"

"We don't have much spare change. Your salary would remain the same, but with an expense account of— What would be reasonable, Jesse?"

"I don't see how you could take anybody to a ham sandwich in New York on less than"—he looked up at the Founder for approval—"a hundred bucks a week?"

Robert Welch stood up after nodding his head. "I have to copy-read my report on the missile crisis." He extended his hand.

Woodroe took it.

After two hours' debriefing by Jesse on the situation in Dallas, Woodroe went to his hotel room, a sandwich and a beer in hand from the local delicatessen.

On the phone he gave Leonora the good news. "It's now confirmed. I'll be staying in New York. So don't pack my bags, Lee."

"I wouldn't pack your bags, Woody, unless I was going off somewhere with you. Maybe Budapest?"

Woodroe winced. "That's a bad memory, Hungary. One day I'll tell you about my first night—my only night, actually—in Hungary."

"Did you misbehave?"

"Not by Miss Rand's standards. It was . . . consensual."

"Can't wait. Woody, be sure to watch at 9 P.M. the president's fireside chat. Joan Mitchell has a contact at CBS and got an advance copy. Our movement is having some effect on the White House. Your people at John Birch are hitting hard on big government; *ours* at the NBI are also hitting hard on big government.

"Anyway, the president's going to say that we *have to have* tax reductions effective January 1, 1963. He's going to announce that Walter Heller, his chief economic adviser and chairman of the Council of Economic Advisers, has so advised him, so the administration's tax-reduction program is 'top priority.' JFK will say, here is his language exactly—I have the speech—that 'the case for a tax cut is independent of recession and rests on the long-continued existence of the gap between capacity and spending and the absence of any reason to suppose that the gap will close itself.' How do you like *that,* Woody?"

"I like it fine. Maybe we can sign Kennedy up!"

"First we'll give him twelve lectures by Nathaniel."

They spoke a full hour. Finally, "Just think, Lee. I won't see you again—till tomorrow."

"Unless there's a Communist takeover."

"Fuck you, Goldstein."

"Well, you've practiced at that, Raynor. Good night, my love."

27

WOODROE WROTE TO MARVIN Liebman. Liebman's command station on Lexington and Thirty-eighth Street was only nine blocks from the Birch office. In the letter, Woodroe recalled their meeting in Sharon at the founding of YAF and congratulated Liebman on the success of the big YAF rally at Madison Square Garden, less than two years after Sharon. Liebman was friendly and talkative on the phone about the prospects for 1963. Woodroe was in turn talkative. He told Marvin he was eager to exchange thoughts on the anti-Communist enterprise. He told him that he had had direct experience with the Communists in Hungary, that he had graduated from Princeton in 1961 and had gone to work directly for Welch, and that he had been at Oxford when General Walker was there, and could they meet for lunch?

Sure, Marvin said. What about tomorrow?

That was no good. "I've got to be in Princeton." He would not disappoint Professor Romney. "Friday?" Liebman suggested. They made the date.

The arrangement was as usual. Woodroe would go to the apartment on Nassau Street. Professor Romney's seminar ("Go West, Young Man," it was informally dubbed) ended at five. "We'll have cocktails and then dinner, skip the sherry," the professor told him. "I'll have a few minutes on my painting. I'm still having trouble with Mount

Olympus, though I've sketched it three times and have *National Geographic* photos of it. They were an improvement on what you sent me. But thanks, anyway. I already told you. It continues to elude me. Did you stare at it as a boy? I'm sure you did. Perhaps the common experience accounts for our elevated view of all matters. Maybe you will give me a critique. Bring your sunglasses—I have used very bright colors. The Soviet feint into Cuba in October was a mighty precedent. Foreign powers, if they are sufficiently hostile, now know they can with impunity bring nuclear weapons to U.S. beaches and vacation for a few weeks. I received your postcard from Memphis last October. You sounded as if you expected to spend the rest of your life trying to get back to Dallas."

Woodroe arrived early enough for squash with his friend Elmer, who was now a senior. They had competed vigorously in squash for two undergraduate years. Elmer Gantry (his parents—they married at age nineteen—had thought it a huge joke to name him after the popular novel deriding clerical hypocrisy) was very solemn in the matter of his squash game, and absolutely unconcerned about all other matters, including foreign policy. He told Woodroe that Communism "would take care of itself after a while—everybody will get tired."

"Tired like those zippy missiles the exhausted Commies sent around?"

Elmer shrugged and walked over to his side of the court.

A half hour later Woodroe didn't give evidence of it, affecting nonchalance, but he was privately elated that he had won the game. He enjoyed Elmer's company, and enjoyed defeating him in squash. He showered, put his pants and jacket back on, and walked over toward Nassau Street.

Not having visited Romney since before his trip to Texas, Woodroe knocked before entering the apartment.

"Come in. That you, Woodroe?" The voice came from above. Theo Romney was hard at work at his painting.

Supper was brought in by the student delivery service. Romney asked for more details about what Woodroe had seen and heard in Dallas and Oxford, and then turned to the broader question.

"It looks to me as though the Communists are retaining the initiative," Romney said. "They've given us a kind of ultimatum—no more blockades. They've won on every front—Bay of Pigs, Berlin, missile development, and they're cranking up an initiative in Southeast Asia. The Republican Party is having a hard time articulating a foreign policy. No matter what JFK does, Americans love him. I don't know whether you people in the Birch Society can do anything to call public attention to how it's going, but your man Welch has to be careful."

"About what?"

"About giving the impression that everybody in the United States is a Soviet agent."

"He doesn't say that."

"I know. But he gives that impression. Tell me about your girlfriend...Leonora?"

"Yes. Leonora Pound. She's an...objectivist."

"You told me that. She works for Ayn Rand. I read *The Fountainhead* a while back. You read it?"

"Of course. It was easier going than *Atlas Shrugged*."

"I told you I haven't done that. Maybe I'll take it along if I ever do another mountain hike. I think what it's telling you is that steep mountains are nothing for true believers."

"You mean true *non*believers."

"Yes, I know Rand is a worked-up atheist. Nonfaith can move mountains, is her motto."

Woodroe smiled and poured another glass of the red wine. "She's certainly consistent in her antistatist positions."

"Yes. And from what I've read, she wants the conservative philosophy to be as...inhuman as the characters in her books. She wants to contend against the Communists by urging us to use reason. I've got nothing against reason. Do you, Woody? Though I can't remember your using any reason in my class."

Again Woodroe smiled. He had scored the highest grade in Professor Romney's class and he knew that he had earned it.

"The trouble with reason," Romney said, "is that it hinders you from understanding people who act unreasonably. And it keeps you from talking with people you need to talk to to make progress in the world."

"People like who?"

"People like voters. President Kennedy is going to run again and the Republicans are going to have to come up with somebody who can—reasonably—call for a harder line against Khrushchev, and they're not going to be attracted by any movement pledged to inhuman policies. It isn't going to help the Republican candidate—that'll be Nelson Rockefeller, I assume—to read *The Fountainhead*. Perhaps your Mr. Welch will convince Rockefeller that Miss Rand is a secret agent."

"Oh, cut it out."

The older man smiled and reached for the flashlight in the bookcase. He wanted to shine it on the mountain peak he was worried about. He still hadn't caught Mount Olympus, and he knew it.

Marvin Liebman, famously affable, liked meeting with one or two people at most. Often his work required him to meet with ten or a dozen, notably at the committee board meetings. But these he managed to hold down, and always succeeded in doing so because the trustees and directors of all his groups had confidence in him.

The central figure in Liebman's life was Charles Edison, the elderly son of the great inventor. Edison, sometime secretary of the navy, had once been the Democratic governor of New Jersey. After the war, he had turned his attentions to the struggle against big government at home and the Communists abroad.

His hearing gravely deteriorated, his health shaky, the widower Edison left New Jersey to live in the Waldorf Towers hotel, one floor removed from General Douglas MacArthur, one floor from former president Herbert Hoover.

Edison distributed his money cautiously, but he was usually there to encourage Marvin Liebman. There was always a prospective mailing to an inchoate committee to protest whatever. In recent years, there had been President Eisenhower's invitation to Khrushchev to visit the United States—Liebman initiated a committee to oppose the visit. South Korean prime minister Syngman Rhee had unilaterally released South Korean prisoners under United Nations detention—after the UN Security Council condemned Rhee, Liebman initiated a committee applauding him. Students at the University of California in Berkeley had mounted Operation Abolition, urging Congress to discontinue the work of the House Committee on Un-American Activities—Liebman backed the congressional committee and produced a film on the operations of the California lobby. Castro had announced his determination to bring socialism to Latin America aided by the Soviet Union—Liebman had a Committee for the Monroe Doctrine. All these political ventures needed modest capital to launch them. Charles Edison was there to advance it.

Marvin was always amused by untoward incidents in his complicated life. At lunch, puffing on his cigarette at Paone's restaurant, where he liked to eat and where the editors of *National Review* so often lunched, he recounted to Woodroe that Governor Edison had asked him to screen for General MacArthur a documentary one of Marvin's committees had made on the subject of the territorial advances of the Communists in Asia and Europe. It was called *The March of Marx*.

"Imagine, being responsible for taking a projector to MacArthur's own suite. Governor Edison was there, but my hands were so shaky I could hardly thread the film. But I did, and then I said, as though

I was good at that kind of thing, I said, 'General, Governor, whenever you say!' 'Go ahead,' the general said. So I pushed the play button and *pftt!* The bulb exploded; I just got some black smoke. What to do? The general pushed a button of some kind and a colonel—Colonel Whitney, an aide—came in. MacArthur pointed to the projector and the colonel came over to look at it. He got down on his knees and smelled it. For a minute I thought he was smelling me. Mind you, I was on the floor, on *my* knees—"

Woodroe laughed. He delighted in the company he was cultivating.

After the story was done (the Waldorf couldn't come up with a replacement bulb; Marvin slinked home, carrying the wounded projector; "MacArthur never made another request to see *The March of Marx*"), they talked about conservative activity in New York City. The heart of it, Liebman said, "is right over there on Thirty-fifth Street. Buckley, James Burnham, Bill Rusher, Whittaker Chambers—until he died last year—Frank Meyer, Russell Kirk. The *National Review* gang. Then there are a half dozen key *activists*. They appear on various of my committees. Two young lawyers, Dan Mahoney and Kieran O'Doherty, they're related by marriage, have started a state Conservative Party. The new party will try to get some voice for conservatives in state politics, which is dominated by Nelson Rockefeller and Jacob Javits." He spoke of the powerful figure just reelected governor of New York, and of the influential liberal Republican beginning his second term in the Senate. "Jack Javits might as well be a Democrat. You say you're a Bircher. Are you a crazy Bircher or a—"

Woodroe grinned. "A noncrazy Bircher?"

"I couldn't have put it better myself. Well, just answer me one question: Do you think Dwight Eisenhower was a Communist agent?"

"No."

"Do you think Earl Warren is a Communist?"

"No."

"Well, what are you doing in the John Birch Society?"

Woodroe was sensitive on the questions. He thought he knew how to contend with them. "We're both Republicans, you and I. What are we doing as members of a political party that has let government grow larger and failed to stop the Communists in Cuba and Hungary and China? So we have a big tent. The JBS is the biggest anti-Communist organization in the United States and has a lot of important conservatives backing it—"

"I know, I know. And a lot of the same people contribute money to my organizations. But that Ike hang-up of Welch's—"

"You know, *The Politician* is not an official Birch Society publication."

"It might as well be."

"Marvin, that's not right. Nobody—remember, I'm an employee and have been for a year and a half—nobody is asked even *to read* the book, never mind taking an oath to subscribe to its conclusions."

"Well, Woodroe, no point in dragging that out. What you want from me, I can see, is something to do in the anti-Communist movement in New York: YAF, the Committee of One Million, the UN Reform Committee—all those. Here's the thing. We can't put any Bircher up front with these groups, at least not up there with the governing trustees. Though"—he laughed and lit up again—"*I* am de facto the governing trustees! But there are a couple of people I couldn't afford to antagonize, and wouldn't want to antagonize."

"Governor Edison?"

"Yes. And, of course, the *National Review* people. Now, listen, Woodroe, I've trusted you. You are not going to report to Belmont what I've just said to you about the JBS?"

"I understand. But I have to report that there is this . . . feeling around in New York about the JBS."

"Sure. You can do that. Now here are the names of a couple of people in New York"—Liebman scratched on the pad with his fountain pen, always at hand—"you *can* tell Belmont about. They're anti-Birch and don't care who knows it. Here's something useful you can do. Get in touch with student conservatives in colleges here. Every college has maybe three or four conservatives—Hunter, Columbia, CCNY, and of course Fordham and St. John's have quite a few. So see what they're up to. Give them things to read. Not *The Politician*! Poke around.

"Here's something else. One of my committees is called 'Keep South Vietnam Free.' That's an endangered part of the world. Ho Chi Minh obviously intends to sponsor terror operations against the South. There's a young South Vietnamese teacher in town. We brought him over for a few press conferences, got him here with the help of Diem's sister-in-law. That's Madame Nhu. They call her 'The Dragon Lady.' The young man's name is Than Koo and he's staying with an uncle who emigrated a few years ago. Look him up. Maybe your boss would like a story on him."

"Does he speak English?"

"Yes. And French. Do you speak French?"

"A little. I studied it in Salt Lake and Princeton."

"Well, you should be fluent!" Marvin said. "Let me know how it works out for you." He passed over a slip with a telephone number. "I'll call him and tell him to cooperate. But maybe I won't tell him you're with the John Birch Society. I'll just tell him you're interested in doing a story on him. After all, that's what he's here for, to attract attention to South Vietnam."

Marvin turned grave. "I thought there was a good chance of a nuclear war in October. That's how serious the foreign policy situation is."

They shook hands. Woodroe walked out of the restaurant; Liebman stayed to make a phone call.

When Woodroe reached his office, he was surprised to learn from Tish, his secretary, that General Walker had called.

He went to his office and called Dallas.

It was very odd. The general spoke to him as if Woodroe were still in Dallas, living around the corner. Maybe, thinking Woodroe was still in town, he had simply told his secretary, "Get Woodroe Raynor on the phone."

The general spoke discursively, as though the two were having lunch.

Yes, Woodroe said, yes he had read Khrushchev's statement that the Cuban precedent—the withdrawal of the Soviet missiles—would not restrict the Kremlin in any future decision relating to the security interests of the Soviet Union. But Woodroe said, "Khrushchev may feel he has to say that kind of thing, don't you think so, General?"

"You know what, Woodroe, I don't do this with many young people. But I'd like you to call me Ed. It isn't as though we were both in the military and I was talking to a subordinate."

"Well, I'm honored . . . Ed."

"I've always been governed by my own intuitions. I don't mind telling you that when Helena brought you into the picture I had my people do a little background check. And I learned about your stay in Austria. And the fact that you were shot up. How old were you then?"

"Nineteen, sir."

"Well, that's old enough to go to war. We'll visit soon. Tomorrow I'm off with the Reverend Billy James Hargis. You know him?"

"I know he's president of . . . I can't remember the name of it. A fundamentalist college in Tulsa."

"That's right. And he's a great televangelist, a powerful speaker, the Reverend Billy James. We're doing a joint speaking tour. Let's make a date for when I get back. Just a man-to-man evening. We won't even invite Helena."

Woodroe was stumped. Should he tell him he wasn't in Dallas anymore?

"Doesn't have to be tomorrow, or the next day, but I'll put it down, and I'll call you. God bless America, Woodroe."

"God bless America, General. Ed."

The call ended. Woodroe was perplexed.

Should he call Helena? He discarded the idea. To tell her about this call, he sensed, would be something on the order of betrayal. Clearly General Walker had intended a purely personal talk.

He would just wait. Perhaps there would be no next call from— Ed. But there would be, on the eighth of April.

28

THERE WAS A HORN AND HARDART Automat near Than Koo's address in Queens, and Than suggested it as a meeting place for the interview with Woodroe at five the next day. Woodroe told Mr. Than he would bring along a copy of *Newsweek* magazine to facilitate recognition.

Woodroe didn't know exactly what to expect, but he was surprised by the youth of the Asian emissary who, with a slight bow of his head, introduced himself as Than Koo.

The shirt collar was too large for his neck. Patches of his blue cotton jacket, glazed from use, reflected light from the neon Automat sign outside the window. Woodroe asked Mr. Than if he would like something from the Automat fare—"after all, it's teatime." In the Automat's famous individual compartments, the food was exhibited and priced. Customers would insert nickels and dimes and quarters, in the sums required, to spring open the door and permit access to the cavity with the selected item.

Than Koo said he would take some tea. He looked up at Woodroe questioningly. "And perhaps"—he pointed to a cinnamon roll, for sale for "three nickels," or "one dime and one nickel." Woodroe had changed a dollar and his hand was full of silver. They walked then to the beverage bar and Woodroe paid for one tea and one coffee.

"Well, Mr. Than, you go ahead and tackle your cinnamon roll and I'll talk, because I'm just taking coffee. Then when you're ready, *you* can talk. Okay?"

Than Koo bowed his head and began with his fork to dismember the roll.

"I'm from Salt Lake City—you know where that is?"

"Of course. Mormon country. I am a Mormon."

Woodroe confessed his astonishment at hearing this, but remembered his promise to give Than a chance to eat and went on to tell his own story. "I was a Mormon missionary in Austria. And I had a very close view of the Communists at work. They were suppressing Hungarian freedom initiatives. They finally made their point, Mr. Than, by running Russian tanks over students."

Through a full mouth, Than managed to say, "We use Chinese tanks."

"Then I went to Princeton. I was one of the founders of the Young Americans for Freedom. That's an anti-Communist, anti-socialist youth organization. We were for Senator Barry Goldwater in Chicago, 1960, when they nominated Richard Nixon."

Than nodded as he finished his roll.

"After graduating, I went to work for the John Birch Society. Marvin Liebman thought I shouldn't tell you that. The John Birch Society is heavily attacked in America. People think our anti-Communism is . . . extreme. And Mr. Welch has some positions of his own which are, well"—Woodroe smiled: he had got used to the little Welch qualifier—"his own."

Than Koo wiped his mouth with his napkin, then put it down and shoved it out of the way.

He explained that Madame Nhu—wife of the chief of security, General Nhu, and sister-in-law of President Ngo Dinh Diem—was his sponsor on this trip to America, that he had met with reporters in Los Angeles and Chicago, and that Madame Nhu was familiar with the John Birch Society, which after all was named after a Christian martyr in China. He, Than Koo, was honored to meet a member of this anti-Communist society, in particular to meet someone who had seen the Communists operate in Europe and knew what they did, and how.

Than Koo, twenty-eight years old, told the story of his education at a French Catholic school in Hué. After the defeat of the French in 1954, he had been sent to college and had attended a secretarial training school. Then he had been drafted by the government and placed in service with a security detail in the North which endeavored to protect farming hamlets from the Vietcong.

He told of his experience at Thom An Van Thuong. "It is twelve kilometers east of the eastern mountain range that flanks the Ho Chi Minh Trail, where all the supplies are brought down for the Vietcong. It was there that, when the barbed-wire gate was opened at daybreak to let the farmers out to the fields, someone banged at my door and reported that the chief councilor had been found dead at his desk, his throat slashed. The office stapler had been used to tack on the back of his neck a sheet of paper with 'IMPERIALIST LACKEY' written on it."

The murder/execution had to have been done, Than explained with deliberation, by one of the residents of the hamlet, and there were only eighty-five. He had sent his little squad on to its rendezvous with the next hamlet, north, but stayed back himself to attempt, by interrogating the villagers, to try to establish who, with late-night access to the councilor, had murdered him.

He had been interrogating one suspect that night in the hut maintained for visiting military. "I was taking notes when the blow on my head came."

He woke in a Vietcong detention cell. "Then it began"—he lowered his collar to reveal the scars on his neck. "I don't know how many days it was, but one morning, blindfolded, I was taken to a crossroads and I was exchanged for three Vietcong prisoners. I was in very bad condition. In the hospital, my nurse had been five years in Utah in college and nursing school. She had become a Mormon, and I fell very much in love with her. We were married. Then—"

With his little finger he stirred the tea and, for a moment, stopped talking.

"—then when walking to the hospital one night—I was back on duty and we lived our happy nights together in a room in her uncle's house—she was shot. It was not yet dawn, she was on the early-morning shift, and when they found her there was, again, a message on her neck. The same words, 'IMPERIALIST LACKEY.'

"I wanted to try to chase down the Vietcong who did this, but my major sent me to Saigon. They needed men who could speak English, and also French.

"That is where I met Madame Nhu, because I serve directly under the general, her husband, who is in charge of intelligence. It was her idea to send me to America for three weeks. I hope to tell the story of the Vietnam that tries to be free."

"Is the Diem government hopeful?" Woodroe asked.

"Everything depends on American aid. The Vietcong crop up everywhere, and their supply routes seem impossible to block. But President Kennedy has of course sent observers to Vietnam and they give us much encouragement. It will be a long struggle—did you see, Mr. Raynor, the declaration of Ho Chi Minh yesterday?"

Woodroe hadn't seen it.

"He denounced American intervention in the South and pledged *ten years* of guerrilla action against South Vietnam, 'if necessary.' On the same day he said this, our government uncovered the huge cache of Communist Chinese weapons, north of Banmethuot."

Woodroe was moved by the old young man with the sad eyes. Impulsively, he said, "Mr. Than—"

"I wish you would call me Koo."

"Well, yes. Koo—I'm Woodroe—are you free to come with me to Manhattan for dinner?"

"I am entirely at your disposal."

"I want you to meet a very special lady." Woodroe went to the telephone.

They traveled, Than Koo talking, Woodroe listening attentively, the twenty minutes to the Thirty-fourth Street subway station, and then walked over to Paone's restaurant. Lee was waiting.

They ordered wine and, tackling his risotto as best he could while speaking, Koo told his story, and tried to tell the story of his beleaguered country.

Later, back in the apartment, Woodroe said that as he viewed it, Vietnam was the next contest in the struggle for the world.

Lee agreed. She said that the cause of a free South Vietnam was a holy cause, in her eyes.

29

NATHANIEL BRANDEN had hoped that, somehow, divulging their secrets might be put off. But put off forever? He had to force himself to think through to the consequences of—thinking. Thinking about *this subject*. Thinking. Reasoning. These were supremely critical skills required of the Designated Successor.

Ayn and he had talked on the subject hours and hours and hours, lying together in adulterous sheets. They had made their love, up until that last Monday, on the large sofa in the living room. It was as safe from intrusion as human quarters could be.

Yet, Nathan reflected, how safe could any quarters be? There had been that man in London who had somehow materialized one morning at breakfast time *in the bedroom of the queen of England!* If somebody could get through to the sovereign bedchamber in Buckingham Palace, which was probably guarded by, what—a thousand foot guards? Foot guards with those forbidding bearskins on top of their heads. . . . True, in the afternoon hours between two and six, *nobody* entered Miss Rand's studio. Frank O'Connor worked in his own quarters upstairs and knew never to interrupt his wife at work; the cleaning lady was gone after washing the lunch dishes; and when Ayn was at work in her private quarters, only those specifically told to be there rang at the door. And that had meant, in the last year or two, only one person, Nathaniel Branden, her collaborator.

Then, a week ago, Frank O'Connor had gone to Boston to visit the museum there and to approach a dealer whose name had been given to him. Frank would show him slides of his artwork. Maybe the dealer would take Frank on and find a market for his paintings. In any case, he would spend the night in Boston and go then to see a second dealer in Hartford, getting back to New York the next day.

On Monday afternoon, Ayn's eyes were especially luminous when Nathaniel came in, as expected, at three. But this time she led him upstairs into a room he had never laid eyes on, a bedroom with a king-size bed and not less than six oil pictures of Ayn on the walls, one of them showing her bare-breasted, the Ayn of twenty years ago. The shades had been drawn and Nathaniel could savor the scent. Today her lover was being welcomed with synesthetical concern for all the senses, only the music missing. But as he lay and later groaned with writhing and release, he brought the full force of his mind to transmuted, voluptuarian elation in this physical union with the very woman who had created John Galt and Dagny Taggart and Henry Rearden, and had touched down her scepter on him, Nathaniel, igniting his mind, and his own scepter, which paid, now, devoted service.

But she was right.

There was *necessarily* a hypothetical risk of detection. That would be very bad. Very, very bad. What would be worse, worse than the detected relationship, would be the deception. That she would deceive Frank, her husband and companion; that Nathaniel would deceive Barbara, his wife and companion and, however incompletely, his lover—that would hurt most awfully. Their pride would be forfeit. No.

The alternative would be painful, but it had to be done. Tomorrow.

She would instruct Frank and Barbara to come to her studio at four o'clock.

Barbara came in and then Nathaniel, who turned his head slightly to one side, toward poor Frank, lonely on his large sofa on the left.

Nathaniel looked away. He could hardly expect to get relief from training his eyes on the husband of the woman he was sleeping with.

Addressing Barbara, Ayn got right to the point.

She said that Barbara had undoubtedly sensed it on the trip to Toronto and during the ride back in the car, that an irresistible flowering was taking place, a great union that expressed rejection of Platonist mysticism and acknowledged the primacy of reason, because it was human reason that compelled this union: she had found in Nathaniel, and he in her, a being who incorporated ideals all of them sought.

Now this union, Ayn said without pausing, had nothing whatever to do with other unions in which they had entered, she with Frank, whom she loved dearly. Contrary to her habit of looking square into the face of a person she was addressing, Miss Rand now kept her eyes straight ahead.

And, of course, as much was so in the union of Nathaniel and Barbara—

"That's nice of you to say so, Ayn, since you were matron of honor at our wedding."

Ayn ignored Barbara's comment. Nathaniel was glad for Ayn's ability to speak endlessly. By doing so now, she was having the customary hypnotic effect on her assembly, going on and on about heroic sentiments and about organic needs and about the simultaneity of love at different levels.

After a half hour Nathaniel permitted himself a look at Barbara. She had that clenched-jaw look. Nathaniel prayed that there would be no tears. He'd have found them unbearable. He turned his eyes to Frank, who looked like a schoolboy having problems with his new chair. *What Frank most wants right now is a drink,* Nathaniel guessed. Poor, poor Frank. What could he do if he left Ayn? He could hardly survive as a painter. There were no reserves left in this nice sixty-five-year-old derelict, if he were to remove himself from his great mother ship, the SS *Rand,* fully armed, fully provisioned, in which he had quarters, even if, now, he would have to share them.

Ayn now brought up practical matters.

Nobody, *ever*, was to know about the ongoing arrangements.

She wished, for herself and Nathaniel, only one afternoon of solitude every week.

There was to be not a hint of the dissolution of their marriages—it was hardly suggested that she would propose marrying someone twenty-five years younger. But now they would have to acknowledge realities; deal with them, the products of reason serving the truly moral purpose of self-fulfillment.

On the subject of self-fulfillment, years later, Nathaniel Branden would write several books.

30

THE SUCCEEDING CALL from General Walker was perplexing. He said he wished to "spend a little time" with Woodroe. He had learned that Woodroe had been transferred to New York by the Society. "That, of course, is their business. But Helena—Mrs. Crowder—wants me to go on a very special mission. In order to undertake what she has in mind, I would need some deep consultation with you. I understand she has cleared the request with Bob Welch, so let me know, Woodroe, when you will get here."

"Could I ask about the—the nature of my mission?"

"It is very important to learn to be very careful when talking over the telephone. My phone is almost certainly being tapped. And probably your phone is being tapped. So I won't answer the question. But ring me, Woodroe, about when you are arriving, or leave word with my office."

"Sure will . . . Ed." With practice, the pause before using the general's first name was now almost unnoticeable, a mere hint of Woodroe's instinctive problem in addressing fifty-year-olds by their first names, let alone major generals. Let alone Edwin A. Walker.

It hadn't even occurred to Woodroe that his telephone might be bugged. But if it was, it would surely be his office line. Maybe one day he could figure out how to sweep a phone.

Meanwhile he had the lunch date. Leonora wanted him to meet Leonard Peikoff. Peikoff was a first cousin of Barbara Branden, and a gifted philosophy student. Woodroe was in awe when told that

186

Leonard had been admitted, at age seventeen, as an original member of the Collective.

"You ought to know, Woody, that Lenny—call him 'Leonard,' he doesn't like 'Lenny,' but cousin Barbara began calling him Lenny when he was a baby and still does. Leonard is not . . . well, not teeming with social graces."

"You mean he's a nerd?"

"Well, yes, sort of. No, not even sort of. He is one. But . . . you should meet him."

They walked together into the little cafeteria at Fortieth Street. Leonard was thin and tall, seemingly without shoulders. His neck simply winnowed its way down to his torso. He wore thick glasses, and a loose sweater against the April nip. In his left arm he cradled a swollen notebook.

He shook hands and put his notebook on the table. The three filed by the buffet, sliding their aluminum trays along the railing. Leonard selected a carrot salad and chicken stew. Back at the table, nibbling at her ravioli, Leonora said, "Woody, I've told Leonard we're good friends and that you work for the John Birch Society. Leonard is a *terrific* expert on objectivism. It is embarrassing to me, how much he knows. He came to Miss Rand not long before I started doing volunteer work for her and he's now almost a Ph.D. The most useful thing *I* do is grade papers for Nathaniel."

Without a smile Leonard said, "That's not exactly the case, Woodruff—"

"Woodroe," she corrected.

"That's not so. Leonora is quite adept in our studies. She is a very good student. Do you, at the John Birch Society, study much in objectivism?"

"Not directly," Woodroe said. "What we've done is arrive at similar conclusions to yours on matters of public policy. We are very much opposed to the growth of the state."

"You run the danger of the sorcerer's apprentice."

Woodroe smiled at the taunt.

Leonora missed it. "What's the sorcerer's apprentice?" She turned, quizzical, first to Leonard, then to Woodroe.

Woodroe explained, affably, that the apprentice is the guy in the fable who tried to duplicate the work of the sorcerer but got one thing wrong, so everything was screwed up. "Paul Dukas wrote a... whatever it was, tone poem, caprice, étude—piece of music—called 'The Sorcerer's Apprentice.'" He turned to Leonard. "You mean, one has to know the *objectivist foundation* for believing in individual liberty, free of statist impositions?"

"Something like that." Leonard resumed eating. Leonora managed to communicate her empathy to Woodroe. But she might as well persevere. "Leonard, talk a bit on that subject, why an objectivist foundation is so necessary to... well, to correct thinking on freedom."

Without looking up at Woodroe, Leonard explained that the term human freedom was everywhere loosely used, giving no evidence that the user recognized its integral connection to the whole view of life, provided by objectivism. Human freedom is the actualization of reason done by an open mind unimpeded by metaphysics or mysticism. Religion, which is of course the mysticism of the mind, obstructs the work of reason, which is why the call for human freedom based on anything to do with divinity gives freedom a superstitious foundation.

Woodroe did not pursue the subject, pursuing instead the advertised rhubarb pie, rhubarb being a center of attraction at the Raynor household in Salt Lake. When he got back to the table, Leonard had gone.

"He is tutoring some undergrads."

"I'm glad I'm not one of them."

"I see what you mean. But listen, he's a straight-A student."

"Objectively qualified. Listen, I've got to go to your apartment, after lunch, to use the phone. Looks like I'm going to have to make a quick trip to Dallas."

"Why?"

"That's what I have to find out about."

"Well, you have a key." They kissed lightly and, at the corner, went off in separate directions.

He got through to Jesse Andrews.

"Jess, are you up on this request by General Walker that I go down to Dallas?"

"Yes."

"What's *that* all about?"

"That's a—there's a big oilman there. Russell Daugherty. He gave the Dallas Chapter five thousand dollars last year. Helena's been working on him for a big-time donation, and he's dangled fifty thousand in front of her. But he said he wanted to hear from General Walker himself why he should invest that much money in JBS."

"So?"

"Well, that seemed easy to arrange, but no. The general said that the future of the Society depended on its appeal to young people and that in his judgment you were the best representative of a young Bircher he could imagine. He'd agree to take on Daugherty only after a session with you. He talked about 'joint planning' and the 'emphasis on youth.'...You know, Woodroe, the general doesn't always make things absolutely clear."

"Uh, yes. Jess, do you assume your phone is bugged?"

"Well, sure. There are certain things I would not discuss over the telephone."

"But this isn't one of them?"

"No. There isn't much anybody can do with what I've mentioned to you."

"Should I assume my phone at the office is bugged?"

"It's wise to assume that. Bob Welch has one phone here with a scrambler. He uses that a lot."

"So I'm just to book passage on my American Express?"

"Yes. Dallas will reimburse us."

"Do I need to speak to Bob?"

"No. He's pretty busy. You got any problems?"

Woodroe thought to tell Jesse that Woodroe's problem would be with Mr. Daugherty if he asked how many twenty-five-year-olds Woodroe was bringing into the movement. Never mind.

"Well, that's it, then. Thanks, Jess."

"Hope everything else is going all right."

"Yeah. Oh, I think I've got a mole in the Nathaniel Branden Institute. Guy called Peikoff." Woody grinned.

"Doesn't hurt to have contacts. Let me know how it goes with General Walker."

"I will. So long. Say hello to the Founder."

He hung up the line and let his eyes roam about Lee's comfortable living room, with all the conventional arrangements. But if you looked hard you might find a personal touch, like the little framed photograph on the bottom shelf of the bookcase, a photograph of a container of pills. But it wasn't just pills, it was The Pill. Why keep a photograph of it, he had once asked her?

"Why have a photograph of the Statue of Liberty?" she had countered.

He let the matter drop.

But now he leaned down, pulled out the photograph, and looked at its back side. Was there a date there, telling when it was framed?

There wasn't.

Might there be such a date on the pillbox in the bathroom?

Probably.

But he wasn't going to let his curiosity take him that far.

31

WOODROE CHECKED INTO the Hotel Clover, called his old number at JBS, and chatted for a minute with Jody. "I know you're not here for long, Woody, but I hope you can come by and say hello to the gang. We sure miss you. You're probably calling for Mrs. Crowder?"

"Yes. Is she there?"

"No, she was here this morning. She's got a bridge tournament. Do you want me to leave a message with her at home?"

"Yes. Just tell her I called."

"Okay."

His next call was to General Walker's number. Christine, the secretary, told him the general was not available, but that Mr. Raynor was expected at 4011 Turtle Creek Boulevard for supper at 6:33. "Is that okay?"

"That'll be fine."

He spent two of the three hours left of the afternoon in an extraordinary extravagance these days: he sat in the armchair and read. On the plane, he had gone through the latest issue of *National Review*, looking out, at first, for animadversions on Mr. Welch or the Society. He lingered to admire essays by Richard Weaver and Russell Kirk, and an exchange on the compatibility of tradition and libertarianism between Frank Meyer and Brent Bozell. He reflected on that nest of influential and productive conservatives in the office a mere block away from Ayn Rand's apartment. He would take Marvin Liebman up on the suggestion that it would make sense for him to meet the people over there. "They won't shoot at you, Woodroe."

"They already have, Marvin."

But he yearned, mostly, to read the remaining chapters of Anthony Burgess's *A Clockwork Orange,* that surrealistic, obscene, fascinating novel about deranged young men and their crazy antics, made almost endurable by the skillful language of the eccentric author. At five, Woodroe donned shorts and walked the three blocks down Houston Street to the park off Dealey Plaza. He did his jogging around and around the small green, the azaleas in full bloom. Perspiring, he returned to the hotel, showered, and called for a cab. He knew the general's fetish on punctuality, so, arriving a few minutes early, he walked about, his eye on his watch, until exactly 1833. He knocked on the door.

"You Misser Reinorr?"

He nodded. "Yes, ma'am."

"The general will come quickly. Very quickly."

Graciela showed him into the living room/office. At the corner was a desk, facing into the living room. The bookcases beside the desk were filled, mostly with pamphlets and back issues of *American Opinion.* A dictating machine was prominent. Behind the sofa, a glassed showcase displayed the general's decorations. Woodroe would be told, later in the evening, their identity, and the circumstances of General Walker's having got them—using a wooden pointer common to military instructors, the general would describe them to him. On either side there were photographs of men in uniform and of the golfer Bobby Jones. The general would in due course identify each one of them and comment.

Woodroe was struggling to make out the inscription on the photograph of Admiral Nimitz when his host came into the room.

Ed Walker looked down at his watch. "I am a minute or two late. I apologize." He wore dark green slacks, a cream-colored sports shirt, and a blue sweater. "Played a little golf this afternoon. I'm getting there. My goal is 84. I shot 85. But I'm a good loser."

"You haven't done much losing in your life, Ed."

"That's right. Not until I ran into—the contemporary Washington. The Washington of postwar America. There's a better way to put that: the Washington created by the postwar situation, where our leaders gave away Eastern Europe, China, North Korea, Berlin, and Cuba. I'm going to have a drink. How about you, Woodroe?"

"Yes. Could I help?"

"You can not only help, you can make your drink *and* mine. Graciela will give us dinner, but she can't mix any drink that doesn't have tequila in it. I want a bourbon on the rocks with a little bitters. You'll find all that stuff over there." He paused for a moment and Woodroe walked to the bar.

"But Graciela will give us a good Mexican dinner. Good idea, I thought, eating at home. In a restaurant, you never know who's going to come by, use up a lot of time. Did you visit at all with Helena?"

Woodroe shook his head and began to explain, but the general interposed.

"I like Helena. She's a good American. But she doesn't really understand the, well, the seriousness of the whole situation. She really wasn't much use after the Oxford business. In fact, I think she retreated a little on account of it." Woodroe was mixing the drinks. "I get around and a lot of people get messages to me, and I think the word was, *Let's cool it a bit on General Walker.* And you know she has a husband. Jerry. He's a cynical rich-guy kind of Texan. I've been to his house. Reminds me a little of General—I won't mention his name. He was in Germany with me, a stand-by, don't-ruffle-any-feathers type, and he got really heated up on the whole business of my indoctrination course."

He was standing upright now, his drink in his left hand, the wooden pointer, retrieved from the side of the door to the kitchen, in the other hand. "When I began to really notice what was going on was just after that"—he pointed to one medal. "That's the Hyères. H-Y-E-R-E-S. We had to provide cover for the invasion, north Italy. . . ."

Graciela, at the door, made him stop before he had completed his second drink and his account of the Little Rock military intervention. "It was ordered by the same General Eisenhower who was in command of the battle of Europe, if you can believe it, ordering me to lead troops to invade, that's the right word for it, to *invade* Little Rock, Arkansas, U.S.A. But let's sit down for chow." He walked through the door.

At supper—Bohemia beer, tacos, enchiladas, tamales, fried beans, tortillas, chicken, and a candied pear with ice cream—General Walker continued the narrative about the encroachment of Communist pressures on the country. "The Supreme Court—above all, the Court, *think Earl Warren*—but also the executive, the Congress, though there are *some* good Americans there, and even"—he sighed heavily—"the military. Let's take our beer back to the living room. Graciela likes to clean up and get out of here. *Muy buena la cena, Graciela. Hasta mañana.*"

An hour later, Woodroe was wondering at what point the subject of youth and the John Birch Society and the conservative movement and Mr. Daugherty would come up. The general was working on his third beer, sitting at his desk. Perhaps, Woodroe thought, he should interrupt him at some point and get on with the business of the next day.

But the general stopped his own talk suddenly, stretching out the collar ends of his sports shirt. "You know what, Woodroe, I have a sauna downstairs, like so many Texans. It gets hot? They take a sauna. I was thinking, why don't we go down and take one together? We can—"

The shot pierced the window and burrowed into the wall, an inch to one side of his head.

The general froze for the briefest moment. And then went instantly into action.

"Turn off your light!" The general reached up for his own overhead light. Woodroe snapped off the lamp by the sofa. *"I'm going upstairs for my pistol."*

Walker bounded up the staircase. Woodroe felt his way through the dark room and hallway to the front door, opened it, and saw the taillights of a car speeding up Turtle Creek Boulevard. The general was downstairs, pistol in hand. He groped his way to the door and peered about.

"They've gone. *Bloodsucker!* He's gone. We got to decide what to do about this. Come on inside."

The lights turned on, he sat again at his desk. He turned to examine the bullet hole. "Looks like maybe a .30. I've had a lot of them fired at me in my day." He looked over at his unfinished beer on the desk. He carried it over to the sink at the bar and poured out what was left of it.

"Tell you what. I'm going to call Bob Morris. He's my lawyer. He's also the president of the University of Dallas."

He dialed the number. "Bob, this is a real emergency. I need you like right now. . . . Right. At home." He hung up.

"He'll be here in less than fifteen minutes."

Woodroe said nothing, nor did the general. They'd wait for Bob Morris.

General Walker cleaned and oiled his pistol.

32

THE HEADLIGHTS BROKE the silence.

General Walker was at the door and let Robert Morris in, ruddy face, crew-cut hair, a man-in-charge.

Walker introduced him curtly to Woodroe, they sat down, and General Walker told what had happened.

Morris's questions and instructions were fired out.

"What's the young man doing here?"

"Raynor is going to lunch with me tomorrow with Russell Daugherty, who's ready to make a big contribution to the John Birch Society. I wanted a young man there to enter the case for young people. Raynor was at Oxford."

"Rhodes scholar?"

"No. Oxford, Mississippi."

"All right. Now, Ed, the *reason* you didn't call the police right away—put this in your mind—is *the denial of your civil rights at Oxford.* You thought it best *to tell the whole story to your lawyer,* so you called me up for advice, since I'm handling the Mississippi picture. Calling the police—remember this—wouldn't have been of immediate help because the killer car had gone. That's all you have to say. Now we got to get *him*"—he pointed to Woodroe—"out of here."

"Why?"

"It's past eleven o'clock at night. Let me handle this, Ed. Now. . . ." He paused, putting one hand on his brow. He spoke quietly, as if to himself. "How in the hell do we get him home?"

"We can call a cab, can't we?"

"We don't want *any* traceable traffic coming to this address. Cabs keep records. They have a record of somebody leaving after the shooting. Who? Why? We want to avoid all that."

"He can have my station wagon," Walker said.

"What do you do for a car tomorrow?"

"I got my other car, my Buick."

"Okay. Let's get it right. Raynor was here and left after dinner. You were alone when the killer fired. *Let's move.* Let's get Raynor out of here, then we'll talk some more. After that I'll call the police."

General Walker led Woodroe outdoors and into the two-door garage. He turned on the overhead lights and fished out the right key from a drawer.

"We meet with Daugherty at 1215 at the Petroleum Club. Drive the car to the door. They'll park it for you. You can give me the parking slip at lunchtime."

"Okay. Okay, Ed. That was a hell of a thing you went through tonight. Good luck with the police."

They waited for the police.

Bob Morris had deliberated, driving to Turtle Creek—whether to divulge the information he had gotten that afternoon from his old friend in the FBI. It was not something Ed Walker, on this night, would welcome hearing. But Walker was his client and also his friend.

"Ed, you've been traveling around with Billy James Hargis—"

"The Reverend Billy James Hargis, Bob."

"Yes. Let me shoot it to you. I won't tell you where I got it and you're not to ask. Billy James—"

"Dr. Hargis?"

"Yeah, yeah. Dr. Hargis performed the marriage of a couple of the students from his college—"

"Why not? He can marry, a reverend."

"Ed, quiet a minute. Two students he married have testified about how he took the bride and the groom in his car and went on the honeymoon with them."

"Shared a car?"

"The testimony is that he slept with the girl during the honeymoon—"

Walker looked up, traces of a frown on his face.

Morris continued: "—and the next day he . . . he screwed the guy."

General Walker's eyes widened, illuminated by the strokes of flashing red from the police car arrived outside. A detective, with three policemen, pounded on the door.

33

THE TELEPHONE IN HIS HOTEL room rang just after eight in the morning.

"It's Mr. Welch, Woody." The phone operator at Belmont put him through.

Robert Welch's voice was strained and he spoke rapidly. "The shooting made the late edition of the *Globe*. They didn't have much detail, just that the police found nothing that could help in tracking down the killer. The attempted killer. Did you hear about it from the Dallas press? What are they saying? Probably a mouthful."

Woodroe was uncomfortable with deception, but he was not going to tell Welch a story that conflicted with what Mr. Morris and General Walker had told the police. So he answered indirectly.

"Yes, the television is full of it. They've got cameras posted outside the general's house."

"Did he get from you the briefing he wanted? For the Daugherty lunch?"

"Yeah. Yeah. Yes, Bob. I think we're all squared away on that. I'll talk to Daugherty about, you know, young people, and what we have to do to wake them up."

"Good. I wonder who in the *hell* shot at him last night. You can bet your bottom dollar it wasn't an American patriot."

"I guess we'll have to wait to find out, Bob."

"Yes—*if* the police and the feds can be persuaded to look hard enough. Well, good luck with Daugherty. I'm glad you'll be meeting

with Revilo Oliver later in the day. He is quite a man, and his contributions to *American Opinion* are vital stuff. He's probably the
leading expert on Communist terrorism. Only he doesn't think that's
the right word for it, and he's probably right: Communists don't act
spontaneously, the way terrorists do. It's always, *always* a part of the
big picture for them. You can bet it was one of their people did it last
night. Call me when you get to New York."

It was a fairly long haul, Dallas to Chicago on Eastern, two hours and
twenty minutes. Then an hour's wait for the American commuter
flight to Urbana, forty minutes. Coming down the ramp of the plane,
Woodroe delighted in the spring air. In Dallas it had already been hot.
In New York it was still cold. In central Illinois, the inside lights were
coming on, but there was daylight enough to make out the trees at
either end of the hangar, the topmost leaves golden in the setting light.
He walked with his briefcase the considerable distance to the hangar
and looked about for the baggage claim area.

"Are you Mr. Raynor?"

A huge man was there. His black hair was parted in the middle,
his mustache, showing a trace of gray, trimmed down above the corners of his mouth. He was dressed in a gray suit; his blue tie, with
white polka dots, was tidily knotted about his neck, just below the
prominent Adam's apple.

"Professor Oliver?"

He smiled, genuine cheer in his expression.

"Grace—that's my wife—heard that you were booked into the
Urbana Hotel and vetoed that." They spoke while walking toward the
baggage claim. "Women have the right to exercise certain prerogatives.
She decreed that you were to use the spare bedroom in our house."

Driving off, Woodroe's bag in the trunk, Revilo Oliver said that
it had been quite a night on Turtle Creek Boulevard in Dallas, as, of
course, Woodroe knew.

"Yes, sir." Woodroe assumed Oliver knew nothing about Woodroe's whereabouts when the pistol was shot. "I had lunch with the general today. Perhaps Mr. Welch told you. We were trying to make the case for JBS with an oilman."

"Daugherty. Russell H. Daugherty. Founder of Principio Oil Company in Venezuela. Mr. Daugherty is one-half part—no, one-third part—instructed in the matters that concern us. I hope you succeeded with him. But did the general reveal anything interesting? I have not spoken with him today, and not with Mr. Welch since late this morning."

"No. No, sir—"

"Call me Revilo."

"Well, that's a tall order. But okay, Revilo."

"Do you know what a palindrome is? Probably not, since you went to school in Princeton, where they know nothing. Perhaps more than at Harvard or Yale, but that's not very much."

"Actually, I don't."

"A palindrome is a word or phrase whose letters can be written out in reverse sequence, replicating the original. The most recognized example is, 'Able was I ere I saw Elba.' If you trouble to reverse the order, you have the same idiotic phrase. My name, 'Revilo Oliver,' forms a palindrome. My father was delighted by wordplay. He was not a scholar, but I was able to amuse him, in his last years, with any number of palindromes in Greek and Latin and Persian."

"How many languages do you . . . have you studied?"

"I have a preternatural ability in language." They had pulled into his driveway. He opened the trunk and let Woodroe pull out his own bag, beckoning him into the hallway. "Come here, into my work study. I will show you what I mean about languages."

Woodroe was surprised that Revilo needed a key to enter his own study.

His desk surface formed a long U, stretching the length of the room, rounding, and coming back, parallel. There were three chairs on casters, and twelve typewriters, each with its dustcover, evenly spaced on the surface, with room for papers and books in between.

"I can readily slide a chair over to whichever keyboard I am working on."

"They are all different?"

"The typefaces are different. Different symbols and accent marks and hieroglyphs. We have"—he pointed to the first—"English. Next to it, Middle English...Latin...Classical Greek...Modern Greek...Aramaic...Egyptian...Arabic...and, of course, Italian, French, German, and Spanish."

"Oh my God."

"It is unusual, of course, but then my field is classical philology. Yes, many disciplines. I am very careful with the typewriters. And I make it a point never to make a mistake."

"Uh—" Woodroe's protest was interrupted.

"I assume *you* type, Woodroe?"

"Of course."

"I had an experience as a very...young man, I guess you'd call a twenty-year-old. I went to see Vladimir Horowitz perform, and, as an encore, he played 'The Flight of the Bumblebee.' You know it? Rimsky-Korsakov?"

Woodroe nodded.

"It is a piece that requires total precision of the fingers, as the notes are all thirty-second notes. I thought it extraordinary that he hit no wrong notes. In consequence, that evening I made a resolution. If Horowitz could play 'The Flight of the Bumblebee' without making any mistakes, I should be able to type my work out without making any mistakes. After all, I am free to pause, if I wish to deliberate on the next word or phrase. Horowitz—pianists—do not have that option."

"So you have made no typing mistakes?"

"I did once, ten years or so back. My old friend and contemporary at the graduate school, Willmoore Kendall, was remarried. I was best man. Kendall's friend William Buckley was the other usher. The three of us had a bachelor dinner. Buckley brought out, at the room in the club, a bottle of cognac, some extravagantly old and rare brand, and Willmoore led in many toasts to his next-day bride and other matters. I came home that night and sat down to write out the toast I would myself give the next day at the wedding lunch. I could not believe it when I found that I had typed T-S-O-A-T."

"For 'toast'?"

"Yes. Imagine! I went straight to bed, and renewed my oath the next morning. But we will talk over a glass of wine, you and I. Follow me and you will meet Grace, and be taken to your room."

They sat in the ample living room and Grace fussed over both men, bringing in from the kitchen a variety of crackers and celery and nuts. But then the doorbell rang. She went rapidly to the door and led the caller, who could not be seen from where Woodroe and Revilo were seated, to a room adjacent.

Grace returned, but after a few minutes was back at the door, admitting a second caller.

There was a third, a fourth, and a fifth.

"Grace, you just attend to them. We'll be all right, Woodroe and I. We have a lot of ground to cover."

Mrs. Oliver left, and now Woodroe could hear a steady, soft whine. Revilo explained. "We have in a fresh speech delivered by General Walker, and another by Billy James Hargis. The tape was sent to us from Dallas. Our friends here in Urbana were alerted, and we are making copies of that tape for them, but can do only one at a time."

They were called to dinner, served spaghetti and Italian bread, a tomato salad, red wine, canned peaches, and brownies.

"There's coffee for you in the living room, Revilo," Grace said. "I must go out now to my JBS meeting. Can I do anything for you, Woodroe?"

He said no and thanked her.

Revilo Oliver leaned back in his chair. "One thing we can absolutely exclude. It is that the man who tried to kill General Walker last night was simply a killer-opportunist. From what happened, it is clear that this was not a case of robbery. In the first place, General Walker hasn't very much to rob. In the second place, the isolated target—the shot through the window, aimed directly at his head—cannot have been, in any relevant sense of the word, random. It had to be someone who sought to kill Edwin Walker."

"Who would wish to do that?"

"You mean, does he have personal enemies? I exclude that. His enemies are ideological enemies. They are those who saw, in recent months, a man of danger to the Left. A man of action. In point of fact they have seen this in him in recent years. It was in April 1961, two years ago, that Edwin Walker was detected in the treacherous act"—Revilo beamed his appreciation of the language—"of teaching his troops about the Communist conspiracy. Now we are in April 1963, and someone decided *all of this had gone far enough.*"

"But Communists don't just, well, go around shooting odd people."

"True, they prefer entire populations. But your point would not be persuasive if told to Leon Trotsky, if he had survived the second attempt on his life in 1940. The survival of General Walker is intolerable for the Communist International."

Woodroe dug in. "Revilo, come on. I mean, there are *quite a lot* of anti-Communists in America who would take precedence over Ed Walker. I mean, we've got—in the Senate alone—we've got McCarran, Jenner. We've got J. Edgar Hoover. We've got MacArthur—"

Revilo held up his hand. "You argue like the editor of *National Review.*"

"Buckley?"

"Yes. Buckley was once one of us. I knew him well. I spent two weeks sailing with him on his boat one summer. He would typically give all the reasons why another explanation than the one that looms at us is the more reasonable one. Buckley was my guest, just two years ago, sitting where you are seated, a month or two after the insidious attack on the John Birch Society was published in his magazine. He was very jolly, that is his manner, you know—"

"I have never met him."

"He said to me, 'Revilo, *why* would we publish our dissent on the John Birch Society, except that we thought it true and helpful?'

"I said to him"—Revilo was speaking calmly, and with great precision—"I said to him, 'I can think of three reasons.' Of course, he asked me what they were.

"'Number one,' I said, 'is the possibility that *National Review* was paid a large sum of money in return for denouncing the Society.'

"He asked, 'What is your explanation number two?'

"'A second explanation,' I said to Buckley, 'is that you were *forced* to take that position by the directors of National Review, Inc.'

"He smiled at me, as if the two explanations were too implausible even to dwell upon. He asked what was explanation number three?

"I told it to him. In as many words: 'Explanation number three, Bill, is that you are actually on the other side.'"

The telephone rang. Revilo rose to answer it in the kitchen.

He came back. "That was Grace. She is at the meeting of her chapter, and they have begged her to bring me there to discuss the shooting yesterday. I'm sorry, but I have no alternative."

From his correspondence tray, he took out a copy of *American Opinion*. "This just arrived. You can take it up with you. I will of course see you in the morning. Either I, or Grace if your flight leaves when I am teaching, will drive you to the airport. I am very pleased to meet you."

Woodroe thanked him.

He yearned to use the telephone, to talk with Theo. To talk with Lee. To talk about his evenings, yesterday's and today's.

He looked hard at the telephone in the living room and spotted the recording device alongside.

So he took his copy of *American Opinion* upstairs. And, using his notepad, he wrote out a letter to Professor Romney. He spent a half hour on it, pouring out his thoughts and experiences. He told him that he had been there when the shot was fired, told him the sequence of Revilo Oliver's conversation. He thought to ask, in his postscript, about the fate of Mount Olympus. "I'll try to come soon to visit you."

34

WOODROE FELT HE HAD BEEN away from New York more than just three days. He went from LaGuardia right to the JBS office. Tish, his secretary, was ready for him. "Murray Kempton called. He heard you were in Dallas with General Walker on Wednesday. Wants to talk with you. . . . The chapter head in Buffalo wants you up there to address their meeting, you pick a day, but give them at least a week's notice. . . . Marvin Liebman called. He'll set up a lunch with a couple of the *National Review* people, just say when. . . . Helena Crowder called, she was very happy, Woody." Tish looked down at her pad. "She said, 'Daugherty came through.' She said you'd understand. . . . You're to call Leonora."

Woodroe went to his desk and started in. Reaching Lee, he told her he'd be at the apartment before 7 P.M. "I'll bring the cake," he said, but a little lifelessly.

When he showed up at Apartment 11E, he didn't have to use his key. His elbow against the buzzer, she was quickly there, and threw her arms around him. Like old times, he had to put down his cake and wine.

She walked him to the sofa. "You sounded bad."

"It didn't really hit me till very late last night. The bullet missed General Walker by only a couple of inches. So it was nowhere near me. Just, maybe, thirty-six inches. I've never been shot at before— *Wait, what am I saying!*"

"You *have* been shot at before?"

"Yeah. Shot at, and hit. In the hip. And had my bandage changed by Vice President Richard Nixon. . . . I'm letting off steam. But I don't much feel like talking about it. But I *will* talk about it. And I'll tell you also what I was doing before they shot at me, if you want. But maybe let's have a drink first. I think I have a chill."

"Who's *they?* Who shot at you?" Leonora went to the refrigerator for ice.

"I'm talking about the Hungarian Communists at the Andau Bridge. They were trying to block the refugees at that little exit point. Finally they succeeded by blowing up the bridge. We had got to the safe side, on the Austrian bank. My Hungarian buddy then shot at them. They shot back. They got both of us, him through the head."

"And what were you doing before they shot at you?"

He took a swig of his drink. "I was trying to find my lady, but she was busy betraying her countrymen."

"What do you mean, 'your lady'?"

"I loved her just so very much, Lee. A week earlier she had taken my cherry, in her tiny farmhouse, while we applauded the radio and the talk of an anti-Communist revolution. I went back to look for her almost every day, bicycling from Andau, where I worked, back across the bridge to Hungary, looking for her. I never did see her again. I suppose she's alive. That was six and a half years ago. Maybe she's Commissar of Youth, in charge of coping with Hungarian virgins. One at a time."

"Ease off, Woody."

"Sorry."

"Do you want to talk any more about—your lady?"

"Not really."

"Then we won't. There's that kind of thing happening in non-Communist countries too. No, not *that* kind of thing, the kind of thing you're talking about. What I mean is . . . Let's just call it Sex. That's what's going on."

"You've got to do better than that. There's *that* kind of thing going on in every block of New York City."

"I'm talking 36 East Thirty-sixth Street."

Woodroe put down his drink.

"Miss Rand? Nathaniel?"

"Look, let me just tell you what happened. Two nights ago, the night you were with General Walker, I had dinner with Leonard Peikoff at Jack Dempsey's on Broadway. We had a pretty quick meal, Peikoff-style, and he got up to go just when my coffee was being served. I said, 'You go ahead, Leonard. I'll finish up and then leave.'

"I couldn't see down the other end of the bar, but as soon as Leonard was gone, Frank O'Connor walked over. He said—you don't know Frank; he's that way, timid, polite—he said could he sit down? I said of course.

"Well, three drinks later, which was I don't know how many drinks after his first drink that day, he was talking about Ayn and about Nathaniel, and suddenly I put it together." Woodroe stared at her and started to speak. She stopped him.

"It was hard enough to imagine, but harder to believe. He didn't say it in just that many words—he wouldn't have been able to say the cow jumped over the moon in just that many words. But I got to where I knew exactly what he was saying—that he had found out, that afternoon, that Ayn and Nathaniel are lovers. And that they. . . do it at Thirty-sixth Street. And that Barbara knows about it. Oh yes, and that if Frank protested, he would be out on his ear, and would I like someday to go up to his studio and see his paintings?"

"Oh my God."

They were silent.

"A lot of people stop by at Dempsey's," Woodroe said.

"Woody, I don't think he'd have told *anybody else* at Dempsey's about it. I can't imagine he has told anybody *anywhere*. I'm a girl, an insider at the Institute, assistant to Barbara Branden, and he needed to tell somebody. He had had a lot to drink. *In vino veritas*. Though

God knows, the whole business is unimaginable. Woody, what *is* unimaginable is that he'd tell it to anybody who would pass the word on to Ayn."

"Why would he tell you?"

"I don't know. I don't even know if, the next day, he even knew he *had* told me."

Woodroe said nothing, opening distractedly that day's *New York Times* on his lap. Then, "What does this do to your... understanding of objectivism?"

"It does something to it, though I'm not sure what. I guess Ayn is doing self-fulfillment." She looked up sharply. Would Woodroe release a smile of derision? "Woody, let's listen to Milton Berle on television. He's on at eight. Maybe he'll joke about—"

"Life. That's a good subject to joke about."

Woodroe put down the paper and went to the kitchen to make the salad, his regular assignment at Apartment 11E.

BOOK

FOUR

35

I T WAS NOVEMBER 10, 1963. Attorney General Robert Kennedy sat in the Situation Room at the White House with press chief Pierre Salinger and presidential aide Dave Powers. The question pending was what would be the city-by-city itinerary of the president's projected foray to the South.

The attorney general was not in a playful mood. "The American people are all for Jack. Right. But listen hard. The Roper poll published last week tells us that 59 percent of American voters say they voted for Jack in 1960. Great! Except only 49.7 percent of American voters actually did!"

"Things are going fine," political expert Dave Powers said. "*Almost* everywhere. The problem is the South. And it *is* a problem, Bobby. A lot hangs on the presidential visit we're talking about, Florida and Texas. There are plenty of people out there who are steamed up about the whole Vietnam business and the assassination of Diem—"

"You're talking about the right-wingers—"

"Yeah. But the Republican Party is—looks like—it might *become* a right-wing party."

"You discounting Rockefeller? Scotty Reston wrote a couple of days ago that Rockefeller had the same chance of missing out on the Republican nomination in San Francisco next summer that he has of going broke."

"That's funny," Powers said. "James Reston extending his powerful hands over history through his column in the *New York Times* and decreeing what will happen within the GOP. But—"

"We could beat the shit out of Rockefeller," Bobby mused.

"I think that's right," Powers said. "But there's a lot of feeling out there for Goldwater, and I personally don't think Reston's right, that Goldwater can just be counted out with Rockefeller on the scene."

"Hang on." Attorney General Robert Kennedy reached into his briefcase and pulled out a memo from his brother. Scrawled on top in JFK's handwriting were the words, *"Bobby, have a look at this. I don't like it."*

The presidential note had been written over a Xeroxed sheet reproducing a page from the *Congressional Quarterly.* The *Quarterly* reported an AP poll of the Republican delegates who had officiated at the 1960 convention. They had been asked by the pollster, Who did they think would be nominated at the San Francisco Republican convention next year?

"*Sixty-five* percent of the delegates," Bobby read from the text, "predict that Rockefeller will be nominated. But get this. *Seventy-two* percent said they'd *prefer* to see *Goldwater* nominated." He tapped his fingers on the table. "Goldwater. Just imagine that. Barry Goldwater. Goldwater is, like—*a Birchite.* Might as well be a *member* of the Society."

"Naw," Pierre Salinger said. "He just plays around with them. I mean, any GOP politician coming out of Phoenix *has* to be nice to the Birchers."

"We've got to do two things. Get the word out to our people that the Republican Party is in the hands of the Radical Right. At the same time, pressure the GOP *not to let in* the Radical Right. We don't want them nominating Goldwater."

Salinger said, "Circulate the Len Nadasdy letter. Remember? He was head of the Young Republican Federation. After he lost out to the Goldwater Right this summer, he wrote a letter to Goldwater and sent a copy of it to the *St. Paul Pioneer Press*. He urged Goldwater to disown the radicals in the Republican Party before it was too late. He said"—Salinger read from his file—"*'Why not do it now, disown the radicals, openly and clearly, rather than waiting until Rockefeller or, even worse, Kennedy forces you to do it in the heat of the campaign?'*"

"There's plenty of ammunition out there we can use," Powers said. "The report by California's Stanley Mosk on the John Birch Society has been leaked to the *New York Times*, and to friendly people in this part of the world"—he smiled, a little sheepishly—"and the *New York Times Magazine* is going with it on Sunday."

"I haven't seen that," the attorney general said. "Let me have it."

Powers handed over a galley. Kennedy ran his eyes down the article denouncing the Society and hinting that it had a death hold on the GOP. Turning a page while humming a song, he said, "This is good stuff. The president should have this. Hang on." He picked up the telephone and rang the appointments secretary. "Ken, the president got anybody with him right now? . . . Good. Keep other people out. I'm coming in." He put down the phone.

"I'll take this upstairs. Wait here, guys."

He was back in a few minutes.

"He liked that. The president liked that. Now, Barry Goldwater can be mean, we're finding out. Pierre, did you see what Goldwater said at the western GOP meeting, the one in June?"

Salinger shook his head.

"Goddammit, I have to act as a file clerk for the press secretary?" Bobby picked up the phone again. "Get me Elmer Horowitz. . . . Elmer, bring me, to the Situation Room, the file on Goldwater's speech at the western conference."

In a minute he had it. He opened it and turned a page. "Here it is. I'll read the part I'm looking for. *'Not long ago, Senator John Kennedy stated bluntly that the American people had gone soft. I am glad to discover he has finally recognized that government policies which create dependent citizens inevitably rob a nation and its people of both moral and physical strength.'"*

"That's *mean*," Powers agreed. "Still, I'm saying: We're not going to be in a race against Goldwater in 1964; it'll be Rockefeller. But we should prepare for all possibilities." Powers returned to his point. "We've got to make a bigger *effort* in the South. Bill Rusher of *National Review*—he was very prominent in the conservative takeover of the Young Republicans in San Francisco—Rusher has quoted one southern senator in his magazine, didn't say who he was, but I think we could guess without any trouble. Quoted this senator as saying, 'Goldwater and Goldwater alone can carry enough southern and border states to offset the inevitable Kennedy conquests in the big industrial states of the North and still stand a chance of winning the election.' That's what Rusher reported to the YR Council. Besides"—he looked up at the head of the table—"in Dallas, Bobby, we've got a ton of millionaires, and a lot of them are going to come to *any* lunch or dinner that's held there featuring the president of the United States."

Bobby Kennedy reflected on it.

He got up from his chair. "Okay," he said to Salinger. "After Florida, schedule Dallas."

36

L EONORA WAS AT THE SHERRY Netherlands in New York, helping to prepare for the twelfth of Nathaniel Branden's twenty scheduled lectures. She had adjusted the two chairs at the head of the room to just where, she knew, Miss Rand liked them, hers and Nathaniel's. Chester, the hotel clerk she worked with, called out to her from the other end of the room. "Miss Pound. *Miss Pound!*" Chester ran down the aisle between the chairs, some of them still banked against the wall, and Lee found herself all but running toward him. Out of breath, he told her President Kennedy had been shot in Dallas.

"Is he dead, Chester?"

"He's been taken to the hospital. But . . . they think he's dead."

Lee thought quickly. "Unless I call you in fifteen minutes, cancel the seminar."

She needed to get to Woodroe.

His phone was busy. She winced. She tried to assemble her thoughts. The Dallas people reviled President Kennedy, at least a lot of them did. And they had all but assaulted Adlai Stevenson a few weeks ago when he was in town lecturing on the United Nations, to which he was U.S. ambassador. Woodroe, as a Bircher, was an upfront right-winger. *He had to be protected.* She dialed again. Still busy.

First things first. She dialed the NBI number, which, thank God, answered. It was Barbara.

217

"Barbara, I told them at the hotel the seminar would be canceled unless we called back—"

"Lee, what's going on?"

She didn't know?

On the other hand, it had been only, what, three minutes since Chester had given her the news? And *he* didn't know for sure whether the president was dead.

Barbara flicked on the television in her office. "I've got it now on TV. Hang on. . . . Yes." There was a quaver in her voice. "Kennedy is dead." Another pause and, "Yes. Of course we'll cancel the seminar. I'll get hold of Nathaniel. He's with . . . Ayn."

One more call to the JBS office; still busy. Lee gave up. She'd go there. Walk the nine blocks. Unless a cab passed by, and one did.

By the time she got to the seventh-floor office she was angry.

"Don't you ever get off the phone?" she said, striding by Tish, who had operator's earphones on.

Tish shrugged and, using her hands, made a sign of helplessness. She pointed an index finger down the little hallway. That meant Woodroe was in.

She opened his door without knocking. Woodroe was on the phone.

She stepped up to his desk and slammed her wrist down on the telephone plunger.

"I was talking to Helena."

"I'm surprised they allow any Bircher in Dallas to use the phone. Now listen, Woody, and don't contradict me. You can tell already. There are people boiling mad, and they're looking for scalps. Right-wing scalps. They've already decided that the president was the victim of the Radical Right. You're coming with me to the apartment and we're both going to pack overnight bags. Then we're going to the garage at Thirty-ninth Street, where I rent cars for Nathaniel and Frank. And we're going to get out of New York City. Out to where anybody looking for Birch meat can't find you."

They drove north on Route 22. "This is the road I traveled going to Sharon," Lee said. "I guess you did too."

It didn't greatly matter which motel they checked in at. "Far enough to be just plain out of the way, but not so far we'd be out of reach of television coverage. You remember Mrs. Coley in Sharon? At her house she didn't get *any* TV signal."

They stopped in Dover Plains at a roadside motel.

Woodroe kept the engine running while Lee went in to check.

Did they have television in the rooms?

Yes.

Was there a restaurant?

In the back.

In their room, Lee sat in the armchair, Woodroe on the bed, his shoulders against the headboard. On the screen was a dizzying whirlwind of pictures centered on the assassination. Every few minutes there were shots of the president smiling as he entered the fateful car, Jackie on his left wearing the pink hat that would be famous. Up front, Texas governor John Connally, and the driver. Then the entourage arriving at Parkland Hospital. The gurney carrying the stricken president in. Then forward to twenty minutes later and the shot of the doctor, announcing that the president was dead. Then Air Force One, waiting for its godforsaken passengers, one of them dead in a coffin. Then shots of a movie theater. Of a police car approaching the theater. Of a handcuffed young man being bustled into a police car. Of cars with sirens sounding. Of the outside of a police station. The voice of a U.S. marshal, insisting on silence, all but blinded by the flashbulbs. Finally he could make himself heard.

One Lee Harvey Oswald had been charged with the murder of Patrolman J. D. Tippit. Tippit was a member of the Dallas police force, found dead a few blocks from the Texas Theater, in which the alleged assailant was detected and taken away in handcuffs.

But was that the same guy who killed Kennedy?

The police chief said that a second arraignment was expected later in the evening, and would be given to the press in an orderly way.

Obviously it was Oswald.

But if it was Lee Harvey Oswald who did it, who *was* Oswald? And what was he up to? *Killing John Fitzgerald Kennedy?* The most personable, the most—enchanting president, chief of state, anywhere. In a matter of minutes, it seemed, the idol of the Western world.

David Susskind was giving background on Channel 13, the educational television channel in New York. He reported that the "consensus"—"How do you get a consensus in eight hours?" Lee thundered—"around the country" was that the assassination had been done by a right-winger inflamed by the "odium" the president was held in, again, in "right-wing circles." In Phoenix, a reporter sometime after 10 P.M. flashed the news that an unidentified gunman had pumped two shots through the window of a John Birch Society office. A witness had heard the shooter cry out, *"You killed my man!"* The young man in charge of the National Draft Goldwater Committee in Washington closed down the office. He was visibly reluctant, when the microphone was thrust on him, to comment on the assassination, but the enterprising reporter, who had acted on a rumor that the Goldwater office would be closing down, finally prevailed on him. Lee Edwards told the reporter that threatening phone calls had come in back-to-back and that Goldwater secretaries had received death threats.

"Death threats like what?" the reporter persevered, pursuing Edwards right to the door of his car.

"Like?" Edwards's face showed exasperation and a measure of fright. He let it all out finally: "Like, they're saying, some of the callers, *You sons of bitches, you killed him!* Exasperation like that."

NBC viewers saw then the doleful face of a bishop in Wisconsin who had summoned his parishioners for a special vesper service.

The camera closed in on his words. "I know that very often, each of us did not just disagree, we poured forth our vituperation. The accumulation of this hatred expressed itself in the bullet that killed John Kennedy this afternoon. I think we know this and I think it has made us realize just how dreadful we people can be."

Woodroe closed his eyes and thought hard on those words. Was he in fact engaged in peddling mortal hatred? Was the JBS? Was Bob Welch?

The NBC camera moved back to the airport, back to Dealey Plaza, back to Parkland Hospital, back to the Texas Theater.

Lee said she was going downstairs to bring up something to eat. Twenty minutes later, carrying a package, she worked the door open.

"Quiet!" Woodroe hissed, absorbed.

She turned toward the television set, easing her package of food and drink down on the bed.

"Lee Harvey Oswald was a member of the Fair Play for Cuba Committee"—the police chief was reading from notes. *"He is a former marine who in 1959 renounced his citizenship and emigrated to Communist Russia. But in February of this year, Oswald reclaimed U.S. citizenship."*

"My God!" said Lee. "It was one of *them*."

37

THE BUSINESS OF POLITICS did not end, could not end, with the assassination. The king is dead. Long live Lyndon Baines Johnson. But of course there were dissenters. The Grand Old Party. And the question for many was: Who would contend against the new king in November, a year away?

William J. Baroody, age forty-eight, liked to think of himself as more than just a think-tank executive. He was proud of the American Enterprise Institute he had taken on. It was now twenty-one years old and, by covenant and practice, was as forthrightly devoted to the promotion of free markets and to opposition to statist government as it could be without arousing the Internal Revenue Service. It was, after all, the IRS that vouchsafed the precious tax-exempt status, required by most prospective donors contemplating gifts. What the AEI did was undertake research on projects Baroody thought useful to right-minded students of economics and politics. It sponsored and conducted seminars and made modest grants to graduate students of what the AEI deemed the right persuasion who needed economic help to pursue their studies.

But churning in the big, convivial, cunning Armenian was a consuming desire to get his hand into street politics. Specifically, he wanted a creative hand in effecting the nomination of Barry Goldwater as Republican presidential candidate in San Francisco, six months down the road.

Goldwater liked Baroody (everybody liked Baroody) and agreed to detach the better part of two days of his planned fortnight in Palm Beach with his wife's family to a very private meeting with Baroody and four others nominated by Baroody and individually approved by Goldwater.

They were Jay Gordon Hall, a discreet lobbyist for General Motors whom Goldwater knew and had been advised by in matters dealing with labor legislation; Stephen Shadegg, the journalist, writer, and man of affairs who had managed Barry Goldwater's successful campaign for the Senate in 1952; Russell Kirk, a young yet already eminent historian and political scientist whose book *The Conservative Mind* was continuingly influential and who wrote a fortnightly column for *National Review*; and William Buckley, *National Review*'s editor and founder, whom Goldwater had several times met and shared a platform with.

There was one negative injunction. Baroody placed a conference call with the participants early in the week: No direct exhortation to run for president.

Baroody's endearing swagger worked also over the telephone. "Goldwater has *not* said he would seek the Republican nomination, and *has* said he won't make his mind up on the matter until some unspecified time in the next few months. Just understand, between us: He *has* thought about the nomination, and he *has* decided to seek it.

"Now, that doesn't mean he mightn't change his mind. One thing we want to do is—encourage him. Treat him as if he *hadn't* made up his mind. But do it without seeming to be egging him on. And very much on the agenda is the whole Radical Right business, especially the John Birch Society. Jay, you have some special something to tell us on that score, right?"

"Right, Bill."

"So see you in the sunny climes of West Palm Beach. As Ralph Emerson said to Walt Whitman, I greet you at the outset of great careers! Kingmakers!"

The guests were housed in small oceanfront suites in the mammoth Breakers Hotel, uncrowded this week in January. The hotel had shuffled off its Christmas patrons and was preparing now for the guests who would come in February and stay, many of them, through Easter.

Baroody had set up a comfortable meeting room with sofas and armchairs and a couple of card tables, as required for the six participants. They had been instructed to dress informally. The senator, predictably, would appear in his Arizona-style jeans, including the leather belt with the silver border and turquoise buckle. Steve Shadegg, also from Arizona, was similarly dressed, though without the great Aztec belt. Informal dress was no hardship for Russell Kirk, who, for all his cosmopolitan travel, lived and worked in the rural north of Michigan, surrounded by lakes and great trees and a thousand books. The code proved unsuited to Jay Hall, denizen of that studiedly withdrawn little division of the General Motors Corporation whose concern was for public policy as it affected GM. In the warm Florida weather, Jay was persuaded to put his jacket aside, but the best he could do with his tie was to loosen it. Buckley appeared in his usual Ivy League off-duty garb: khaki pants, blue button-down shirt, and light gray sweater.

They sat down and had coffee, awaiting the senator.

"Don't have to save any coffee for Barry. He doesn't drink it," Baroody said pleasantly.

"You're right about that, Bill." Goldwater had walked into the room and put down his cowboy hat. He greeted everyone. "Steve, Jay, Bill, Dr. Kirk."

Baroody never seemed pressed, and so for a half hour the conversation touched informally and engagingly on events of recent days. On the last day in November, President Johnson had appointed a commission to investigate the assassination of President Kennedy. Its chairman was Chief Justice Earl Warren. "That will confirm to Bob Welch that the whole thing was a Communist operation," Goldwater wisecracked. "But there's not going to be much fooling around on *this* subject. It's a pity that Communist son-of-a-bitch Oswald had to go and get himself killed. We need to find out if there are any ties there."

Baroody encouraged talk on the implications of the sudden end of John Kennedy. He knew that Kennedy's death had greatly affected the political Goldwater. A few weeks after the assassination, Goldwater had said over drinks one night that he couldn't see the American people tolerating three presidents in twelve months' time. "The 1964 election will take place less than one year after Dallas. So are the American people going to want Kennedy...Johnson...Goldwater in the space of twelve months?"

The thing to do, Baroody thought, was to emphasize that Kennedy was *gone* and that Johnson was headed in the wrong direction for America. Baroody cited, with amusement shared by Goldwater, the one-sentence editorial in *National Review* in December. "The editors regretfully announce that their patience with President Lyndon Johnson has been exhausted."

Goldwater was coming around, and every reference to Kennedy as *yesterday's* news helped. The Warren Commission would emphasize not the tragedy but *who* and *what* were responsible for that tragedy.

But then Jay Hall said he thought it would be of general interest, and of very great interest to the senator, to discuss a report done for the benefit of the leaders of the United Auto Workers, the Reuther brothers. "It's secret. But the White House has a copy of it and—*is acting on it*. Let me give you the guts of it. It's twenty-one pages long, but I have parts of it pulled out."

He handed a sheaf of papers to each participant. "You'll notice they are numbered, 'cause I'll have to have them all back. Remember, this is a supersecret private report to the Reuther brothers. The United Auto Workers are to the left of the American labor movement generally, but the UAW dominates union industrial policy. The Reuthers are interested in November 1964: Johnson versus—versus whoever is nominated by the Republicans."

Hall brought up his own copy and read, "'The Radical Right's forces are bounded on the Left by Senator Goldwater and on the Right by Robert Welch.'"

"So I am a left-winger!" Goldwater grinned. He turned to Buckley. "Will you people read me out of the party?"

Everyone laughed. Hall went on.

"The report says, 'It is late in the day to start dealing with these problems.' It says the same thing several times. Now, here is something else I have, and something not even Baroody has got hold of. It's a White House report *reacting* to the Reuther report. It's written by Lee White of Attorney General Bobby Kennedy's staff. It outlines proposed means of combating the American Right. (1) Curb right-wing activities in the armed forces. (2) Get the attorney general to classify a few ultraright outfits as 'subversive,' in the same way the attorney general has identified some Communist organizations, ever since the 1930s, as subversive. (3) Get the IRS to review the records of these organizations—like the John Birch Society and YAF—and see if some damage can be done through discreet publicity. And (4) get the FBI to plant some informers in these organizations."

There was silence.

Goldwater said, "Steve, Bill, why don't you people get on this? Steve has his contacts in the press, Bill has his magazine."

"Barry, you're right. But"—Baroody dramatically covered his eyes with his open hand—"we need to look into our own stable here for a minute. So I think between now and lunch we should talk about . . . the John Birch Society. Bobby Kennedy has singled it out for criticism, and everybody guessed the JBS was what JFK was talking about in his speech in California in November 1962. I'm wondering, Barry, whether you shouldn't just step forward and . . . shrug off the John Birch Society."

Round and round they went. Shadegg several times reported on how many of his friends in Arizona were members of the Society. "They don't know that Welch thinks Ike is a Communist, and if they knew they wouldn't care."

Jay Hall worried about the fragility of the conservative movement within the GOP, which was dominated by such liberal stalwarts as Governor Rockefeller. "With the administration and, who knows, even the FBI going after our people—you saw the list. It's not only the John Birch Society and General Walker and Ayn Rand. It's George Benson and Fred Schwarz, the Volcker Fund, the H. L. Hunt outfit, what's left of it—"

"*Facts Forum*," said Buckley.

"Yes, *Facts Forum*. I just don't think we should give ground here."

Russell Kirk vigorously disagreed. "It's not a matter of giving ground, Jay. It's a matter of not ce-ceding" (Kirk spoke with an occasional stammer) "ground we don't want. It's not like giving up Quemoy and Matsu, which would be surrendering Taiwanese islands to mainland China. In giving up John Birch, we're not giving up anything we *should* want."

At 12:30, the maître d'hôtel came in, followed by two waiters, two trays of food, and a bar.

"Tell you what," Baroody said, "let's get off this subject at lunch. There's a lot else to talk about. Like the increasing cost of Johnson's government and—good sign—presidential economic adviser Walter Heller urging tax reduction."

"Yes," said Shadegg, pausing to signal to the waiter, *scotch on the rocks, a twist of lemon.* "There's a whole lot the GOP has to concern itself with. But on how it should deal with the Radical Right is something we—you especially, Barry—can have a lot to say about."

Baroody turned to Buckley. "What are you thinking, Bill?"

"What *I've* got to worry about is whether any of those FBI plants have gotten into *National Review*!"

Reviewing his notes at the end of the afternoon, Baroody said that Kirk and Buckley would continue to expose the weaknesses of the Birch Society, but without calling for its corporate rejection from the conservative movement. "And you, Barry, you're willing to go, but only with criticizing Bob Welch. Steve, you've said you'd do a survey in Arizona and tell Barry what you came up with. Tell me too, will you, old buddy? Jay, you'll look for an opportunity to get a copy of the Reuther report through conventional channels. Barry will look for an opportunity to get somebody from the administration to demand a congressional hearing. Ask some questions. Those questions *need* asking. There's the First Amendment somewhere around, supposed to protect dissent."

The assembly dispersed. Buckley was off to give a speech at St. Augustine and would be back late that evening. Kirk had a lecture to prepare, and a chapter for his new book. Baroody went to Peggy Goldwater's for drinks and supper.

They'd all reassemble the next morning.

38

T HE WARREN COMMISSION hearings into the assassination of John F. Kennedy were conducted in different cities, always in utmost secrecy. Witnesses were permitted counsel. And of course, as the chief counsel for the commission, J. Lee Rankin, had said on the first day, "This is not a criminal proceeding. There is of course abundant evidence that Lee Harvey Oswald fired at the president, but the commission will be bound by no presuppositions. The commission proposes to unearth anything we can that will be useful to an evaluation of the whole, tragic event."

Before it was through, the commission heard 552 witnesses, issuing an 888-page final report with twenty-six volumes of transcripts and exhibits.

Present on the first day of the hearings was the entire panel. Its chairman, Earl Warren, had been a Republican state attorney general in California, governor of that state, and vice presidential candidate with Thomas Dewey in 1948. He had been named chief justice of the United States by President Eisenhower. Other commission members were the venerable Richard Russell from Georgia, a Democrat but a conservative; Republican senator John Sherman Cooper of Kentucky; Democratic congressman Hale Boggs from Louisiana; Republican congressman Gerald Ford of Michigan; former CIA director Allen Dulles; and banker and diplomat John McCloy. There were six assistant counsel under Lee Rankin.

One of the witnesses in 1964 was General Edwin A. Walker. The examining counsel was Wesley J. Liebeler.

After legal preliminaries, Mr. Liebeler asked biographical questions:

LIEBELER: Where were you originally born and raised, General?
WALKER: At Center Point, Texas. I was born in 1909, November 10. Center Point is in Kerr County. It is C-E-N-T-E-R P-O-I-N-T, Kerr County, Texas. That is sixty miles west of San Antonio.

Mr. Liebeler asked about the event in Dallas of April 10, 1963. It had been established that the assassin Oswald had shot at General Walker that day. Oswald had lived only forty-seven hours after killing the president, having been shot down at the police station by nightclub operator Jack Ruby.

LIEBELER: Do you have any other information that would indicate any connection between Ruby and Oswald?
WALKER: I think the two boxes in the post office are very interesting.
LIEBELER: Well, are you suggesting that because two men, Jack Ruby and Lee Harvey Oswald, both happened to have post office boxes in the same post office, that that suggests there is some connection between them and indicates a conspiracy to assassinate the president?
WALKER: The boxes were rented the same week.
LIEBELER: You think that suggests a conspiracy between Oswald and Ruby to assassinate the president?
WALKER: That suggests a possible relationship. I think the fact that Rubenstein—
LIEBELER: You are referring to Jack Ruby?
WALKER: Rubenstein was his original name. I was saying, that the fact that Rubenstein shot Oswald suggests plenty. I am

convinced he couldn't have shot him except for one basic reason, and maybe many others, but to keep him quiet. That is what shooting people does. I think the whole city of Dallas is very interested in that. I would be interested. I would be interested in information on a Professor Wolf, William T. Wolf.

LIEBELER: Who is he?

WALKER: The first man we found in the newspaper that seemed to have come to a strange death after the attempted shot at me.

LIEBELER: I am not familiar with the circumstances surrounding that. Would you tell me about Dr. Wolf?

WALKER: William T. Wolf is a professor who was supposedly burned up in an apartment fire, which seems impossible to have burned a man up, a normal man with his normal faculties, because the apartment, he couldn't have been trapped in it on the first floor.

LIEBELER: Did you know Dr. Wolf?

WALKER: Never heard of him until I read about him in the paper, and I believe I read about him eight days after they shot at me.

LIEBELER: You think there is some connection between Dr. Wolf's death and the shot at you?

WALKER: No; but I think there is some connection with respect to what is going on in Dallas.

LIEBELER: Well, now, does this relate to the possibility of a conspiracy between Oswald and Ruby to assassinate President Kennedy?

WALKER: I think many unusual deaths in the city of Dallas might show some indication of what is going on, to include what happened on the twenty-second of November. And I would refer you to one other, a professor by the name of Deen. His name is George C. Deen.

LIEBELER: What has that got to do with the assassination of President Kennedy? What are the facts about it?

WALKER: It seems rather mysterious that a young doctor of psychiatry at Timberlawn would, so far as I can tell, only show up in the obituary page.

LIEBELER: What happened to this fellow?

WALKER: He was reported died of natural causes, I believe, or certainly nothing more than that, according to the obituary, so far as I can find.

LIEBELER: Er, we . . . General Walker. Are you familiar with the organization known as The Minutemen?

WALKER: In general terms.

LIEBELER: Do you know of any connection between The Minutemen and the assassination of President Kennedy?

WALKER: I do not.

LIEBELER: Do you know of any conspiracy or connection on the part of any so-called right-wing organization and the assassination of President Kennedy?

WALKER: I do not.

LIEBELER: Do you know of any connection between any of the people who associate themselves with and who, shall we say, follow you as a political leader, and the assassination of President Kennedy?

WALKER: No. People that follow me are for constitutional government. This, shooting the president, is absolutely in violation of constitutional government. Very destructive to what we stand for.

LIEBELER: I asked General Watts to bring whatever records you have that would indicate your whereabouts in October and after that in 1963. Particularly, I want to know whether you were at a political rally or meeting that was held immediately prior to the visit of Adlai Stevenson to the city of Dallas in October of 1963.

WALKER: Yes, I was the speaker on the day before Mr. Stevenson appeared in the auditorium. I was the speaker in the same room and the same platform on October 22.

LIEBELER: How many people would you say were there at that rally?

WALKER: The room holds about 1,700 seats, and there were about 1,300 to 1,400 filled.

LIEBELER: Were you aware of the fact that Lee Harvey Oswald claimed to have been at that meeting?

WALKER: No, sir; I wasn't.

LIEBELER: You didn't know he was there at the time?

WALKER: I don't know yet.

LIEBELER: In any event, you didn't know then?

WALKER: Certainly didn't.

General Walker testified for three and a half hours.

"This guy thinks I'm a Communist," Warren said to chief counsel Rankin after looking over the transcript of General Walker's testimony.

"He had me convinced you were," Rankin laughed.

Chief Justice Warren pretended he got the joke.

39

MARVIN LIEBMAN'S APARTMENT on East Forty-fourth Street exhibited his current passions. His intense ideological involvement in the cause of a free China had taken him to Taiwan several times. Acquisitive by nature, he came back with artistic souvenirs, which evolved over the months into oriental rugs, tables, chairs, paintings, tapestries, wall decorations, mirrors, and cuisine. His China period meant chopsticks were served to his guests at dinner. But there were knives and forks within reach, which maladroit guests could turn to, and when they did, that was okay by Marvin, who always aimed to please and to be hospitable.

Seeking to indulge a fancy, sometime in 1963 he took to painting oil canvases. He was too restless to persist in the development of his marginal skill, however. He did not exhibit his own work, satisfying himself instead by buying oil paintings, one after another, and hanging them on three walls of his apartment on which they fit so tightly that the blur on first walking into the room was of a single wall-sized canvas by an eclectic artist who would not let his endless canvas close down until he had come up with the kitchen stove; and if you looked hard for it on the east wall of Marvin's room, there it was: a little oil painting of a stove, done in Florence, the embers illuminating the heating plate. Right over it was the bottom banana of an eight-foot-tall, eight-inch-wide canvas depicting a fruit tree which climbed up Marvin's wall like a beanstalk, hitting the ceiling with a pineapple, through which Marvin had hand-painted an arrow in order to give substance to the presumptive skills of the lithe Greek archer whose bow was strung at maximum tension diagonally across at the other end of the room, one of his feet apparently resting on the head of Marvin's beloved mother, whose portrait Marvin had commissioned with his very first earnings as a lobbyist for Conservative America.

Dressed in a painter's smock, he welcomed Lee Pound and Woody Raynor and asked if they would like a mai tai. Marvin himself didn't drink, but he took pleasure in mixing drinks for others. The news was that the Warren Commission would issue its report the next day, and Marvin told a funny story. His friend Oscar Dystel, the head of Bantam Books, had made a boast to his colleagues at a convention of book publishers. He was acclaiming new techniques which had streamlined book production. The Warren Report would be issued at noon on Friday. Dystel's boast, on behalf of Bantam, was "to have the Warren Report available, to sell, in London at twelve noon on Monday!" Everyone thought him mad. Having lined up every typesetter in the East Coast, pledged to work day and night beginning at noon Friday, he came upon the problem of preprinting the covers. If the report turned out to be 300 to 500 pages long, the preordered cover would be for a book one-half inch thick. If 500 to 750 pages, one inch thick. If over 750 pages, two inches thick.

It surely was not too much to ask of the Warren Commission, About how many pages would the report *be?* He put in a call to chief counsel Lee Rankin, asking for just that little lead.

"Lee Rankin," Dystel told Marvin, "is a ... schmuck! *He would not tell me. So?* So I have ordered one million covers one-half inch thick, one million covers one inch thick, one million covers two inches thick." Dystel joked, said Marvin, that if the commission report turned out to be longer than 900 pages, "he will simply edit it down before sending it out."

They laughed pleasurably and Marvin insisted they have more mai tais. "Chiang Kai-shek gave me the ingredients for these mai tais you're drinking and had a colonel with dry ice take me to the plane to keep them dry—no, to keep them wet—on the trip home."

"*Really?*" said Lee. She was briefly taken in.

"Sounds like altruism to me, Lee."

"Oh, shut up, Woody."

"Well, we'll put that one away," Marvin said. "I was joking about Chiang Kai-shek—though I did visit the sacred man and one-day liberator of Communist China."

"We can all drink to that," Woody said, as Lee raised her glass.

But Marvin said then, "Straighten me out, Lee, on your objectivist objections to altruism. I mean, don't we all do things for others?"

Lee addressed Marvin rather heatedly. "When I tell people I'm opposed to altruism, they go crazy. They think it means I'm opposed to kindness, charity, benevolence, and respect for the rights of others—and yet *altruism* means none of those things."

"So," Marvin said, "if you do good things for others, then you're not an altruist?"

"Not unless the sacrifice you make for others means surrendering *yourself,* abandoning the kind of self-fulfillment that is the key to true liberty."

"Aw, come on, Lee," Woodroe broke in. "Let's look at Marvin. He fought for Zionism in the early days of Israel. He was a smuggler, brought in weapons to Israel on two runs, was so seasick"—Woodroe had been shown a draft of an autobiography Marvin was working on—"he very nearly died. But he did it again. Finally he was sent home, and in Greece, where he was getting the arms for Israel, he ran into the Communists, who were selling—he could see—the same arms to the Palestinians. He quarreled—let me know if I have any of this wrong, Marvin—and decided that what he wanted to fight was the Communists, so he came back here and has been doing that for six years."

"Eight years."

"Now he obviously lives well. His various committees pay him to do the work he does. But he didn't live well when he was tossing his stomach up in a freighter going through stormy weather to Haifa."

"As long as someone feels he is doing what he wants to do, then he isn't an altruist."

Marvin interrupted. "Suppose I don't want to spend my life on anti-Communist work but I feel—a *calling* to fight against the Communists on as many fronts as I can. Am I an altruist then?"

"Yes," Lee said. "And you are contaminating freedom. You're putting someone else's interests—the anti-Communist cause—on a higher order than your own. In that way, you are rejecting the moral dimension of liberty."

"Balls," Woodroe permitted himself.

She looked around at him. Her eyes blazed. "Look who is offended by definitions he thinks are nothing but . . . balls. Here's a guy who works for the John Birch Society, whose head—whose '*Founder*'— whose *godhead*—thinks Eisenhower and Warren are Communist agents. If he's so allergic to '*ballish* thought,' why doesn't *he* pull out?"

"Lee—Marvin, I've told her this before, and you must have heard it. Working for Welch even though he has a crazy idea doesn't mean that the whole effort isn't worth it. Like, you're a Republican and Ike fails to bring effective help to the Hungarians when they strike out for liberty. That doesn't mean you stop being a Republican, does it? Lee can be an 'objectivist' and still believe in sacrifice and—I'd call it altruism—"

"*I* wouldn't," she snapped. "Just like you couldn't be a Christian and disbelieve that Christ rose from the dead—"

"I believe that," Marvin said. "But I guess we should change the subject, go back to the Warren Commission."

"No," Lee said. She paused and looked up. "You say you believe that about Christ?"

"Yes," said Marvin. "And I'm taking instruction. I'm going to be baptized. And Bill Buckley will be my godfather."

Dinner was announced by the housekeeper.

Marvin said that he wouldn't pretend the food had been brought to him directly from Chiang Kai-shek, but it *had* been brought to him directly by Chiang's ambassador to the United Nations.

That brought laughter, and at dinner they spoke of the Republican nomination coming up, and the high prospects for Barry Goldwater.

40

I N LATER YEARS, MANY questions would be asked about the Warren Commission Report on the assassination of John F. Kennedy. David Belin, a staff investigator and highly respected lawyer from Des Moines, was severe in his criticisms of evidence withheld from the commission and of leads unpursued.

His criticism had to do with CIA knowledge of Oswald's doings between the time he returned from the Soviet Union, in June 1962, and the day he shot Kennedy, seventeen months later. CIA Director John McCone's motives in withholding this information were correctly discerned in later years. It was as simple as that President Johnson—and in this he represented, though without consultation, the thought of senior legislators, Democratic and Republican—did not want to enliven speculation that in shooting Kennedy, Oswald was acting explicitly or implicitly on instructions from Moscow or Havana. If, Lyndon Johnson one day reminisced to a biographer, it had come out in that period that the assassination of President Kennedy had been the work of the Soviet Union, "we'd have had to tear those fuckers apart limb from limb, never mind nuclear war."

Much later research confirmed that Moscow had no hand in the assassination and that Premier Khrushchev ardently hoped that there would be no evidence of any Communist official's ties to Oswald of a kind that might engender suspicion.

But angry as he was that Oswald's past contacts with Communists in Mexico had been papered over, David Belin was adamant that accumulated research absolutely and conclusively established (1) that Oswald had fired the first bullet, which was aimed at Kennedy, and the second bullet, which killed Kennedy; (2) that no other shot had been fired that day in Dallas at noon in that area; and (3) that there was no evidence whatever that anyone other than Oswald was involved in the bane of November 22, 1963.

But the findings of the Warren Commission did not satisfy everyone. Sometime after Oliver Stone's film *JFK* was distributed, nearly thirty years later, a poll reported that 70 percent of the American people believed that someone other than Oswald had been involved in the shooting. The term "grassy knoller" was used to depict those who insisted there had been another assassin, and that he had operated from the elevation of a grassy knoll in the Dealey Plaza green. In order to substantiate the suspicions of the grassy knollers, staff investigator Belin pointed out, it would be necessary to make corollary assumptions. It had to be that the police had suppressed evidence; that perhaps the ballistics experts had erred on the matter of the officiating weapon, the Mannlicher-Carcano rifle; that Oswald's shooting of Officer Tippit was a part of a larger design; that Ruby had shot Oswald to prevent him from giving evidence that might be incriminating to those who had things to hide; and that the conspiracy to cover up the assassination involved the chief justice of the United States, the director of the Federal Bureau of Investigation, the president of the United States, and the autopsic surgeons in Washington to whom the corpse had been turned over.

If indeed it really was the corpse of the president! Some people wondered.

Those were, mostly, suspicions by members of the political Left. On the political Right, suspicions came primarily from John Birch Society spokesmen. Most prominent of these was Professor Revilo Oliver, who wrote of the Warren Report in *American Opinion*, the official JBS monthly.

Oliver's was a very long article. He undertook to explain to the membership what the Warren Commission had done and what it had not done. He devoted many thousands of words to a general orientation of what was happening to America, and how to approach any investigation of the assassination.

Woody took up the issue eagerly when it arrived in the mail.

"Lee Harvey Oswald," the Birch Society article began, "was a young punk who defected to the Soviet [Union], taking with him the operational codes of the Marine Corps and such other secrets as a fledgling traitor had been able to steal while in military service. He was then trained in sabotage, terrorism, and guerrilla warfare (including accurate shooting from ambush) in the well-known school for international criminals near Minsk—"

Did he, Professor Oliver, have specific knowledge of an agency in Minsk where such training is given? Professor Oliver had been asked that question when testifying before the commission. Oliver had answered airily that he did not have specific knowledge that *Minsk* even existed.

"—and while there," the article in *American Opinion* continued, "[Oswald] married the daughter of a colonel in the Soviet military espionage system (and probably also in the secret police). Oswald took up his duties as an agent of the Conspiracy. In April, 1963, he was sent to Dallas, where he tried to murder General Edwin Walker. The failure does not reflect on the assassin's professional training: General Walker happened to turn his head at the instant the shot was fired.

"In November, Oswald was sent back to Dallas, where a job in a suitably located building had been arranged for him. He shot the President of the United States from ambush, left the building undetected, and would have escaped to Mexico but for some mischance. He was stopped for questioning by a vigilant policeman, whom he killed in a moment of panic. Arrested and identified, he, despite his training, was so vain as to pose for photographs while triumphantly giving the Communists' clenched-fist salute."

It seemed to Woodroe that Professor Oliver was carried away in his certitudes. Where had it been established that the Communists had gotten Oswald his job in the Texas School Book Depository? That his flights to Mexico had been arranged?

Glued to the text, Woodroe read on with intense curiosity. Oliver did not falter.

"Obviously, something went wrong in Dallas. The identification of the murderer was a near-miracle. I shall not be greatly astonished if, in the course of the Conspiracy's frantic efforts to confuse us with irrelevancies, it should be disclosed that pay-offs had been made by Jakob Leon Rubenstein, alias Ruby, and other members of the underworld that panders to human vice and folly.

"It is quite true that the Communist Conspiracy, through the management of great broadcasting systems and news agencies, through the many criminals lodged in the radio and the press, and through many indirect pressures (such as the allocation of advertising and harassment by bureaus of the federal government), have a control over our channels of communication that seems to us, in our moments of discouragement, virtually total. As was to be expected, a few moments after the shot was fired in Dallas, the vermin, probably in obedience to general or specific orders issued in advance of the event, began to screech out their diseased hatred of the American people, and, long after the facts were known to everyone, went on mechanically repeating, like defective phonograph records, the same vicious lies about the 'radical right' until fresh orders reached them from headquarters."

Woodroe could hear Revilo Oliver saying the words. And he knew that he would not have made any typographical errors in composing his article on that typewriter in the room with the battery of typewriters.

The phone rang.

"Have you seen *American Opinion*?" Jesse Andrews wanted to know.

"I'm reading it right this minute."

"Well, it's going to cause quite a sensation, quite a fuss. We sent it out to the AP, and Revilo is giving a press conference at Urbana at 5 P.M. There might be something on the television news. Just checking."

"Thanks. I'll let you know what I think of it after I've finished."

Revilo was drawing his conclusion based on the reversal of fortunes he wrote about.

"But the significant fact is that there were enough honest American newsmen, in the United States and abroad, to make it impossible to conceal the Conspiracy's connection with the bungled assassination. That is very encouraging.

"All that could be done at the moment to obscure the Communist's mischance was to stage an elaborate spectacle with all the technical virtuosity seen in a performance of *Aida* in the Baths of Caracalla or the amphitheatre at Verona, supplemented with the cruder devices of Hollywood's expert vulgarians. Every effort was made to incite an orgy of bathos and irrationality."

Woodroe had to admire the technical virtuosity. Revilo's language!

"Regardless of office, political violence is always shocking and a warning of impending collapse. The Roman Republic was doomed as soon as it became clear that the wealthy and high-born renegade, Clodius [*sic*], could send his gangsters into the streets with impunity; when the decent people of Rome tried to protect themselves by hiring gangsters of their own under Milo, that was not an answer: it was a confession of defeat. The assassination of Kennedy, quite apart from consideration of the office that he held, was an act of violence both deplorable and ominous—as ominous as the violence excited by the infamous Martin Luther King and other criminals engaged in inciting race war with the approval and even, it is said,

243

the active cooperation of the White House." Woodroe let his eyes close for a moment.

Oliver continued. "It was as deplorable and ominous as the violence of the uniformed goons (protected by reluctant and ashamed soldiers) whom Kennedy, in open violation of the American Constitution, sent into Oxford, Mississippi, to kick into submission American citizens, whom the late Mr. Kennedy had come to regard as his livestock.

"Such lawlessness, regardless of the identity of the perpetrators or their professed motives, is as alarming as the outbreak of a fire in a house, and if not speedily extinguished, will destroy the whole social order. That is a fact that all conservatives know, for it is they who read the lessons of human history and understand how hard it is to build and how easy it is to destroy—how perishable and precious are the moral restraints and the habitual observance of them by which civilization shelters itself from the feral barbarism that is latent in all peoples."

Woodroe was dumb with fascination. Where was Revilo headed?

"The foregoing are two good and sufficient reasons why Americans were shocked and grieved by the assassination in Dallas. Let them suffice us. It is imperative that we do not permit ourselves to be confused at this critical time by a twisted proverb and residual superstition. Taboos are for barbarians, who indulge in tribal howling and gnashing of cheeks and breast whenever a big chief dies or an eclipse portends the end of the world. We are a civilized race.

"I have mentioned but a few of the hundred reasons why we shall never forget John F. Kennedy. So long as there are Americans, his memory will be cherished with execration and loathing. If the international vermin succeed in completing their occupation of our country, Americans will remember Kennedy while they live, and will curse him as they face the firing squads or toil in brutish degradation that leaves no hope for anything but a speedy death."

An hour later, he telephoned Jesse.

"I've finished the Oliver article."

"That's something, isn't it?"

"Yeah. I'm resigning from the John Birch Society. I'll put it in writing."

He hung up the telephone.

41

THE YOUNG ECONOMIST and idealist Murray Rothbard was one more of that seemingly endless list of excited readers of *Atlas Shrugged* who, on reading it, wrote to Ayn Rand to profess gratitude and enthusiasm for the novel. Rothbard's letter was learned and lyrical, even poetic, his enthusiasm unmitigated. "I have just finished your novel today. I will start by saying that all of us in the 'Circle Bastiat'"—Rothbard's think group, honoring the memory of Frederick Bastiat, Libertarian—"are convinced that *Atlas Shrugged* is the greatest novel ever written. You have carried the novel form to a new and higher dimension." A meeting with Rothbard was buoyantly arranged, at which, however, not everything went well. Nathaniel Branden was present and thought he had spotted in Murray's face something he later described as fear and malice, though it was more than Rothbard's features that brought on the ensuing disharmony.

The meeting took place at the Rand power center, her legendary studio, at which the Collective continued its sabbatical worship. Murray was infatuated by the novel but didn't think its author divine, and he was young enough, and self-reliant enough, to let his feelings show. This irreverence brought on more than the usual consumption of cigarettes by Rand, as she deployed her forces.

Murray Rothbard had set the stage by declaring that he was a libertarian and *therefore* an anarchist. But this was a huge, oblique leap in Rand World, and not a little arrogant. There were plenty of self-styled libertarians around, certainly including Miss Rand, who was their queen mother; but she was not an anarchist, indeed she disdained anarchy. So then, who had the property rights here?

Nathaniel Branden, in search of definition, challenged Rothbard. Without *some* government, how did Rothbard propose to ensure individual rights? Rothbard answered, "With private, competing defense agencies." That reply was brought to Ayn Rand and precipitated her withering comment, everywhere reiterated in Randian circles, "You mean, as in civil war?"

The Randian movement was in pretty full swing in 1964, seven years after the publication of *Atlas Shrugged*. The nascent libertarian political movement had not yet been organized nationally. Its scattered disciples at the beginning were not seeking to pick factional quarrels with the Objectivist legions. John Hospers, a devoted student of Rand and an estimable philosopher, would one day soon step forward as the first presidential candidate of the Libertarian Party, but even then the party, like the conservative movement at large, was riven by personal and ideological disputes. Hospers, and others, labored to make antigovernment thought and resolution a national movement. They encouraged thoughtful discussion in magazines and teaching seminars, imitating, if unevenly, such programs as Nathaniel Branden had so successfully launched in behalf of objectivism. But they were always heavy-laden by the unanswered question, *What is the charter of libertarianism?*

That was a question Woodroe and Leonora frequently asked themselves, sometimes when dining at home in the apartment, sometimes in the company of other members of the Young Americans for Freedom, or with Marvin Liebman, or with editorial associates of *National Review*. "Two-hundred-proof libertarians," Leonora said, quoting a learned friend, Professor Ernest van den Haag, "oppose *all* taxes and *all* public services. That has to mean that they oppose public courts, laws, police, armies, roads, parks, education, and public health. Well, that lets me out, Woody, and you too, right?"

"Yes. I wouldn't want to rely on a private volunteer defense force to stop the Soviet military who moved in on Budapest."

"On the other hand," Lee made the point, "there's a certain, well, poetry in putting it that way, isn't there? Like . . . well, like paradigmatic political thought. How things *ought* to be—no government, etc.?"

"But Rothbard and Hospers and those people aren't writing in the spirit of the utopians. That is the point," Woodroe stressed. "And Miss Rand insists *she's* not a utopian. She says she's prescribing for the modern world, effective more or less immediately."

"Ayn," Lee ventured, "is a . . . fabulist."

"Would she like it if she heard you use that word about her?"

"I don't think so, because it might suggest she was otherworldly. She . . . isn't. She insists she isn't."

Woodroe nodded. "I know. So we're left wondering, What does the libertarian movement have to say to the GOP? Anything? What will the libertarians, if they get around to selecting a spokesman, testify to if they present themselves to the Republican Platform Committee in San Francisco?"

"That's not so hard. You have to begin somewhere. You come out for a reduction in all federal enterprise—"

"Including defense?"

Lee paused. "Yes, that's a tough one. We want to stop the North Vietnamese in their war against the South. That isn't going to get done by Murray Rothbard and his volunteers. Still, you can go on about federal aid to education, health, Social Security, you name it—"

"Public monuments?"

"Adam Smith said that was a proper concern of government."

"The libertarians wouldn't say that, would they?"

"Guess it depends on whom you ask."

It went on and on.

In the late 1950s and early 1960s, disputes raged between satrapies in the libertarian/anarchist/Randian world. There was only one pope, and he was Ayn Rand. Her edicts were dispositive. Her (ritualized) excommunications of heretical followers who wandered off the dogmatical trail, or were thought insufficiently servile, had the desirable effect of finality within the Randian communion. But such folk, in exile, did not cease to exist or, even, to exercise influence.

Where possible, the Randian ultramontanists preferred to have persuasive grounds for trials and convictions. They did not always succeed, and strategic loyalties were frayed. Kay Nolte Smith was expelled for making unauthorized changes to a few lines of dialogue in a public performance of Rand's play *Penthouse Legend*. Some confederates deemed her sentence (expulsion) inordinate, even eccentrically severe, given the long years Kay had put in as a faithful disciple. Four years later she was told she would be readmitted, but now she declined ("I had come to my senses"). The formidable John Hospers was ruled out of bounds. On taking leave of Rand, he recalled, "along with the pain and desolation, I felt a sense of release from an increasing oppressiveness." He was now glad for relief from "the web of intellectually stifling allegiances and entanglements" that were a part of Rand life.

In Murray Rothbard's case, the tinderbox was a scholarly paper in which he cited as the source of certain ideas he was advancing on the subject of causality a scholar who had written in the Middle Ages. Rand Inc. pounced on this, insisting that the inspiration for that thought had been Ayn Rand, not a mere Aristotelian of centuries back. Rothbard was summoned to Rand's chamber, where formal censure had been scheduled, but Rothbard simply declined to show up. The Collective proceeded without him, expelling Rothbard from the Objectivist circle. In turn, Rothbard took to registering his own dissatisfactions with Rand and Randianism, broadcasting his criticisms of her. And so it went.

The Rand people did not like it that Murray Rothbard soon acquired—the Randians would say, cultivated—the cognomen "Mr.

Libertarianism." To begin with, chubby, hardworking, obstreperous Rothbard was a relative upstart, a highly productive scholar, to be sure, but damaging to the usefulness and integrity of objectivism because of his anarchist propensities. The Randians believed, along with most libertarians, that limited constitutional government was necessary, and therefore tolerable. But Rothbard pressed his fight against *any* government at all, going beyond even where his patron, the august Austrian seer Ludwig von Mises, had gone. Mises, after all, had written, "Government as such is not only an evil but the most necessary and beneficial institution, as without it no lasting cooperation and no civilization could be developed or preserved."

Some sensed—correctly—that Miss Rand's growing aversion to association with "libertarians" reflected less her opposition to any proposal by a libertarian group than her resentment of the apparent willingness in some of her subordinates to proceed without her explicit benediction. Keith Edwards, who represented the Nathaniel Branden Institute in Detroit and was active in nascent libertarian politics, made one attempt to understand Rand's objections to what he was doing, but was rebuffed. Ayn Rand's exfoliated position was that no political party could succeed unless explicitly based on her philosophy of metaphysics, epistemology, and ethics. Early followers had heard her use the term *libertarian* freely and approvingly, but now she associated the term with defective, unruly—and therefore excommunicable—disciples; so that Murray Rothbard—and even John Hospers—became the enemy. Now Rand would use, with equal contempt, the terms *fascism, Communism,* and *libertarianism.*

The House of Rand could not tolerate this swirl of individualists who, whatever their misgivings about government, declined to be governed by the thought and the pronouncements of Ayn Rand. The libertarians would not organize into a political party until many years later, but in the political contest dead ahead, they rallied behind Barry Goldwater, as did Miss Rand.

42

L EADERS OF THE YOUNG AMERICANS for Freedom arrived in San Francisco in the high spirit of loyalists, triumphing over morganatic contenders with impure bloodlines, here now to see their hero crowned. YAF chairman Robert Bauman, elected to the post after the untimely death of Bob Schuchman at age twenty-four, held a press conference. He jubilantly told a questioner that young Republicans who had been deprived of the nomination of Barry Goldwater four years before, in 1960, were now in San Francisco "to see it happen." This, he said, was the "catalytic moment" for a Republican Party accepting the proud mandate of enduring conservative principles.

But the catalytic moment had obstacles to overcome. And these proved overwhelming.

By the time the nomination was in hand and Goldwater officially named, the public image was of a presidential challenger askew, wobbling through a convention floor strewn with questions, denunciations, challenges, and unanswered questions.

And the question of the role of the John Birch Society was everywhere.

Senator Mark Hatfield, from Oregon, gave the keynote address. The Goldwater camp was apprehensive about him. But after all, he was a "moderate," and moderates needed to have a voice at the convention.

Senator Hatfield leapt right into the question of factionalist boarding parties. "There are bigots in this nation who spew forth

251

their venom of hate," he declared. These groups must be overcome, he said, including "the Communist Party, the Ku Klux Klan, and the John Birch Society."

The applause was uncertain.

Former president Dwight Eisenhower was there, an earthy champion of the capitalist ethos—he was a paid commentator, hired by ABC News. But of course his own moment at the convention was as premier spokesman for the party, the Republican who, only four years earlier, had occupied the White House, to which he had been reelected after a first term. When General Eisenhower addressed the convention, he too warned against "radicalism of *any* kind, whether of the Right or the Left." He exhorted the delegates not to "stain our image by consorting with radicals of any kind."

Yet the dramatic moment in Eisenhower's speech was not his admonitions against radical suitors. He spoke a sentence which, in the advance text, had not caught the attention of anyone as conveying anything extraordinary. His words were, *"Let us particularly scorn the divisive efforts of those outside our family, including sensation-seeking columnists and commentators—"* Before he could finish the sentence, the San Francisco Cow Palace Convention Hall was wild. Shouts of approval, sustained applause, hoots of compliant, excited, jubilant, reproachful accord spoke the raucous voice of a convention avenging hours, days, weeks, and months of print and TV commentators who had scorned the emerging GOP, imputing to it reckless inclinations in foreign policy and, in domestic policy, an indifference to civil rights for blacks and a primitive resistance to federal concern for social welfare.

That night, Youth for Goldwater had a dinner. There were one hundred guests, each paying $3.75 for the chicken. The cash bar sold chits; a beer cost twenty-five cents, vodka or bourbon, one dollar.

"ANY SURPLUS IN THE ACCOUNT WILL GO TO THE GOLDWATER CAM-
PAIGN," a typewritten notice taped against the side of the bar pledged.

"Are we supposed to finance the campaign by boozing it up?"
asked Dick Cowan jocularly.

"Not a bad idea," YAF chairman Bauman winked, bringing his
glass to his lips. "After all, we've got a whole lot to celebrate."

"And a whole lot left to do," Tom Phillips, another cofounder,
interposed.

It was with concern for what was left to be done that a half dozen
young veterans convened after dinner in Bob Bauman's suite at the
St. Francis Hotel. All of them, except David Keene, had been present at the founding of YAF. They had survived wasteful, internecine,
opportunistic, factional wrangling, but all of that at this moment was
merely bad memory. Now they were united, hoping to bring off at
the convention and on election day what had brought them to
Sharon, Connecticut—the very idea of a national youth federation
that would change American politics.

"There are three subjects we want to talk about," said Bauman.
"One of them is the civil rights question, a second is the need to
fight hard on the anti-Communist movement in Vietnam, and the
third is how to handle the John Birch Society problem. Let's start
with this last one, which was pretty much the highlight of the
speeches today by Hatfield and Ike. Woody, clue us in."

Woodroe Raynor had worked as assistant to Goldwater press
chief Karl Hess for two months. He spoke off the record and told
his young colleagues that the fight over how to deal with the John
Birch Society was going on in the inner council of Goldwater headquarters. "It features Bill Baroody, Clif White, Denison Kitchel, and
Dean Burch."

"Dean Burch? Is he any relation?" Cowan always looked for an
angle that would permit levity.

Woodroe smiled. "Yeah, Dick. But Dean is an ambiguist. He changed his name to B-U-R-C-H. Burch and Kitchel are both from Arizona and they're pleading with Goldwater to leave the organization alone, just maybe let out a peep or two against Bob Welch."

"The trouble is, Welch isn't the only wild Birch leader," said Carol Bauman, Chairman Bob's wife. "There are others. For instance, what about people like Revilo Oliver?"

"There's no way Goldwater's going to—no way people could expect Goldwater to go down the list of Birch Society members and say yes on him, no on him," Woodroe said. "The question Goldwater faces is whether to make a *corporate* disavowal—which is what Baroody is urging."

"How would you hope he'd go, Woody?" Keene asked.

Woodroe paused for a moment. "That runs hard up against my own history, and you all know about that, at least, about parts of it. And Leonora here knows about it in some detail. Right, Lee?" He looked over at another cofounder of YAF. "Lee lived through a lot of it. On the other hand"—he smiled broadly—"I've lived through a lot of objectivism."

"Hey!" Dick Cowan said. "We ought to call on Hatfield and Ike and demand they go back to the podium and denounce Ayn Rand!"

"*John Galt lives!*" David Keene intoned, his lips framing a solemn warning against blasphemy, his eyes alight with amusement.

"No offense, Lee." Cowan got back on the road: "Go on, Woody."

"It's just a plain fact that a lot of people are members of the John Birch Society who don't much care *what* its Founder or anybody else says in *American Opinion* but would care *very much* if the Society was publicly criticized by Candidate Goldwater. They don't want to hear from Goldwater the same kind of thing Ike got cheered for when he criticized 'sensation-seeking columnists and commentators.' These people are out there waiting for Goldwater's speech, and if he condemns the Society by name, they're going to be . . . forgive the language, Carol, Lee"—Woodroe was momentarily a proper Mormon—

"plenty peed off. We're not here to formulate moral advice for Goldwater, I say. We know he doesn't himself believe the kooky things. Whether he denounces the Society is a political question.

"So to answer your question, Bob, if I were in his inner council, I'd urge him *not* to go for the corporate rejection. But maybe I'm a late learner on this subject."

Back to Bauman. "Thanks, Woody. Let's ask Tom Phillips to sound off on the foreign policy plank."

"It's going to be good. The language renounces any notion that the Communists are leveling off, tending to accommodation. And it makes an important issue of the Vietnam scene. Last November, when JFK died, the U.S. had seventeen thousand so-called advisers on the Vietnam scene. The Johnson administration keeps putting off a hard position on Vietnam, and Goldwater's going to have to challenge him on that, the doctrine of containment."

"I thought we were for liberation, not containment?" Woodroe corrected him.

"Of course you are, and we are, and James Burnham's *Containment or Liberation?* guides us all on the subject. But the challenge in Vietnam is a challenge to *containment.* If the North Vietnamese Communists overwhelm Saigon, that makes for the first territorial Communist victory since what they set out to do in Korea. And that containment line has to be held."

"Well, no disagreement on that. Alfred, give us the outline of the thinking on the civil rights business."

"The attitude the liberals/moderates are asking for," Alfred Regnery said, "is what Catholics call *internal assent.* What they're saying is: Goldwater voted against the civil rights bill and said his reason was that the bill arrogated unconstitutional powers.

"But now what they're saying—Hatfield, Eisenhower, Rockefeller, Scranton—is: The country is behind the civil rights bill, it has been passed by a substantial majority, it hasn't been ruled unconstitutional and isn't likely to be. *Therefore,* we want from Goldwater an endorsement of the *ideals* of the bill, equal rights for everybody. He's advanced those ideals abstractly, but he is going to have to do that now wholeheartedly *in the context of the civil rights legislation.* He's got to back off from the states' rights people, from the General Walkers and the interpositionists and—the segregationists."

Leonora let out an approving *"Right."* She went on: "Let's face it, there are people out there who don't have in mind so much states' rights as that they don't want a Negro sitting in the same classroom with their children."

"So do we back the constitutional principle, or say—*Whatever the deficiencies of the bill, it aims in the right direction?* We should say just *that,*" Bauman summarized.

"I think that's right," Lee Edwards said. "And maybe, Bob, you could write out just the right wording to convey all that and still encourage the delegations in the South and West to stay excited about Barry."

"Well," Bauman acknowledged, "there are problems."

"One problem," said his wife, Carol, "is how to get some sleep before the 8 A.M. Young Republican rally."

"Do I hear a motion to adjourn? There being no dissenters, I declare this meeting adjourned."

"Don't forget *sine die,* Bob. You're a lawyer, after all."

"Not quite. I'll be a lawyer in about . . . one year. Er, adjourn *sine die.*"

43

THERE WERE VOTES, ON THE FLOOR of the Cow Palace in San Francisco, on the myriad attempts by what the press called the "moderate wing" of the GOP to record victory in something—*anything,* it sometimes seemed—that might serve as a rebuke to the reigning Right. The proposed amendments all failed, in part because the convention was under control of Goldwater enthusiasts. In pride—and vainglory—they voted against anything they thought would contaminate Goldwater's coronation. Their obstinacy was egged on by the antagonistic auspices of the amendments. They came in—all of them—as amendments sponsored by the other side: the forces of William Scranton, the governor of Pennsylvania. And Scranton was, after all, the (defeated) enemy.

When, just six weeks ago, in June, Governor Rockefeller was defeated by Senator Goldwater in the California primary, it was inevitable that *somebody* would have to step in and contend against Goldwater. Richard Nixon was the obvious figure, but he had sensed the inadvisability of the race. He was handicapped by his smarting defeat at the hands of Democratic governor of California Pat Brown just two years before. And then, too, Richard Nixon was the Republican who had been nominated for president in Chicago in 1960, at the time the little band of Goldwaterites was pressing for its own candidate. The Goldwaterites were now in charge. Nixon was a cool observer of the political balance of forces. He would wait, and make his play for the presidency another time.

But somebody had to oppose Goldwater. That left William Scranton, the blue-blooded, handsome, rather reserved governor of Pennsylvania. Very early on, a test of delegate strength had shown that as things were going, Scranton would not prevail over Goldwater. Putting their desperate heads together, several of his aides acted to try something dramatic, if risky. A letter to Goldwater was composed. "Dear Barry," it began. And it was signed "Bill." The letter, ostensibly the work of Governor Scranton, detailed Goldwater's disqualifications to contend for the office, let alone to serve as president of the United States. The indictment was done in language appallingly hostile, coming as it did from a brother-in-arms in the Republican Party. The invidious letter ended, "In short, Barry, 'Goldwaterism' has come to stand for a whole crazy-quilt collection of absurd and dangerous positions that would be soundly repudiated by the American people in November."

Scranton aides proceeded to slip a copy of the letter under the bedroom door of every single GOP delegate.

Reading it on Sunday, Goldwater rubbed his eyes in disbelief.

So—it was said—did William Scranton when he first read his own copy.

Scranton immediately passed out the word that he had never actually laid eyes on the text before it was sent out—it had been composed by staff and signed by an aide who was authorized routinely to affix Scranton's signature on form letters.

"Talk about fitness to serve as president!" Karl Hess fumed to his aide, Woodroe Raynor, at breakfast. "I wonder if Bill Scranton's aide is also authorized to sign petitions for a declaration of war."

It was, under the circumstances, imprudent of the anti-Goldwater people to proceed to use Scranton as de facto sponsor of the three amendments that followed, bang, bang, bang. The first, formally proposed by Senator Hugh Scott of Pennsylvania, Scranton's convention manager, called on the party to "repudiate" the efforts of "irresponsible extremist groups such as the John Birch Society."

The second was offered on the floor by Joseph Carlino, Speaker of the New York State Assembly, a Rockefeller-Scranton delegate. It called for "enforcement" of the 1964 Civil Rights Act, declaring it a federal responsibility to superintend equal rights for minority members in voting, education, jobs, and accommodations. Yet the existing platform draft had already called for "full implementation and faithful execution" of the new law.

What Carlino had done was not only to use the dread word *enforce,* but to call for a public rejection of Goldwater's legislative record. When he voted against the civil rights bill in June, Goldwater had charged that the bill usurped states' rights and exceeded constitutional limitations on federal power. An analysis of the bill had been done for the senator by his young legal friend in Phoenix. William H. Rehnquist (who years later would be chief justice of the United States) had judged it unconstitutional. The motion by Carlino, if now accepted, would have humiliatingly rejected Goldwater's conscientiously drafted constitutional analysis.

And then Christian Herter, who had served President Eisenhower as secretary of state, filed a third amendment, again manifestly under Scranton auspices. It reaffirmed exclusive presidential control over the U.S. arsenal of nuclear weapons. This maneuver was designed to bring attention to Goldwater's having said in a primary campaign exchange that there were hypothetical circumstances in which contingent authority to use theater nuclear weapons might be given to senior military officials in the field.

"I say it's spinach and the hell with it," said Goldwater delegate head Sam Lopez, addressing the Arizona caucus before the vote. "They're just trying to embarrass Barry."

That was the finding of the majority: To hell with the so-called moderates; they're just trying to embarrass Barry.

One or two close members of Goldwater's staff, the Scranton amendments having been defeated, counseled some kind of rhetorical propitiation by Goldwater in his acceptance speech. A conciliatory draft was thereupon prepared. Goldwater read it, judged it anemic and servile, and tossed it into the wastebasket.

Professor Harry Jaffa, a political science scholar and a close student of Lincoln, sent over to Goldwater's hotel a memorandum reminding the candidate that Lincoln too had been accused of "extremism" and had handled the charge coolly and effectively, relying, in effect, on Aristotelian logic. Jaffa's insight, on Goldwater's instruction, was worked into a fresh draft. When read by vice presidential nominee-to-be Bill Miller, and then by primary campaign manager Clif White, and then by Goldwater intimate Dean Burch, the Jaffa text aroused uniform alarm. But Goldwater had had enough. He drew out his pen and underlined twice the two provocative sentences. *These were the words he would speak.*

His staff could think of nothing else to do except hide the text from the press until the last moment.

Goldwater had correctly sensed in the mood of the majority of the delegates a desire for a show of historic triumphalism. He began, "Anyone who joins us in all sincerity, we welcome. Those who do not care for our cause, we don't expect to enter our ranks in any case. And let our Republicanism be so focused and so dedicated as to not be made fuzzy and futile by unthinking and stupid labels."

FIRE ONE: *"I would remind you that extremism in the defense of liberty is no vice."*

FIRE TWO: *"And let me remind you also that moderation in the pursuit of justice is no virtue."*

The utter jubilation of the delegates corresponded almost exactly to the utter dismay of senior Republican figures. Scranton, of course, as also Rockefeller. And—most perilously—Dwight David

Eisenhower. He was appeased the following morning only when Goldwater, calling on him at his suite, reminded him that in 1944 extremist measures were thought appropriate to the reconquest of Europe.

The happiest man in America that night was the scholarly Professor Jaffa, watching it all at home on television, confident that Candidate Goldwater was showing the kind of strength and self-confidence Abraham Lincoln had shown in one of his own dark hours.

44

SENATOR GOLDWATER WAS BACK in his beloved desert home six days after the San Francisco convention. There had been a stop in Chicago and a few days in Washington to catch up on Senate duties.

The electoral tradition, back then, called for a hiatus in the electioneering activity of presidential candidates between their nomination and Labor Day. The pause gave the candidates six weeks of relative peace, time to deliberate on the campaign, devise strategy, schedule public appearances, and raise money.

Goldwater's staff rented office space in downtown Phoenix, and the candidate spent time there, reluctantly. Goldwater enjoyed working, whenever he could, out of his ample house, on the hill above Paradise Valley. Working there, he had the recreation of an hour or two with his beloved ham-radio facilities in the garage wing of the house.

His own study was decorated with Indian artifacts and framed family photographs. Featured there were native Arizona Indians, men and women, boys and girls, at work and at play. The cactus motif was omnipresent—in outdoor plants, for the most part, springing up, inexplicably, in the seemingly moistureless hot sand; sometimes as cactus flowers inside Arizona's adobe dwellings. Goldwater kept in his office a modest pile of his acclaimed book of photographs, which he would inscribe and give to special visitors. Routine visitors got only *The Conscience of a Conservative,* his political book.

He wanted just two men at his side to help him with special problems he had put to one side, problems he needed to face, however minor in the grand scheme of things. He would give time, of course, to consider the speeches Karl Hess and his assistants would draft, addressing issues on which he intended to campaign. He needed to give attention to a letter from Prime Minister Alec Douglas-Home of Britain, who, in writing Candidate Goldwater, had observed protocol by sending a copy of his letter to President Johnson. The prime minister asked about positions a President Goldwater would take on pending questions of state that touched on British policy on NATO, on Africa, and on diplomatic relations with China.

And then there was the dangling matter of Ayn Rand.

Goldwater had read *Atlas Shrugged* and had written to Rand to compliment her on it. She had been copiously grateful, Goldwater remembered. In her acknowledgment she had spoken of the possibility of a meeting with him, offering to travel to Washington for that purpose. Goldwater had not followed up on her offer, in part because he felt that if she traveled from New York to Washington just to see him, he would need to give her several hours of his time. He had heard that she was a difficult woman; he did not court a visit.

On the eve of the primary campaign in February, his aide Judy Eisenhower (unrelated to the former president) had reviewed Goldwater's files, intending to give him to read over anything that might prove useful in the primary season. On one letter, written several years before, Judy had underlined the sentence "I regard you as the only hope of the anticollectivist side on today's political scene, and I have defended your position at every opportunity."

The attached note from Judy said, "Senator: This lady is not only the author of the novel you liked so much, *Atlas Shrugged*. She is the active and *absolute* boss of the movement called 'Objectivism.' She and associate Nathaniel Branden operate what they call 'Objectivist' seminars and they are sprouting up all over the country. She's a highbrow type, but they also vote, and *capitalism* is her *thing*."

Goldwater had noticed Judy's memorandum just weeks before the critical California primary fight against Nelson Rockefeller. It would not hurt at all if Ayn Rand used whatever influence she had there, which Goldwater assumed would be considerable. California had been her home for many years and all cult figures in California had a following. He sent her an inscribed copy of *The Conscience of a Conservative.*

She had replied with a four-page letter analyzing the book. On receiving the letter, he had run his eyes over it and concluded that it had no bearing on the work he needed to do immediately. But he did owe her the courtesy of a thoughtful response, admiring her as he did as a novelist and thinker.

Accordingly, on the fifth day of his brainstorming sessions in Phoenix, his agenda for that morning included "DISCUSS RAND LETTER, Hess, Burch."

He sat back in his chair behind the desk, his hands clasped behind his head, his bolo tie loose under the collar of his bleached blue shirt. Dean Burch, tall and slight of build, sat behind his makeshift desk at the left, facing Goldwater. Karl Hess, age forty-one, jovial as always, his dark hair full, framing his new steel-rimmed glasses, sat at the other corner behind a table with mounds of paper scattered about.

"Okay," Goldwater said, "let's go on the Rand letter."

Hess looked up. At that moment the morning sun streamed in from the window at one side, illuminating Goldwater's graying hair and his rugged profile.

Hess said, "Barry, you know, you've got to be the handsomest man in *the whole world*. That's probably the *real* reason Ayn Rand said you were the only hope of the anticollectivist side. You remind her of Howard Roark and John Galt."

"Cut the bullshit. Remind me, Karl, who are they?"

"They're the heroes of her books, *The Fountainhead* and *Atlas Shrugged*. You got to understand this, Barry. Rand sees herself, and so do a lot of others—I'm tempted myself—as coming up with the central philosophical justification for capitalism, which is self-interest. She thinks she has a claim on the thinking of the GOP and I, well, I think she's right."

"We were talking about her heroes, Karl."

"Yes. Well, Rand's heroes have to be tall, handsome, determined, heroic, and unbribable."

"I don't know whether I'm unbribable. Nobody ever tried. Isn't that right, Dean?"

"That's right, Barry. But we did try to do a little bribing in New Hampshire."

"Much good that did. And anyway, as I told you back then, you can't outbribe Nelson Rockefeller, so there's no use trying. Okay, Karl, so she read my book. What didn't she like?"

"Well, she was being a polite lady, Barry, so she said that your most screwed-up chapter had to have been written not by you but by a ghostwriter."

"The whole book was written by my ghostwriter."

"And she says *no insult intended,* because—she says—*she's* of course a writer and she knows that people in public life, people unlike her, have to have ghostwriters just to get everything done."

"She's right on that point. You're here, and you've been with me through the campaign. Only we don't call you a ghostwriter, but press chief, and now I'll call you anything you want, as long as you write good speeches."

"Like Brent Bozell's."

"Yes, but Brent's living in Spain, and he writes now mostly about God."

"Ah. Well, that's one of Miss Rand's principal complaints, God. But let me start with the beginning of her letter. She says you were wrong in saying that you hoped your book would contribute to the conservative philosophy because"—Hess reached for his notes—"because *'there is no such thing as a conservative philosophy.'* She also says that the philosophy of the Founding Fathers wasn't the putting together of old ideas. 'It is dangerously misleading to call these principles ancient and tested truths. They were new, untested, and unprecedented.' She says that was 'the great achievement of the Founding Fathers, the fact that they created a political system *fundamentally*'—that word is in italics—'different from any that had ever existed before in the whole of human history.'"

"Well, that's true, in a way."

"Right. She says that American conservatives have to stand for capitalism and that if they don't, *they're done for.*"

"I agree."

"But wait. To subscribe to capitalism, Rand says, requires a complete acceptance of it, and you made a fundamental mistake because you wrote that people had to have *faith* in capitalism. Not so, she says, there's only one reason for capitalism and that's *reason.* She has a good way of formulating this part of her argument. She says that *socialism* is a faith—because people are taken in by it, thinking it will produce idealistic things when in fact it produces nothing but poverty and restrictions on freedom."

"We certainly buy that, don't we, Dean?"

Burch nodded his head.

"Now she starts to bite. She says that any appeal to faith has the effect of subtracting from the appeal to reason. And when you do that, you dilute the understanding of capitalism." He paused. "It's this simple, Barry. She thinks faith is for the birds. She doesn't mind if you have it, as long as you don't *ever* suggest that freedom and capitalism are related to faith."

"Have you got my acceptance speech handy?"

"What are you looking for?"

"The passage about our Maker."

"I liked it a lot," Karl chuckled. "That's why I wrote it. You said, 'The Good Lord raised this mighty republic to be a home for the brave and to flourish as the land of the free—not to stagnate in the swampland of collectivism, not to cringe before the bully of Communism.' You laid it on the line about the failures of Communism, and Rand is certainly enthusiastic about your anti-Communist positions. She quotes, in this letter, what you wrote about the Berlin crisis. Want to hear it?"

"Provided it's not too long."

"It's just a paragraph. Here it is—she exactly identifies it as paragraph 2, page 101, *The Conscience of a Conservative.* 'When the Soviets challenged our rights in West Berlin, we handed them a victory by the mere act of sitting down at the conference table. By agreeing to negotiate on that subject, we agreed that our rights in Berlin were "negotiable," something they never were before. Our answer to Khrushchev's ultimatum should have been that the status of West Berlin is not a matter that we are prepared to discuss with the Soviet Union. That would have been the end of the Berlin "crisis." ' "

"She liked that? Good for her."

"Wait, she liked it but then said, 'I find it difficult to believe that that same man would advocate the tenet that material production belongs to man's lower animal nature, without realizing what principle he is establishing and what monstrous moral consequences that principle implies.'"

"What does she mean by all that stuff?"

"What she's saying is that you are capable of thinking very straight—for instance, by analyzing the Berlin crisis the way you did. But that when you wrote that man has an animal nature and that that nature is partly responsible for his productivity, you missed the whole thing, because what is responsible for productivity is the free use of man's reason."

"Hmm. Well, Karl, there isn't anything there we need to implant in our speeches. Let's just write her a nice letter—"

"Hang on, Barry. She's sore as hell at *National Review.* You remember, they published the famous review of *Atlas Shrugged* by Whittaker Chambers. She says in her letter that she never herself deigned to read it, but was told about it. Then she says *NR* wrote two essays about her, one of them favorable, one of them unfavorable, but both misrepresenting her"—he picked up his folder—"'misrepresenting my position in a manner I have not seen outside *The Daily Worker* or *The Nation*. What was significant was their second article. It denounced me for advocating capitalism.'"

"That doesn't sound like our magazine."

"No. Must have been some angle of objectivism the writer was objecting to. But she signs off on *NR* this way, putting it all together: 'This leads me to the subject of the *National Review*. I am profoundly opposed to it—not because it is a religious magazine, but because it pretends that it is not. There are religious magazines which one can respect, even while disagreeing with their views. But the fact that the *National Review* poses as a secular political magazine, while following a strictly religious "party line," can have but one purpose, to slip religious goals by stealth on those who would not accept them openly, to "bore from within," to tie conservatism to religion, and thus to take over the American conservatives. This attempt comes from a pressure group wider than the *National Review*, but the *National Review* is one of its manifestations.'"

Dean Burch said he was surprised, he had read the magazine since its founding and had never thought it a "religious" journal.

"I have too," Goldwater said. "And I was the guest speaker at their last anniversary party. Karl, you're an associate editor, aren't you?"

"Sort of. Right. And I'm a Catholic, so is Buckley, so is Bozell. But Burnham isn't—at least, he isn't now. He lapsed back in his Trotsky days. Though come to think of it, Max Eastman resigned from the editorial board a couple of years ago because of an editorial they published at Christmastime. It was written by Garry Wills and made some reference to Christ as 'the Son.' Eastman said he didn't want to be on the masthead of a magazine that was 'religious.' I think what Rand is saying is that if you believe in God, then your sense of hierarchy, your advocacy of freedom and reason, is . . . upset. Deranged."

"Anything else?"

"Yes, she said she was willing to write a speech for you to give. Funny, she said either you or General Eisenhower could give it."

Goldwater looked down at his desk for a moment. Then he said, "Let's not get involved. Write and tell her I think there *is* such a thing as a conservative philosophy, and that I am an advocate of both religious faith and natural laws. And say hello."

"Wilco."

"What's next?"

"You ran into Woodroe Raynor in San Francisco. He was working in the office and running errands."

"Sure. Woody. Tall, good-looking young guy. A Yaffer. Sharp. Peggy specially likes him. He's still with us, isn't he?"

"Oh, sure. He's working full-time at campaign headquarters in Washington. Anyway, he gave me"—Hess drew the letter out—"a brief memo. It's from a retired historian at Princeton. I gather from Woody that he's somebody who hides his political views, but who's privately very emphatic about them. He is hot on anti-Communist foreign policy and for hedging against welfarism at home. For a while he was a member of the John Birch Society—get this, using an assumed name. But he pulled out of the Society a couple of years ago. Professor Romney is a libertarian and he knows that the fight between Ayn Rand and Murray Rothbard—"

"Who's he?"

"He's a young, academic type. Total individualist, like maybe an anarchist."

"What did he and Rand fight about?"

"Whether there's any life left in the Republican Party."

"Who won? The person who said yes, I hope."

Karl laughed. "Ayn Rand is in favor of backing your campaign. Rothbard is against it, because he says political action doesn't work in a 'statist society'—"

"What's the professor want?"

"He wants to send you a memo every week or two, giving special attention to the long-term prospects of the Republican Party."

"What's so special about that?"

"He doesn't want to write the letters unless you agree to read them."

"Fair enough. You read it first, Karl. Underline the parts you want me to read. What's next?"

"Our thoughts on federal deregulation." Karl looked down on the agenda sheet. "Dean, you've done a memo on that?"

Goldwater turned to Dean Burch, who nodded. "Milton Friedman thinks we should whack away real hard on federal regulations—growing every day, it seems. For instance, how many permits do you need to fly your airplane?"

They moved on to the next item. "What can we offer Bill Scranton?"

45

"*Holy Moses!*" Woodroe cried out in the Elect Goldwater office in Washington.

Olivia Spratt, doing volunteer work at the campaign office, looked up from her typewriter. "What's up, Woody?"

"Be right back." He walked, almost ran, across the hall to the office of Denison Kitchel, national campaign manager. He went through the motions of knocking but in his haste opened the door without waiting to be admitted.

Kitchel was there—and so was Candidate Goldwater, all dressed up to give his dinner speech to the American Legion convention.

Woodroe excused himself hastily. "Sorry, Denny. Sorry, Senator. But I've got big news. I was on the phone with Senator Tower—he'll be introducing you tonight, Senator. He cut off the line for a second, then came back on and said, '*Johnson's bombed North Vietnam!*' Senator Tower got the bulletin from an Armed Forces Committee clerk—"

"I'll be damned. I'm a member of that committee. You got any more details? Denny, turn on the television." Goldwater noticed Woodroe standing irresolute by the door. "Sit down, Woody. We don't need to hog the television, do we, Denny?"

The news came flooding in. The North Vietnamese patrol boats had loosed torpedoes against two U.S. destroyers. . . . President Johnson had ordered retaliation. . . . American warplanes had bombed targets on the North Vietnamese coast for five hours.

Kitchel finally turned the set off. "We've got to decide what to do to your speech."

Goldwater nodded. "I'm wondering: Is Lyndon really deciding to fight back?"

Woodroe discreetly left the room. He went to the public telephone and reached Lee, giving her the news excitedly. "I think maybe we're going to say no to a Communist-backed civil war. This may be a big day, a turning point."

"Provided he sticks with it."

"Yes. But what a day this must be in Saigon! The actual engagement of U.S. military on their side. We have to hope they do it right. Maybe this will stop the whole North Vietnamese offensive.... Did you remember to feed the cat?"

"What cat?"

"Oh! I thought you were Emily. She and I keep a cat."

"Cut it out, Woodikins."

"We'll talk later. Love."

46

GOLDWATER, AFTER THE VOTE, was both disappointed about some features of his campaign, and mad. Not so much the humiliating enormity of the loss (he won only six states and lost 43 million to 27 million in the popular vote)—he had expected that. He was mad at Johnson for imputing to Goldwater secret thoughts on policy which he simply didn't have, and never harbored—for instance, an alleged indifference to racial equality and to the dangers of nuclear war. He was unforgivingly sore about the famous Democratic television spot featuring a six-year-old girl pulling petals from a daisy, the incremental petal setting off a nuclear blast. The only thing that had been missing on the screen was a depiction of Goldwater grinning at the nuclear cloud.

He knew that the extremism charge against him was bound to go on and on. A week or two after the San Francisco speech, he had had what he privately described as "a kissing conference" with General Eisenhower. That was at Gettysburg, after which Goldwater had faced the press and denounced radicals of the Left and the Right. He said that if he had to do a paraphrase of his famous sentences at San Francisco, "I would do it by saying that wholehearted devotion to liberty is unassailable and that halfhearted devotion to justice is indefensible." That had got him a pretty straight endorsement from Ike and a formalistic one from Rockefeller, though you could see Rockefeller's teeth gritted when he said it. But the John Birch stigma stuck, and Goldwater was sick and tired of it.

Goldwater had charged *three* times in the campaign that Lyndon Johnson was "lying" in the matter of Vietnam, that in fact the president had *not* devised a winning policy on Vietnam. This Goldwater profoundly believed. But of course, in August, responding to the rogue North Vietnam patrol boat attack on U.S. destroyers, Johnson had pulled his masterstroke: he had gone to Congress and said, *Give me the authority to do anything I want to do against the Communists in Vietnam.*

They called it the Gulf of Tonkin Resolution, and Johnson carried a copy of its text around in his back pocket for years, pulling it out to display to any critic who thought he had done not enough— or was doing too much without congressional approval.

"He never *did* say what his policy in Vietnam is," Goldwater insisted, late in the afternoon, to Dean Burch and Karl Hess at one of the postmortems a week before Christmas.

"Yeah, but after the Tonkin Resolution you could hardly convince a lot of voters that Johnson was 'soft' on the Communist issue."

"That's right, I didn't. But I've got a *feel* on Johnson and the whole Communist business, just the way I got to feeling the same thing toward the end of Jack Kennedy's years. They haven't learned how to say *no* to the Communists. I don't know how long it'll be, but you watch. The North Vietnamese will take over the South. The Taiwanese will get kicked out of the United Nations. We'll recognize Peking. And? Aw, shut me up, Dean. I'm sitting here stewing, and maybe I'll bore myself to death."

"Until the nuclear bombs land?" Karl Hess always had a smile.

Goldwater laughed. "You know, last week when you birds were vacationing in the Caribbean, I was in Washington for the fundraiser for my deficit and I was in my hotel room at the Hilton when the phone rang. I picked it up, and the voice said"—Goldwater's imitation was dead-on—"'Bar-rree? This is Lyn'dn.'

"I said, 'Fuck you, Lyndon,' and hung up. Two seconds later the phone rang again, an' this time he says, 'Barry, is that the way to talk to the president of the United States?' An' I said, 'What do you want?'

"'I thought you might want to come on over to the White House and have a cup of coffee.'

"I said, 'I don't drink coffee.'

"An' he said, 'That's right, I forgot. Well, come on over and have a shot.'"

Karl loved it. "What did you say then?"

"I said I didn't have time tonight. If I had time tomorrow after the GOP conclave, I'd come around. The thing about Johnson is, he doesn't care *what* he said during the campaign, but he doesn't see any point in having an ex–presidential candidate—never mind that I lost bigger than Governor Landon, and that I don't even have a Senate seat anymore—going around loose, hating Johnson full-time."

"Let's just do it half-time then," Karl suggested.

"Good idea. They call that moderation, right, Karl?"

Dean Burch thought to get into the act. "Full-time would be extremist, right, Barry?"

"Right. Let's have half a drink."

47

AYN RAND HAD NOW ENTERED into melancholy, and the intensity of her sexual passion for Nathaniel eased, to a point that physical union stopped entirely. This did not at first affect their collaboration on Objectivist enterprises. But after a year of this, Ayn took to finding fault in Nathaniel for this and that. Her criticisms were always done in private and were entirely personal in direction— there were no expressed misgivings about the quality of his leadership of the Nathaniel Branden Institute. What he got was simply Ayn in a critical mood. Ayn Rand's critical moods were intense, her language lacerating; and then one day, a year later, it came to him, after heavy concentration on objectivist epistemology, that Ayn was really asking now for a return to sexual intimacy. Nathaniel's problem was that, vis-à-vis the goddess of his faith, he simply could no longer... get it up.

This was by no means a problem he was having with Patrecia Wynand. Ayn Rand hadn't attempted to alter the tall, beautiful Patrecia's first name, which, as far as Nathaniel knew, had always had that odd spelling, but Ayn had had a very direct influence on Pat's last name. It had been "Scott" ever since her wedding two years ago, which Ayn had jovially attended, Pat having taken lessons in objectivism from Nathaniel. After a time, she became an apostle of the movement. She played a dramatic part in a Rand play, delighting Ayn by her portrayal. "Patrecia, what is magnificent is that you have taken the philosophy of objectivism and applied it to the art of acting!" Elated, Pat thought to consider a career as an actress, which dalliance led to the conversation with Ayn in which it was suggested that Pat change her last name to "Wynand."

"Wynand as in the character in *The Fountainhead*?" Patrecia was quick enough to remark.

"Indeed," said Ayn. So from then on it was Patrecia Wynand.

That she was married to Larry Scott didn't seem to matter; Wynand, after all, was a stage name. What did matter very much was that the relationship between teacher (Nathaniel) and student (Patrecia) became ardent—supremely ardent, Nathaniel confessed to his wife, Barbara. Barbara, who had been married to Nathaniel for some years, understood him, and was herself distracted, as it happened, by the affair she was having with one Wilfred Schwartz.

So then there were the inherent complications. Nathaniel's mistress-on-hold was anxious to come back into play, knowing nothing about the mistress *not*-on-hold, and relying—because Ayn was very close to Barbara—on her ex-lover's wife to revive the dormant adultery.

Well, what happened was that Nathaniel just couldn't stand the tension anymore. He spent hours and hours with Barbara discussing and analyzing and objectifying the situation. Desperate, he came finally to a conclusion: *He would have to tell Ayn.*

Tell her what?

Well, certainly not about Patrecia. That would be too much. He would tell Ayn only that the old ardor didn't work for him anymore. After all, she was twenty-five years older than he. He wrote all of this out on notepaper; he would read his notes aloud to her, to make absolutely sure he remembered to say all the things he wanted to say. After all, Ayn had said to him, had said it in the presence of her husband, Frank, and Nathaniel's wife, Barbara, that in entering into the sexual relationship with Nathaniel, she had had no intentions whatever to seek marriage with him; he was a quarter century younger than she, and these age differences couldn't just be ignored. And then Nathaniel had added, in the notes on the speech he prepared to recite to her, a declaration—of utter, perpetual devotion to Ayn as his inspiration, his seer, the great genius of the modern age, and in the truest sense of the word, his perpetual mistress.

He walked down tremulously from his own apartment, in the same building as Ayn's, several floors higher. Stepping into her studio, he waited anxiously for her. She had said she would be there at eight. She came in.

Her expression was severe.

"Go ahead, Nathaniel. What do you have in mind to discuss?"

He read her the notes he had written. Word for word. He did not let his eyes stray from the paper.

Nathaniel had seen her cross before. He had seen her critical. But he had not seen her uncontrollably, titanically, murderously angry. It was like a great tidal wave smashing everything in its path, including skyscrapers, the white cliffs of Dover, and the Maginot Line. When finally he escaped upstairs to Barbara, they wept together. But before they had come near to exhausting their reserves of mutual consolation, the telephone rang, and lo! it was Ayn. She wanted to speak with Barbara.

She did so at great length. Ayn told how she had misestimated Barbara's husband. She had thought him a true man, on the scale of the great men she had created in fiction. He was less than that. Far less. He was despicable.

After one hour on the phone, it was agreed that Ayn would not lay eyes on Nathaniel while he did his work at the Institute. All communications of a professional nature would be relayed through second-in-command Barbara. There would be a period of probation for Nathaniel, said Ayn. That was not easily explainable to Barbara, because after all, the Institute was a Branden enterprise, not organizationally subordinate to Ayn Rand.

The Objectivist scene was strained, but Nathaniel continued with his work. A few weeks later, Ayn summoned him. He was to appear at her studio in two days.

He had dreaded the next, clearly predictable chapter in his dealings with Ayn. At this point, he had concluded ruefully, he would have to tell her all. Tell her that he was in love. He would not tell her that he was actually sleeping with his new love—only Barbara knew that. No one else, including Patrecia's husband.

Nathaniel begged Barbara to actually speak the words, to tell Ayn that Patrecia was Nathaniel's love—but a Platonic love. Nathaniel thought it would be easier if the relationship was disclosed by a woman. Barbara finally agreed. They discussed the best procedure and hit on the idea of bringing in a third party, to reduce the one-on-one melodrama. Barbara came up with a nominee: Allan Blumenthal. Why not? It wasn't more, really, than an experienced psychiatrist could handle. As a practitioner, Allan was professionally equipped to handle problems. And he was a member of the Collective. Who better than Allan Blumenthal?

Barbara called on her old friend and undertook to brief him on the entire story, chapter by chapter.

Barbara counted on Dr. Blumenthal, Ph.D., M.D., psychiatrist. He could surely take it all in.

He would be told now that Ayn and Nathaniel had become lovers, that Frank and Barbara had been advised of the arrangement. That during the recent period, sexual activity between Ayn and Nathaniel had ceased, owing to Ayn's depression. But that now Ayn had asked to revive the sex. Nathaniel had then told her he could not continue as her lover. Nathaniel had fallen in love with Patrecia. Indeed, he was having an affair with Patrecia but saw no reason to say this much to Ayn, but he did feel he had to let her know that he was in love with Patrecia, another woman who was not his wife.

Blumenthal listened to it all, then asked, his mouth set heavily, for a night to think the matter through as well as he could.

Barbara called Ayn and confirmed the appointment for the following day: for herself, Nathaniel—and Allan Blumenthal.

When they walked into the familiar studio room where the Collective continued to meet regularly on Saturdays, Barbara saw that the dutiful Frank O'Connor was also present.

"Where's Nathaniel?" Ayn wanted to know, blowing smoke from her mouth.

Allan Blumenthal took over. "Ayn, I have been asked to have a hand here, and I counseled that Nathaniel stay in his own apartment upstairs until we call him down."

"The answer is no."

So Nathaniel was called down, and sat by the desk on the studio landing.

Ayn had on a little extra rouge, Barbara thought. Allan, middle-size, wearing his usual dark suit, sat down in the same spot he occupied on Saturdays.

He began with some talk about psychological instincts and their bearing on coordinate thought and impulses in men of different ages—

"Get to the point."

Allan nodded his head. He drew breath and said that Nathaniel was in love with Patrecia Wynand.

He added quickly that the last thing Nathaniel wanted was to hurt Ayn Rand, that he was devoted to her. Barbara reiterated this.

"Get that bastard down here!" Ayn instructed Allan, pointing to Nathaniel on the landing.

What happened then was recorded in the memory of the professional, practicing psychiatrist.

It was one denunciation after another by Ayn Rand.

"You are an irredeemably rotten human being. . . . Objectivism never meant anything to you. You passed yourself off as a soul mate, God damn you. You're less than Peter Keating or James Taggart," she said, referring to the weak, evil figures in her two novels.

Blumenthal tried to slow her down, but failed. She followed the imprecations with concrete talk of retaliation.

"Your whole act is finished! I created you, and I'll destroy you! You won't have your career or money or prestige! You'll have nothing! I'll stop the publication of your book! I'll remove your name from the dedication page of Atlas Shrugged! *You would have been nothing without me, and you will be nothing when I'm done with you!"*

She stopped. She approached Nathaniel, coming within inches of his face. "Did you tell Patrecia about our relationship?"

Nathaniel said that yes, he felt he had needed to do so in order to instruct her on the context of the problem.

Rand gasped. Then she backed her arm wide and smashed her open palm against Nathaniel's face, backed it again and hit him again. She shouted, *"God damn you! God damn you!"*

She turned then so that Barbara and Frank and Allan could see her full face.

"Well," she said, wheeling again to Nathaniel. "I have one more thing to say to you. *If you have an ounce of morality left in you, an ounce of psychological health, you'll be impotent for the next twenty years. And if you achieve any potency sooner, you'll know it's a sign of still worse moral degradation!"*

Allan Blumenthal told Barbara later that when he strode suddenly from the studio to the bathroom after Ayn's screed, it was in order to vomit. He didn't say whether the nausea was provoked by his face-to-face encounter with the apotheosis of objectivism.

Whatever. There had been nothing in his experience quite like it, he told Barbara.

"There can't have been anything like it in *anybody's* experience," Barbara replied.

But they didn't proceed as if the whole objectivist business was now demonstrated to be phony. Inertial forces continued in command. The next day Ayn would merely make reference to an administrative problem that had been taken care of: Nathaniel and Barbara would have to fend for themselves; they were off the payroll.

Allan Blumenthal was back at his post on Saturday night, a docile member of the Collective.

48

NATHANIEL AND BARBARA and Allan talked about it—my, how they talked about things, the Randians!—and a few days slipped by. Nathaniel resolved that the moment was past due to address the staff of the Nathaniel Branden Institute and of the newsletter, *The Objectivist.* He had gone an entire month without teaching. They needed to be told something.

What?

What they needed to know, he and Barbara finally decided, was that he and Ayn Rand had had—a parting of the ways. Nothing more than that. Just that.

Why?

Nathaniel was not about to tell the cadre of national Objectivism that he had been expelled from the movement because he had declined to resume sleeping with Miss Rand.

But he had to say something, and here Nathaniel talked himself into a singular act of self-abasement.

What he said to the thirty or forty devoted members of the staff, Barbara seated in front, Leonora at her side, was that he had acted immorally, without fidelity to objectivist principles.

By doing what?

He did not specify. Instead he went immediately to the consequences of his infidelity.

The Nathaniel Branden Institute would dissolve.

There were gasps of surprise and shock.

The newsletter, The Objectivist, *would continue, under Miss Rand. Nathaniel would retire from the board of editors.*

The next edition of Atlas Shrugged *would no longer include his name, alongside that of Frank O'Connor, as dedicatee.*

Barbara Branden was crying. Lee reached over to hold her hand and she too began to cry. Others had wet eyes.

Nathaniel made the point that under no circumstances was anyone to lose confidence in the movement itself. What mattered in life was that objectivism should prevail. *Nothing* done by votaries of a faith had any bearing on the faith itself. Whatever his mistakes, they were his, not to be taken as weaknesses in the structure of the movement he sought to serve.

"I have taken actions I know to be wrong," Nathaniel said. "I have failed to practice the principles I taught to all of you. Ayn is fully within her moral rights in severing our relationship. But objectivism is as worthy of your support as it ever was."

He bowed his head slightly and left the room.

What on earth did Nathaniel do?

Everyone wondered, everyone talked about it. Had he molested a child? Taken and sold drugs? Conspired with the enemy?

Nobody penetrated the real story.

What did happen was that, excepting, of course, his wife, NBI members ended any contact with Nathaniel. He was at first stunned that this should include members of the Collective, intimate friends and fellow apostles for so many years.

But they would have nothing further to do with him.

Whatever he had done—and if he had accurately described it as a betrayal of Ayn Rand, then that is what it had to have been—if his betrayal was so grievous as to have justified such extraordinary measures as Ayn Rand had taken, then these measures must have been condign.

What hurt and astonished him most was that Allan Blumen-thal—the sole informed witness to the drama—joined in repudiating both Barbara and Nathaniel, and placing both in Coventry.

Allan! He had actually *vomited,* he told Barbara, on hearing Ayn's imprecations on Nathaniel. He had gone so far as to wonder out loud whether Rand hadn't in actual fact "created an entire system, including her philosophical system, to deal with her own psychological problems."

Nathaniel had always known it, had even gloried in it, but now he knew directly the unmitigated force of Ayn Rand's charismatic presence.

But two days later, one heretofore unflinching arm of Ayn Rand's system snapped. Ayn was informed that Barbara Branden thought it wrong for Ayn to attempt to stop the New American Library from publishing Nathaniel's book, *The Psychology of Self-Esteem,* nearly complete. Barbara passed the word to headquarters that she thought this measure unwarranted.

Through an intermediary, Ayn summoned Barbara to appear before the Collective to answer for her insubordinate thought. Barbara got Ayn on the phone and said dejectedly but firmly that she was willing to argue the case for Nathaniel's right to publish, argue the case with *Ayn.* But she was *not* willing—she found her voice tightening, in words directed to her mentor, her god, lover of her husband, who was determined now to exact vengeance by destroying her husband's career—"absolutely not willing" to appear before Ayn's court and submit to its members as qualified jurors on the question.

Ayn countered directly. She *ordered* Barbara to appear.

Barbara refused.

Ayn's telephone slammed down.

Barbara was weeping when, minutes later, Lee came into her office. Barbara looked up at her young assistant.

"Come with me to the grill," Barbara motioned her head.

Barbara had to tell *somebody* what had happened in these horrendous, earth-shattering days. She told Lee all of it. She said she was aghast at the "peremptory manner in which Ayn was abandoning the future of the Objectivist movement."

Lee had no rejoinder.

49

I T WAS AFTER SEVEN THAT LEE opened the door to her apartment. Woodroe was anxious about her, and had the news about her mother to give her. Lee had told him several days ago that something explosive had happened at NBI and that the staff had expected to hear directly from Nathaniel with some explanation.

He saw her red face—was it the winter wind? After she removed the ski cap she favored in snowy winter, he could see that tears had swelled her eyes. And now, whatever the office news, he had the doleful message for her.

"Darling, you are to call this number. It's a man who called. It's about your mother."

She walked quickly to the phone.

She spoke in Yiddish. After a minute, she put down the phone. "I have to go to my mother. She is in the hospital. That was my mother's uncle, Samuel."

"Shall I go with you?"

She shook her head. "That wouldn't be a good idea."

Silent, they went down in the elevator. Woodroe hailed a taxi.

"There's something else going on, Lee—right?"

"Yes. I'll tell you about it later." She got into the cab.

At ten, she called to say she would stay the night with her great-uncle and her mother.

"It's bad, Lee?"

She muffled out her words. "Very bad."

The next day Woodroe, unemployed since two weeks after the election, was in Albany for his appointment with Graham Molitor, who did the political hiring for Governor Rockefeller. On the phone, Molitor had been very direct: The governor was looking for a young man with ties to the GOP right wing. Karl Hess, a schoolmate and old friend of Molitor, had recommended Woodroe Raynor.

"Karl said he was pretty sure you were unemployed. After all, Goldwater is unemployed."

Returning from Albany, Woodroe took the subway at Grand Central to Fourteenth Street and walked to Beth Israel Medical Center. The clerk was busy with his crossword puzzle. Woodroe asked where Mrs. Leo Goldstein was.

The clerk looked down at a roster. "She's . . . checked out."

Woodroe was surprised.

"She's been released?"

"She's been released to the Weisser Funeral Center."

"Where's that?" Woodroe asked tersely.

"You can look it up, mister."

He found Lee there. At the funeral chapel she was seated on the left. She wore white lace over her head and the muted blue suit he had last seen her in.

The rabbi was reciting a eulogy. Woodroe sat with three other men, on the right. They wore what seemed a scrap of clothing on their lapels. In the center was the coffin, a pine box draped with a plain black cloth, the Star of David knitted on top.

Moments after his arrival, a chant was begun. *El Maleh Rachamim,* the rabbi announced. Lee's head was bowed.

Woodroe bowed his own head.

He found himself reciting the Lord's Prayer.

50

Woodroe had continued to read diligently the publications of the John Birch Society. His resignation from the Society did not break the habit. He turned now to the latest issue of *American Opinion*.

In February, the United States had undertaken the heaviest air raid to date in Vietnam. This was the first U.S. military action not undertaken as retaliation for Vietcong guerrilla offensives. Six American planes had been shot down since the Tonkin exchange, bringing the total number of U.S. planes lost to forty-three. Three hundred twenty-five Americans had been killed in Vietnam since 1961. Woodroe focused on the stark figures.

President Johnson had testified to a congressional committee that 75,000 Vietcong had been killed in the same period. An additional 2,376 soldiers had arrived in South Vietnam in the new year, bringing U.S. forces there to 46,500. Henry Cabot Lodge, who had run as vice presidential nominee against the Kennedy-Johnson ticket, had been sworn in as ambassador to Vietnam. That told the story: bipartisan support for Johnson's Vietnam policy was urgently desired.

It seemed indisputable to Woodroe that the United States was finally resolved to reaffirm the doctrine of containment against the Communist world.

He opened the magazine. He read it without enthusiasm and greeted with a trace of skepticism Welch's report that the Society was continuing to grow, that it now had an incredible five thousand chapters and a membership in excess of 100,000.

He turned then to Welch's report on Vietnam.

He could not believe it.

Only Robert Welch could have written what he was reading.

There were, as ever, the freighted sentences: Welch's ongoing reliance on the mystique of the *inherent treachery* of American officials at every level.

Woodroe would not, he knew, bring himself to read *all fifteen* densely packed pages of Mr. Welch's analysis of the Vietnam scene. But the hypnotism of the Founder required that he read—here and there even out loud to himself, to capture the actual *sound* of Welch singing his song—a few pages of Welch's analysis:

> *The greatest asset the Communists have anywhere in the world today is the willingness of the American people to be deceived. Even some reasonably informed anti-Communists find it so much easier and more pleasant simply to go along by accepting some action or development as bona fide which, if they would only make themselves stop and think hard about it, they would know was utterly absurd. The mushrooming war in Vietnam, and the predictable uses to be made of that war, form the most horrible current illustration. And, however much we too dislike the job, the truth must be faced.*
>
> *Permit us again to repeat ourselves, this time from a bulletin of two or three years ago. When the press was suddenly allowed to obtain and publish "leaks" that the United States was going to initiate and support the invasion of Castro's Cuba—which later came to be known as the Bay of Pigs fiasco—this writer was asked by a small but informed audience in California: "What's taking place?" I had to reply that,*

having been on the road for a week, I knew none of the details, and could predict none. But that, just from the headlines alone, the Communist formula being used was unmistakably clear, and that consequently I could predict, with complete confidence, the ultimate general results. (1) The anti-Communist opposition in Cuba would have been lured out into the open, betrayed, and destroyed. (2) The United States would have lost tremendous prestige all over Latin America, both for having meddled in the affairs of a smaller nation, and also for having completely fumbled the operation. And (3), Castro would have come out of the whole affair with tremendously increased prestige, at home and throughout all of Latin America, as the Communist David who had decisively stood up and licked the gringo Goliath. I added that obviously the whole operation had been planned for these purposes, by Castro and the Communist influences in Washington. A day or two later the "invasion" got under way. The rest is history. And what on earth makes anybody think that the increased activity in Vietnam has purposes that are basically any different?

Or have we so soon forgotten Korea, where we know now that the Communists at the top, through their influence within our government and their control over the Red Chinese, were pulling the strings and determining the action on both sides? Where we could have won a decisive victory within three months from any time that our generals were given the green light to go ahead? Does anybody doubt that we could have wiped the North Vietnam Communists out of South Vietnam within three months, at any time during the past several years, and made them glad to stay out, if we had really wanted to do so? Or that right now we could make Ho Chi Minh's guerrilla cutthroats, and their Chinese Communist "volunteers" and allies, all put their tails between their legs and run for their lairs, while we set up a permanent and solidly anti-Communist regime in South Vietnam, all within three months if that were really our purpose? If we could not, after our spending forty to fifty billion dollars per year (!!) on our armed forces since the memory of man hardly to the contrary, then treason and stupidity in Washington have been an even more successful combination than even we had suspected.

Why on earth should this Vietnam operation not turn into a larger and longer and more infamous Korea? Does anybody think that there has been any lessening of the power or ruthlessness of the Communist influences in Washington since 1953? Or that the Communists do not use so successfully a formula again and again? Or that any war carried on against the Communists by Robert Strange McNamara or Dean Rusk is going to be any different from the one they sponsored in the Congo—or more recently in the Dominican Republic— where the net result was the destruction or demoralization of as much as possible of the native anti-Communist strength? Can anybody who has studied the career of Henry Cabot Lodge have any doubt about the significances of his return to South Vietnam, as the chief wielder of American power in that area? Or need any clearer proof that any activities planned and presented there by Lodge as anti-Communist measures will be exactly on a par with his treatment of [dismissed anti-Communist] Bang Jensen, or with his treatment of the native anti-Communists in Algeria, while he was Ambassador to the United Nations?

What on earth is the matter with our compatriots in the American anti-Communist movement, anyway? The Communists, by exercising a minimum of discipline and of control by propaganda, over a relatively few thousand beatniks and half-baked collegiate brats, and by passing the word to a few of their highly placed agents, create a left-wing demand that the United States pull out of Vietnam! And this gambit fools the American people into thinking that we are serving some purpose, other than exactly what the Communists want, by what we are doing in Vietnam. Naturally the Communists have been doing everything they could to advance the theme that it is our patriotic and humanitarian duty to "stand firm" in Vietnam, and to keep on increasing our forces and our involvement there as the war is "escalated"—exactly according to their plans—into a greater Korea. What on earth would you expect? For twenty years we have been taken steadily down the road to Communism by steps supposedly designed, and always sold to the American people, as a means of opposing Communism. Will we never learn anything from experience?

Woodroe Raynor thought, *Now is the time for the final renunciation of the John Birch Society under Robert Welch.*

Others on the Right had come to the same conclusion. It came in the next issue of *National Review.*

51

O N THE MAGAZINE'S COVER, the headline read, "THE JOHN
BIRCH SOCIETY AND THE CONSERVATIVE MOVEMENT." It
announced articles and statements by editor William Buckley;
senior editors James Burnham and Frank Meyer; former chairman
of the Joint Chiefs Admiral Arthur Radford; and Senators John
Tower and Barry Goldwater.

The editorial tone of the lead article was severe. The editors con-
densed the swelling case against the Society and its leader. The succeeding issue of the magazine, stressing questions of intelligence,
taste, and judgment, in Woodroe's opinion proved the more deadly.

"In the opinion of the editors [the lead piece had begun] the time
has come to look once again at the John Birch Society and evaluate
its role in the current American political scene."

The magazine cited the Society's attack on U.S. Vietnam policy
as undermining the strategic thinking of the "conservative, anti-
Communist community." Moreover, "the Society has reached a new
virulence, a new level of panic. The current issue of *American Opinion* asserts that *the United States is now '60–80 percent Communist-
dominated.'*"

The magazine demonstrated that every public policy question of
the day, when analyzed by the Society, was framed in a single superintending perspective: the subversive motives of the officials,
named and unnamed, who thought up the policies and sought to
execute them.

The Civil Rights Act of 1964? *"[It was all] part of the pattern for the Communist takeover of America. The whole racial agitation was designed and is directed by the international Communist conspiracy."*

The economy? *"The conspiracy can now produce a total economic collapse any time that it decides to pull the chain."*

The lower courts? *"Do not overlook the fine contributions made by the criminals whom the conspiracy has slipped into lower courts."*

The Supreme Court? *"The theory that the Warren Court is working for a domestic, as distinct from a foreign dictatorship, becomes less tenable every day."*

The federal government? *"Communist domination of many of the departments of the Federal Government is too obvious to require much comment."*

Foreign policy? *"As for Vietnam, one thing is certain: no action really detrimental to the Communists is conceivable or even possible, so long as [Secretary of State] Rusk, [Defense Secretary] McNamara, and [Attorney General] Katzenbach remain in power."*

Summary? *"The important point is that Americans can expect only defeat so long as they are commanded by their enemies."*

The *NR* spread went on with brief statements from conservative icons.

Admiral Arthur Radford, former chairman of the Joint Chiefs, wrote of Robert Welch, "It is disturbing that a man with such ideas could gain such a following in the United States." From the academy, Russell Kirk wrote, "As several conservatively inclined gentlemen have remarked to me, were it not that they feared they might fall victim to the conspiratorial obsession of Robert Welch, they would be sorely tempted to believe that the leaders of the Birch Society are agents of the Kremlin, subtly working to discredit all opposition to Communism by reducing anti-Communism to absurdity." Senator John Tower said that *"National Review's* research graphically illustrates the gulf between responsible conservatism and unreasoning radicalism."

And from Senator Goldwater: "I don't for one moment agree with some Republican leaders that this organization is about to take over the Republican Party, but I do believe that the type of people generally whom I know as members of the group could add effective weight and work to the Republican Party if they cared to, but they should resign from the Society, since Mr. Welch has declined to do so."

In Belmont, there was consternation.

Welch presided over a meeting with three of his principal aides. They went over the *National Review* text paragraph by paragraph.

Jesse Andrews thought such textual exercises ill-advised. He didn't say exactly that to Welch, but in the men's room he spoke nervously to one of his coadjutors. "It's harder to resist the *National Review* thing when it's all put together this way. I mean, Bob would be better off just being—just making the broad case for anti-Communism."

In the end, after a tortured two days spent attempting to devise a written salvo, Welch decided that Andrews's advice—settle for the reiteration of the Society's anti-Communist mandate—should be taken.

"What we have working for us is the loyalty of our members. Let's get the word out to them, the best we can."

The next issue of *National Review* published a counterpunch by JBS loyalists who had written in their protests. The magazine ran a dozen letters.

"So, The Establishment has finally gotten to you! The word is Comply—or else! Or else what? Your magazine will not be distributed by 'accepted' distributors! Cancel My Subscription [hereinafter abbreviated, the editor advised, as '[CMS]']."

"What Robert Welch wrote in *The Politician* [imputing pro-Communism to President Eisenhower] is mild."

"Did you just have to do it? Couldn't you have left it to the Overstreets [Harry and Bonaro, authors of *The Strange Tactics of Extremism*], [Communist Party head] Gus Hall, and perhaps [NBC commentator] Chet Huntley? [CMS]."

"The same old smear method employed by the Liberals is used, namely, condemn the man and what he stands for but don't dare try to refute his facts."

"Since I have just so much hate in me I must parcel it out rather sparingly, and as I understand you I am now to love Russia and hate the John Birch Society."

Some letters were personal. "I am unable to understand whether in this latest attack, you [Buckley, the editor] are just being officious, or whether you periodically suffer from hot flashes, in some form of male menopause. [CMS]."

"I believe I heard that there was some $95,000 involved in your last smear of the John Birch Society. How much did you get paid this time? And by the way, whose side are you on, anyway? [CMS]."

One or two were amusing. "I have heard a rumor that John Kenneth Galbraith is a majority stockholder in *National Review*."

Most were summed up by the one-word charge from a reader in Willimantic, Connecticut, scrawled in large red crayon across his stationery, "Judas!"

Woodroe Raynor put the two well-thumbed issues away in the special file he kept, which included his membership card in the John Birch Society, dated February 16, 1960. Later he added to the folder the handwritten note from Professor Romney. "Woodroe: I welcome these two issues of *NR*. The job at hand is to encourage an anti-Communist, conservative political party—the Republican Party, as history has worked it out—that is unburdened by mind-clogging distractions. The GOP can do better by repelling impurities. A successor to Barry Goldwater as presidential candidate in years ahead will have less to worry about, the horizon will be brighter, our cause more compelling."

Less than ten years had gone by since Woodroe had seen the Hungarians groping their way to another world over the bridge at Andau. He had promised himself, when he saw the bridge go down and felt the bullet in his hip, to do what he could to stand athwart history.

What a huge effort expended, since 1956. And how much he had learned. He resolved to commit himself anew to the struggle, but this time on the front line.

52

OODROE'S PLANS HAVING CHANGED, he called Mr. Molitor to say that after all he would not be available to take
the job for Governor Rockefeller, and thanked him for the trouble
he had gone to. He was left with four weeks uncommitted, and volunteered for work at the Mormon library at Columbia University. It
was there, while he was sorting books one afternoon, that the librar-
ian passed him the message slip. He was to call Lee.

He reached her. She was doing homework for her graduate studies.

"General Walker wants you to call him. He called here when I
was out. When I came in, there was a telegram for you from your
mother saying the general had called Salt Lake—same message, he
wants you to call him."

"Well, that's not a call I look forward to. I'll be leaving here in an
hour. I'll call him from your place."

"Our place."

"Our place."

"Is the work going okay?"

"Fine. I had forgotten what nice people the Mormons are."

"Somebody taught you to be nice."

"I'll bring you a cake. My love."

"Christine, this is Woodroe Raynor returning the general's call."

"I'll put you through."

He heard the general clearing his throat.

"Woodroe?"

"Hello, Ed."

"This is General Walker."

Woodroe was brought up short. Then, "This is Woodroe, General."

"Yes. Well, I wanted to talk to you about the issue of *National Review,* taking the pro-Communist position on the John Birch Society."

Woodroe thought, *Just let it go? Or stand up to him?* But General Walker did not draw breath. "There are several ways of looking at what the *National Review* magazine people are doing. You probably know—maybe you don't know?—that a lot of the people who got together to start up that magazine were Communists. The Vietnamese fellow, I mean the Viennese fellow—Schlamm—is back in Germany. He was a Communist. So was their Frank Meyer, he was a Communist. So was James Burnham—"

"Actually, General, Burnham was a Trotskyist."

"What in the hell's the difference?"

Woodroe gave it a try. "The Communists assassinated Trotsky."

"Lovers' quarrel."

Woodroe didn't want to argue *that* point.

General Walker went on. "The Communists make a lot of mistakes, don't get me wrong. It was a mistake, for instance, to have that feller shoot at me and then kill the president. But the Commies are good at one thing, and that's taking aim at real enemies."

"Like Kennedy?"

"No, goddammit. Like *me.* Killing Kennedy was a mistake. Trying to kill me wasn't a mistake. I don't mind telling you I've wondered about you being there that night."

What was he getting at?

"You've tied up with the so-called anti-Communists in New York, the *National Review* crowd. Liebman—at least he didn't change his name, the way Jack Ruby did—he's part of that setup. And he was a Communist. Maybe you knew that."

"I—"

"There's a lot of them. And a lot of them who *pretend* to be ex-Communists. Why wouldn't they? It's an effective device. Did you ever know anybody in Hungary who pretended to be anti-Communist?"

Woodroe was startled. What could General Walker know about Andau?

"It's a common thing, and now you've got to wonder, how they get out and influence people. You take Arthur Radford. I've served under Arthur Radford. He has been one fine American. But when President Truman kicked MacArthur out of Korea—because our government wasn't going to take a chance on a victory over the Communists—"

Woodroe felt the blood rise to his head. Would the general also find something to question about Goldwater?

"—well, that whole *National Review* operation was hard to understand. After I read the issue on our Society—I guess I got to say, on *my* Society, since you dropped your membership—I put in a call to Revilo Oliver. I know you know Professor Oliver. You went up to see him the day after I got shot at. Turns out he remembers you very well."

"He's—"

"Yes, and he cleared things up for me. He's got a very penetrating mind. I've always dealt with you frankly, the times we've been together. And I'm going to be frank with you now. Professor Oliver has the perspective of a true scholar, and he has a real *strategic* vision, we call it at the Academy, *strategic vision,* and he raised an interesting question: What was it that brought Oswald to my house that particular night, the night you were there? If I had been shot, some tidying up at my place would have been necessary—"

"General Walker, fuck you."

He slammed the telephone down. One minute later, breathing heavily, he dialed the number back. Christine was on the phone. "This is Woodroe Raynor calling back. Tell the general not to call me again—"

He cooled down. He lowered his voice conspiratorially. "Tell him—to watch out for Professor Oliver. He's a secret Communist agent. Christine, that's confidential."

He hung up again.

He'd better call his mother and say it was all right, nothing to worry about, it was just a routine call from General Walker.

53

WOODROE AND LEONORA arrived early at Paone's for Marvin Liebman's party. "Gosh!" Woody said, looking around the table at the ten place settings. "A party for me and Lee—and none of my old Birch associates here, and none of *her* Objectivist associates here."

"They're all Commies," Marvin said, lifting his cigarette to his mouth in time to stifle the grin.

"Or anarchists," Lee grinned. "But no, we won't get into that. You know, I rather wish Barbara Branden were here, though it's been a long time since I've seen her."

"Where is she?" Marvin asked.

"She's off in Los Angeles with Nathaniel, trying to start up an Objectivist organization without Rand."

"An evening without Beatrice Lillie," Marvin commented.

"What's *that* mean, Marv?" Woodroe asked.

"Oh, you poor dears, you're so young and ignorant. Beatrice Lillie, the actress, had a great Broadway one-man—I guess it was one-woman—show. Rave success, ran about six months. The show was called *An Evening with Beatrice Lillie*. A few years later another actress—I forget her name—tried to do the same thing, put on a one-woman show. The review by John Mason Brown the next day in the *Herald Tribune* was a single line: 'An evening without Beatrice Lillie.' Get it, Woodroe? Objectivism without Ayn?"

He laughed. "Yeah, I get it. But Nathaniel is persistent, and California will buy anything, so he and Barbara might make it even *without* Beatrice Lillie."

Stan Evans came in with Dick Cowan and Carol Bauman and Lee Edwards. Leonora introduced her close friend Elsie Norman, who was at graduate school with her, studying psychology.

They all had drinks. They got on to radical movements in America in the 1930s and the big voices of the time. Dick Cowan mentioned the book he had just finished reading, Richard Hofstadter's *The Paranoid Style in American Politics*.

Stan Evans interrupted. He wore a grave countenance when telling amusing stories. "Hofstadter's book," he said, "spoke of three great demagogues back then, Huey Long—"

"FDR was *genuinely* afraid of Huey Long," said Marvin. "He seemed unstoppable back there in 1935."

Evans went on. "Then there was Father Coughlin—"

Again Marvin interrupted. "*I* heard Father Coughlin on the radio, maybe four or five times. He made my mother mad because he was always talking about the Jews, which made me mad too, but he was also always denouncing Wall Street and as a young Communist I thought that was *great*."

Evans persisted: "And there was Gerald L. K. Smith. Gerald L. K. Smith had one great moment: He began that broadcast by quoting what Father Coughlin had said on *his* broadcast the day before." Evans put on his grave voice and suddenly they were all listening to the twangy, deep-voiced Gerald L. K. Smith.

"'Father Coughlin was talking last night about Roosevelt. What he said was, *'Roosevelt, that great betrayer. That in-famous scoundrel.'*' You could hear Gerald L. K. Smith sigh," Evans said. "And then he said, 'I wish *I* had said that!'"

They roared with laughter. Marvin turned the subject to contemporary experiences. He told of going to hear a lecture by Russell Kirk a year ago at a New York teachers' council. "Some teacher got up and said, 'Professor Kirk, what do you think should be done about the rise in juvenile delinquency?' And dear Russell—looking very grave—said, 'I th-think we should start a Birch John Society.'"

They laughed again, and over dinner spoke of the Young Americans for Freedom and its tribulations, of Richard Rovere's and Teddy White's books on the Goldwater campaign, of Buckley's candidacy for mayor of New York. Lee told Elsie to imitate their psychology teacher's morning invocation of God. Elsie said she couldn't do the Polish accent but that the words were always the same: "'Gott help us. I use—*I yooss*—the term Gott only because *only* Gott can stop President Johnson's terrible war against Southvienamese interdependence.'"

They drank more wine, but Lee's free arm didn't leave Woodroe's—arm, hand, thigh.

"Well, ladies and gentlemen"—Marvin tapped lightly for attention, holding down his voice to guard against disturbing other diners. "We're here, as you know, for two reasons. The first is to congratulate Lee. Lee, hold up your ring."

"That," said Marvin solemnly, "looks to me like a genuine diamond. Or is it, Woody? It's too small for me to tell from where I'm sitting."

They all toasted Lee and Woody on their engagement.

"And, of course, the second reason we're here is to tell Woody he will be in our thoughts and prayers—Woody's a Mormon, you know, I'm a Jew—but I'm becoming a Catholic!" Several people clacked their spoons on their glasses lightly. "And, Woody, now that you're a second lieutenant and shipping off tomorrow for Vietnam, I know... we all know"—Marvin paused, lowered his head slightly, and brushed his napkin across his eyes—"we all know that, well, that you know we'll all be thinking of you."

Notes

THE AUTHOR MET WITH the principal figures frequently (Goldwater, Welch, Liebman) and infrequently (Rand, Walker).

Chapters 1, 2, 3

Encyclopaedia Britannica, 15th Edition (Chicago: Encyclopaedia Britannica Inc, 1974).

National Review, November 10, 1956; December 1, 1956; December 29, 1956.

James Michener, *The Bridge at Andau* (New York: Random House, 1957).

Chapter 5

Barbara Branden, *The Passion of Ayn Rand* (Garden City, N.Y.: Doubleday, 1986).

Jeff Walker, *The Ayn Rand Cult* (Chicago: Open Court, 1999). The book has twelve chapters examining aspects of the cult, and an extensive (seventeen-page) bibliography.

Chapter 6

Jonathan M. Schoenwald, *A Time for Choosing: The Rise of Modern American Conservatism* (New York: Oxford University Press, 2001), 62–66.

Fr. James Thorton, "Remembering Robert Welch," available at the John Birch Society website, **www.jbs.org**.

Robert Welch, *May God Forgive Us* (Chicago: Henry Regnery Company, 1952), 105.

Chapter 7

Schoenwald, 61–63.

Robert Welch, *The Life of John Birch: In the Story of One American Boy, the Ordeal of His Age* (Chicago: Henry Regnery Company, 1954).

Chapter 9

Barbara Branden, 185, 296–99.

Nathaniel Branden, *My Years with Ayn Rand* (San Francisco: Jossey-Bass, 1999), 152–71, 197–202.

Whittaker Chambers, "Big Sister Is Watching You," *National Review,* December 28, 1957. Available at: www.potomac-inc.org/aynrand.html.

Letters of Ayn Rand, ed. Michael S. Berliner (New York: Dutton, 1995), 571–72.

Jerome Tuccille, *Alan Shrugged: The Life and Times of Alan Greenspan, the World's Most Powerful Banker* (Hoboken, N.J.: Wiley, 2002), 69–86.

Jeff Walker, 26–28, 278.

Chapter 10

John A. Andrew, *The Other Side of the Sixties: Young Americans for Freedom and the Rise of Conservative Politics* (New Brunswick, N.J.: Rutgers University Press, 1997), 53–74, 221–31.

Schoenwald, 87–89.

Chapter 12

Ayn Rand, *Atlas Shrugged* (New York: Random House, 1957).

Rick Perlstein, *Before the Storm: Barry Goldwater and the Unmaking of the American Consensus* (New York: Hill and Wang, 2001), 114–16.

Schoenwald, 62–66.

Thorton.

Chapter 13

Schoenwald, 61–64, 101–23.

Chapter 14

Facts on File 1962 ["*Facts on File*" hereinafter referred to as "*FOF*"].

Barbara Branden, 306–8.

Nathaniel Branden, 205–8, 213–16.

David Kelley, *The Contested Legacy of Ayn Rand: Truth and Toleration in Objectivism* (New Brunswick, N.J.: Transaction Publishers, 2000), 81–85.

Jeff Walker, 31, 143.

Chapter 15

FOF 1961, 1962.

Andrew, 141–44.

Perlstein, 163–64.

Chapter 16

FOF 1961, 1962.

Perlstein, 147–48.

Schoenwald, 100–23.

Chapter 18

FOF 1962.

Schoenwald, 89–91, 106.

Chapter 19

FOF 1962.

Edwin Walker's press statement: available at www.textfiles.com/conspiracy/walker.txt, reprinted from the *New York Times,* September 30, 1962.

Chapter 20

FOF 1962.

Ole Miss campus map: available at www.olemiss.edu.

Schoenwald, 89–91, 106.

Exchange between Robert F.
Kennedy and John F. Kennedy,
September 30, 1962: "The John
F. Kennedy Tapes: Federal Inter-
vention in 'Ole Miss' Crisis Takes
Shape in Phone Call," *Washing-
ton Post,* June 24, 1983.

Chapter 21

FOF 1962.

"General Walker, Stage II," *National
Review,* October 23, 1962.

Schoenwald, 106.

"Walker Crazy?" *National Review,*
October 16, 1962.

Chapters 23, 24, 25

Barbara Branden, 255–57.

Nathaniel Branden, 7–15, 33, 43,
121–25, 129–33.

Chapter 26, 27

FOF 1962.

Chapter 29

Barbara Branden, 258–64.

Nathaniel Branden, 145.

Chapter 31

FOF 1963.

Details of the Walker shooting from
Edwin Walker's testimony before
the Warren Commission: *Investigation of the Assassination of President John F. Kennedy: Hearings
Before the President's Commission
on the Assassination of President
Kennedy,* vol. XI (Washington,
D.C.: United States Government
Printing Office, 1964), 404–28
[hereinafter referred to as "*Warren Investigation*"].

Chapter 34

Barbara Branden, 258–64.

Nathaniel Branden, 129–45.

Chapter 35

FOF 1963.

Perlstein, 221.

Chapter 36

FOF 1963.

Chapter 37

FOF 1962.

Andrew, 151–57, 165–66.

Perlstein, 156–57.

Chapter 38

FOF 1964.

Edwin Walker's testimony before
the Warren Commission: *Warren
Investigation,* vol. XI, 405,
423–25.

Chapter 39

Nathaniel Branden, 81.

Kelley, 52.

Chapter 40

FOF 1963, 1964.

Revilo Oliver, "Marxmanship in
Dallas," unedited version, February 1964, available at **www.revilo-
oliver.com**.

Revilo Oliver's testimony before the
Warren Commission: *Warren
Investigation,* vol. XV, 718.

Chapter 41

Barbara Branden, 412–14.

Nathaniel Branden, 229–31.

Ernest van den Haag, "Libertarians
and Conservatives," *National
Review,* June 8, 1979.

Jeff Walker, 33–35.

Chapter 42

FOF 1964.

Andrew, 192–93.

Chapter 43

FOF 1964.

Andrew, 194–96.

Perlstein, 377–78, 390–92.

Chapter 44

FOF 1964.

Andrew, 194–96.

Letters of Ayn Rand, 565–72, 627,
629.

Perlstein, 377–78, 390–92, 396–97.

Chapter 45

FOF 1964.

Chapter 47, 48

Barbara Branden, 334, 340–51.

Nathaniel Branden, 208, 219–20,
267, 286, 315–16, 323, 330–45,
350–51, 353, 362–63.

Jeff Walker, xv–xvi.

Chapter 50

Robert Welch, "Protest Neglect of
Our Soldiers Captured in Vietnam," *American Opinion,* August
1965.

Chapter 51

"The John Birch Society and the
Conservative Movement,"
National Review, October 19,
1965.

Acknowledgments

I AM INDEBTED FOREMOST for help in research to Robert Smiley, who traveled to Switzerland and gave invaluable help when off piste. Mr. Smiley is a young television writer, embarked, no one doubts, on a great career. Frances Bronson in my office provided syntactical and motherly help at every stage, and Tony Savage's painstaking work is responsible for the fine final draft. Lois Wallace, my agent for many years, tossed the champagne bottle and got the book under way.

As always, I have relied on friends and family. My sisters Priscilla and Jane. My son Christopher, a critical reader, said about the manuscript almost word for word what I routinely say about his work, and him. Professors Thomas Wendel and Chester Wolford, old counselors, were generous, acute, and encouraging. My special thanks to author Sam Tanenhaus, whose enthusiasm for this book gave it great wings. And, of course, Samuel S. Vaughan, whom I hail again as my patient and talented editor.

In returning to Regnery, my first publisher, I take leave (of absence?) from Andre Bernard, who has so beautifully published, on behalf of Harcourt, several of my books. Alfred Regnery is the son of the late, immortal Henry Regnery, among whose lesser accomplishments was the publication of my first book, *God and Man at Yale*. Jed Donahue, Regnery editor, did a superb and comprehensive copyediting of the manuscript, ably assisted by Regnery's frequent book editor, Patricia Buckley Bozell.